A little blue world, the third planet from the sun. It's home to seven billion people—with all manner of faiths, beliefs, and customs, divided by bigotry and misunderstanding—who will soon be told they are not alone in the universe. Anyone watching from the outside would pass by this fractured and tumultuous world, unless they had no other choice. Todd Landon is one of these people, living and working in a section of the world called the United States of America. His life is similar to those around him: home, family, work, friends, and a husband.

On the cusp of the greatest announcement humankind has ever witnessed, Todd's personal world is thrown into turmoil when his estranged brother shows up on his front porch with news of ships heading for Earth's orbit. The ships are holding the Nentraee, a humanoid race who have come to Earth in need of help after fleeing the destruction of their homeworld. How will one man bridge the gap for both the Humans and Nentraee, amongst mistrust, terrorist attacks, and personal loss? Will this be the start of a new age of man or will bigotry and miscommunication bring this small world to its knees and final end?

# CONTACT

A New World, Book One

*M.D. Neu*

A NineStar Press Publication

Published by NineStar Press
P.O. Box 91792,
Albuquerque, New Mexico, 87199 USA.
www.ninestarpress.com

# Contact



Printed in the USA
First Edition
January, 2019

Print ISBN: 978-1-949909-96-8

Also available in eBook, ISBN: 978-1-949909-88-3

Warning: This book contains sexual content, which may only be suitable for mature readers, and the death of a character.

For my family and friends.

# One: Best Option

MAINTENANCE DRONES PASSED the Speaker General's window as Mirtoff stifled a yawn. How long would they be here this time? The fleet stopped in a holding pattern while repairs were performed, the darkness of space surrounding them. Soft light from the window surround bathed her in a warm glow as she brushed away the few strands of hair that dropped from her tightly braided bun.

The past several months had been difficult, and she'd had little sleep. The suffering of her people weighed heavily on her. Mining Ship 9 had a malfunction in one of its storage bays while on an Ĩ-type asteroid pulling out much-needed water, nickel, cobalt, and platinum. One hundred and fifty people died that day.

She perused her terminal, chairs, conference table, and sofa. At times her office was claustrophobic. *It's bigger than what most of my people have.* She gathered her scattered thoughts and sipped from the now warm cup of *tuma*.

Faa was curled up on the couch. Their gazes met, and a comforting smile filled his face. He closed his big green eyes and nestled his gray, fur-covered head onto one of the sofa's pillows for a nap. His tail shifted gently back and forth.

*He's calm today.*

They'd been inseparable since he was plucked from the wreckage of Agricultural Ship 15 ten years ago when he was a *seyas*. Perhaps a month old. She had been consoling survivors and reviewing the damage. Twelve people died that day, including her sister-in-law.

Faa still suffered from nightmares, but he had always been a sensitive *cádo*. If he could communicate his pain and fear better so she might help him, maybe it wouldn't bother her so much, but the cádo were limited in that manner. She always considered it so unfair to them, particularly Faa.

Sighing, Mirtoff took a final swallow of her tuma, savoring the last of the now warm liquid, preferring it chilled as it should be, but unwilling to cool it again. The sweet, spicy flavors were still there, so the taste was pleasant enough. Turning her attention back to the chaos of her desk and the report-filled datapads, she rubbed her temple. The people and the cádo were weary of traveling through space. It had been too long.

If J'Veesa had intended Mirtoff and the Nentraee people to wander the stars, she would never have created their world, even if it was gone now. They had a home once.

They needed to find somewhere they could build a new life, a new world. They needed off these ships.

She glanced out the window again at the 450 ships carrying her people. How long would it take them to find a home?

Of course, there were other worlds and other civilizations, but none that fit her people and their needs. J'Veesa never meant for the Nentraee to be worshiped like gods; there was only one God, J'Veesa. Many names, yes, but there was only one.

They needed to either find a world void of life or one with a civilization they could work with and learn from. Their first choice was a world with equals on it.

What if they never found one? What if the ships stopped working? What if they were forced to do what some in the military had suggested? What if they had to take advantage of a lesser civilization? Or worse, what if...

"Enough," she huffed and turned back to the reports.

Faa startled and glanced up at her. "Provider?" he asked in a soft murmur. His speech was poor but understandable.

"It's nothing, little one. I'm sorry."

He shook his head and settled back in his chair, his big eyes not leaving her.

She grabbed one of the datapads to review. Agricultural Ship 23 was still under repair, forcing the other agro ships to increase production and require rationing. Again. She sighed.

There was a chirp at the door. *Odd. Is it that late?* Faa's eyes didn't leave her, but his floppy ears perked up.

Her aide, Danu, was gone for the day. The lines of her mouth softened into a smile when the visitor's image appeared on her desk monitor. She tapped a button on the screen, and then the door opened swiftly and Mi'ko entered.

"Vice speaker, tell me you've brought good news," Mirtoff's brows raised, and her lips pulled up at the edges. "Would you like a tuma? It's a little warm, but it's still good."

Faa looked at the vice speaker; his eyes softened and his muzzle twitched. If anything happened to her or her family, she wouldn't be surprised if he chose Mi'ko as his new Provider.

Mi'ko regarded her with his aging, aqua eyes. The wrinkles around his mouth turned up into a smile as he spoke. "No, thank you, Madam Speaker."

He was still in his traditional gray suit. She wondered if he'd been home yet. His brown hair was neatly groomed and pulled back, past his shoulders. His lopsided tieback was coming loose, which allowed a few wisps of hair to fall free.

"I have news," Mi'ko said. "The signals we've been studying have promise. We locked onto the frequencies, followed them, and found more transmissions." He typed on his datapad and a three-dimensional holographic image lifted from the screen, revealing a small solar system. He pointed at the third planetoid, and it zoomed in. "I think this might be what we've been looking for."

Mirtoff sipped her tuma and joined the vice speaker, leaving her work and her frustrations behind. She strolled to the screen on the wall by her conference table. This was a neutral space for her to meet with her staff or the other members of the Speaker's House.

Jumping off the couch, Faa swiftly followed her and lay by her feet. Reaching down, she scratched his head. He often whined about the room being too stifling, but thankfully, not today. The parks and their trees were his preference.

The vice speaker waved the holographic image away, pulled up a different file on his device, and swiped them over to the larger monitor. "It's a collection of speeches. We're halfway through the translations. What we do know so far is there are multiple languages and cultures, which could be both good and bad. It shows high intelligence."

Mirtoff set her tuma down.

Mi'ko cued the wall-mounted monitor as an image slowly appeared. Grainy, at first, but clearing. What came into view were snippets of a dark-skinned being almost like the *U'Ztraee* in coloring. Under the image: Martin Luther King, Jr. "...dream." The being was standing at a podium, speaking:

"Five score years ago, a great American...signed the Emancipation Proclamation. This momentous decree came...of Negro slaves...seared...injustice. It came...end the long night of their captivity..."

The first video ended, and Mi'ko tapped his datapad. "The life forms seem inspired by what it's saying. I'm eager for our linguist teams to finish working on the translations. The beings have a similar appearance to ours, but we will have to clear up the images for better examination."

The next broadcast started. This one showed a pale-skinned being wearing some form of optical assistance device with the words: "United States" under the creature. The life form looked very *Caleen*, sitting in some kind of assembly hall with a gold backdrop.

"I doubt if anyone...except possibly...the Soviet Union has any doubt about the facts. But...the Soviet Government up...Thursday, when...denied the existence...installing such weapons in Cuba...evidence available right now..."

Again, the image faded out as Mi'ko swiped a new file over. "I don't know what to make of that last one. The creatures did not seem pleased." After another pause, the next one started. The audio degradation was more present, and the vice speaker needed to make a few adjustments. There were no images to accompany the speech. The words that came were of a different language and sounded harsh and more guttural.

"The crisis in German economics...is expressed by our economic statistics, but it is above...internal course of our economic life, in...organization...here we can indeed speak of a crisis which... It is the crisis which...between capital, economics, and people. This crisis is particularly...relations between our workmen and the employers. Here the crisis...than in any other country in the world..."

Mirtoff tapped her mug. "Speeches made by the same creatures of different cultures, it would seem. Not an unattractive race, certainly not Nentraee. They can clearly pontificate and bring in masses of their fellow beings. Do we have anything that reflects their technology or knowledge?"

Mi'ko typed out a few commands on the screen. "It would seem so, but we're not sure how advanced they are. We have images of air shuttles, large ocean vessels, and small space vehicles."

The screen came to life, and an older being in a dark suit appeared. It looked Caleen, similar to the other being with the visual aid. However, this life form's pale face had dark circles under its eyes. The corners of its mouth fell as the image filled the screen.

"Nineteen years ago...lost three astronauts in a terrible accident on the ground. But we've never lost an astronaut in flight...And perhaps we've forgotten the courage...the shuttle. But they, the Challenger Seven...the dangers..."

The image changed. On one side, a mix of beings, in blue suits holding helmets. On the opposite side, an image of a ship, lifting off, and within seconds, exploding on screen with the words written underneath: "Space Shuttle Challenger explodes...seconds...liftoff."

Mirtoff's concentration broke when Faa got up and circled the vice speaker's feet. Mi'ko's face softened as he glanced at the cádo, who beamed up at him. Mi'ko was about to lean over to pet him, but Faa moved back over to Mirtoff with a murmured giggle.

"Madam Speaker, there were other speeches with varying tongues, but these are the longest and clearest. We've also tracked broadcasts with flowing qualities similar to our language; we are studying those as well, but those vary greatly and are accompanied by nonverbal rhythmical sounds. They'll offer us the greatest chance at further translation and study." He placed the datapad on the table before continuing. "We have additional images of these beings, but they show a great deal of war, death, and destruction, some natural and some not."

Sighing, Mirtoff turned to the vice speaker, rubbing her temples. Faa nudged against her leg to offer support and comfort. "Images of pain and sorrow don't require any translation, do they?"

Mi'ko's expression dropped as he fussed with his tieback again, trying to straighten it. "No, Madam Speaker, they don't."

Mirtoff stood, causing Faa to scramble off. Gliding back over to her desk, she picked up one of the reports. She frowned. All they brought was bad news. "What else do we know about these creatures?"

The vice speaker cleared the reviewed files with a wave of his wrinkled hand over the datapad. Sitting in front of her desk, he spoke. "We traced the signals and where they came from—sector 19.70a.1027sj. A small solar system, one main sequence star with various planetary bodies; theirs is the third planet with one stable orbiting planetoid."

He pulled up the holographic image of the solar system again and they watched the three-dimensional image lift from the device filling the space in front of them. He tapped a few commands, and the image increased in size.

"Similar to our solar system," Mirtoff sipped her almost forgotten tuma.

Mi'ko picked out the third planet. It appeared to be an oxygen-based planet with heavy atmosphere. It showed up as a blue world with white clouds covering parts of it. Both he and Mirtoff studied the holoimage.

He reduced the size of the holographic image, moved it to the side, and pulled up another image that lifted from the device's screen. It was their fleet.

Mirtoff leaned in closer to see the ships.

*That's all of us. Four hundred and fifty ships. Everyone else left behind dead.*

"Given our current fleet status, lack of resources, and repairs that still need to be made, it will take us between nine and twelve months to reach them, should we go."

He highlighted the ships in red that still needed repairs.

Her eyes closed.

*So many.*

"It would give us more time to study them and their cultures. It would also give us the time needed for our people to learn the basics of their main languages."

"Home, Provider?" Faa asked. "A new home?" He jumped up on Mirtoff, nuzzling her neck happily.

Her laugh filled the office with warmth. "Faa, that tickles. Be a good cádo. Go to your spot."

*He's such a dear one. Always bringing me joy.*

He jumped off and bounced to his place on the sofa. His joy at the prospect of a new home made her smile. Possibly, it was what they needed, but could she be sure this new world would be the right choice?

"You're my top advisor and the vice speaker of our people." Her eyes met Mi'ko's. "What do you think?"

"Madam Speaker, that's your decision," Mi'ko said. "You're our leader. My duty is to provide you with the information I can so you can make the best possible decisions." His brows were furrowed. "However, considering the state of our people and our fleet..."

Her groan was louder than she wanted. *He's right.* "Very well. Pull the information you have, and call the Speaker's House together to discuss our options. I want to know everything about this species. Find images of hope, something we can show to the others. These beings may appear similar to us, but they are not us. They must have something good. Are there more images of them traveling into space? An outpost, perhaps? Something on their orbiting planetoid? Is their technology similar to ours? Anything like that would do wonders."

The vice speaker made notes on his device. The energy in the room shifted. It seemed lighter and the atmosphere more energetic than when he entered. It was a welcome change.

"We'll keep this quiet for now. I don't want to get our people's hopes up. We've been through this before, with bad outcomes."

Mi'ko's face hardened. They had, indeed, learned from their mistakes. "Of course, Madam Speaker. It will be kept within the confines of the government. For now."

Mirtoff leaned forward, her voice becoming quiet. "I don't have to tell you General Gahumed will be difficult, especially if these beings have military technology similar or greater than ours. Let's do our best to anticipate her arguments and have rebuttals in place. We can't afford constant challenges and her pushing for military intervention."

"Of course, Madam Speaker. I'll do my best." Mi'ko stood. "May you rest well." He lingered in the doorway. "Madam Speaker?"

She put down the datapad, allowing the new information to load.

"Regardless of what happens, we can't keep it quiet for long. Our people are restless. They need hope, even if it's a tiny glimpse in absolute darkness."

"May you rest well, my friend," she said and went back to the report.

He bowed, touched the panel next to the door, and when it opened, he strolled out.

"Well, little one, no dinner with Ecra and Suloff tonight," she said. "I have to go over this new information."

The grin on his face fell as did his floppy gray ears. "Provider, no Suloff? No scratches?"

"Sorry, little love. But maybe we'll walk the park on the way home and get something at the promenade." She checked her now empty cup of tuma. *Should I have another cup?* Her head shook in the negative. Instead of having more, she picked up the datapad and scanned the new files over to her terminal.

*Will this be it?* A tingle of excitement filled her chest, but she needed to be the voice of reason and keep things in perspective.

They would have a lot to learn, but Mi'ko was right. She had to make the decision to explore this new world and race. Her people needed hope, something to grasp.

"One step at a time," she whispered. This burden came with being the Speaker General. She had to weigh the options and make the best choice she could. *But would it be the right one? Would it be enough?*

# Two: A Day like Any Other

TODD FORCED THE frown off his face, shaking his head at the email. He didn't need this. Not today. He switched screens and continued to tap away on his laptop.

*I'm not going to let it bother me. I'm in too good a mood.*

His head bobbed to "Photograph" playing in the background. His brain spun with ideas for his new game. The vampire role-playing game finished a couple of weeks ago; he had been working feverishly to get things set up for a new adventure game. For the past few days, he'd had nothing, but today he hit the jackpot. New ideas swam in his head. He had the scenes figured out and knew the direction the game would go.

Smiling over at the window, he saw Bianca, who like any good cat, was a true queen. She glanced out toward the front yard, surveying her realm. Todd and Jerry were her servants, and this was her castle, no mistake about it. She changed position and Todd turned back to his laptop. *How long have I been writing, anyway?*

The news was on; some talking head chattered about the conflict in the Middle East and troops being pulled out to come back home. Todd's lips pursed. *It's rubbish.* There was never anything new to report. One group of people hating another group of people, either trying to kill them or take their power. It was no different anywhere else. Everyone thought they were right, and no one believed in compromise.

"They should blow each other up and be done with it," Todd said, as new images of this week's disaster situation were shown. He shook his head. "When are we gonna get our shit together as human beings and grow up?"

Turning from the TV, he reread the opening scene. Grabbing his diet soda, he took a swallow. He paged down a few lines. It was a start, and it was better than yesterday, having only the outline.

"Hey. Whatcha doing?"

"Jerk," Todd yelped, startled by the voice behind him. Jerry could be a ghost when he wanted to be. It was unnerving at times.

Jerry was a mess from working in the yard, covered in dirt and sweat. Honey-brown hair hung in clumps. It wasn't a flattering appearance for him, chiefly because he was such a handsome guy. Still, with his big dopey smile, it made Todd's heart skip a beat.

"Moi?" Jerry asked. "A jerk?" He grabbed the remote off the coffee table, muted the TV, and turned off the radio.

"Yes, you. I'm just working on my game. I had a great idea for a way to start. I'm gonna have the players in different locations around the world, and their first focus will be meeting up. That way they get to develop their characters and their backstories. Then I figure—" Todd stopped, noting the vacant expression on Jerry's face. "You could care less."

"Those games are your thing, not mine." He kissed the top of Todd's head. "I'm just happy you found something that you enjoy."

"Well, thanks." Todd beamed.

"So, anyway." Jerry pointed to the TV and then the radio. "I wouldn't have startled you if it hadn't been for this noise. I mean, come on." He shook his head. "I can hear the

TV and radio all the way out back, and I'm sure the neighbors are loving it. How do you even concentrate?"

"It helps me focus," Todd smirked. "It's kind of like how you can sleep in your chair with a full can of soda in one hand and the remote control in the other." He jerked a thumb at the window. "So, how's the yard? Are we having fun yet?"

"Loads and loads. We should get a gardener. Let them deal with the mess." Jerry ran his hand through his sweaty hair. He leaned against Todd's shoulder, taking a peek at the screen.

"Now you're interested?" Todd saved the file and closed the laptop. He would come back to it when he had time, probably later that evening when Jerry was watching TV.

Jerry rolled his eyes. "I don't understand you." He rested his hands on Todd's shoulder. "Instead of wasting your free time on these role-playing games, why don't you focus and create a short story, or even a book? I mean, why are you always hiding and avoiding things? Clearly you have the passion and the talent. Hell, why not try to submit it for a movie or TV show? It's good enough." Jerry picked up Todd's diet soda and finished it off with a loud slurping sound.

"'Cause it's not that good. I'm no writer. I just do it for fun." Leaning back on the couch, he took a breath. "Plus, you need an agent and all that crap. It's not like you can submit it and go." He put the laptop on the coffee table. "And I hide from no one."

Jerry shook his head. "One day, I'm going to get into your files and put it together. Then I'm gonna dump it on the internet to see what happens."

"No, you won't!"

"Why not? I love you and you love writing. Plus, it'll get you out of your safety zone. Show how talented you are. Get you out of your crazy HR job."

"If you do, I'll have to sic the kitty on you, and she'll take your sorry ass out and smack you around." He pointed to the white, long-haired cat, who wasn't paying either of them the least bit of attention as she lounged in the window. He brushed white cat hair off his shirt as he stood and stretched. "Plus, she watches all that you do and reports back to me."

Bianca must have known they were talking about her because she turned, glanced at them, and let out a little meow.

"See, told ya."

"Yeah, yeah, whatever. I say we get the kitty and cook 'er up and have kitty stew." Jerry rushed over to the window. Before Bianca managed to escape, he scooped her up into his arms and gave her a sweaty and dirty squeeze. "Who wants kitty stew? Does the kitty want to be cooked in a pot, hmm?" Bianca gazed back at him with unimpressed green eyes. "No telling what the puss thinks, is there?"

"Nope, she's full of mystery. That's why she's a cat."

Jerry gave her nose a little scratch: one of her favorite itchy spots. "I'm gonna do it to piss you off. I'm gonna post your work online," he said, with a menacing glare and a twinkle in his blue eyes.

"No, you won't, because you love me." A chuckle broke from his lips.

Part of him almost wished Jerry would post his work online. It might give him the kick-in-the-ass he needed to take that next step. But then, why rush? There was plenty of time; there always was tomorrow.

Bianca jumped from Jerry's arms to the floor and pranced off.

"Well, bye," Jerry said, the cat walking away with her tail in the air. He dusted off the hair she left behind. "By the way, I got a call from Dan yesterday."

"Was it the snarky bitchy Dan or professional work Dan?" Todd asked.

Jerry laughed.

"What? I just want to know what to be prepared for."

"Come on. We both love his sharp wit and he always makes us laugh."

"Oh, I know. But you have to admit he can be a bit much, at times."

Jerry nodded.

"So, what does he want?"

"He's gonna be here tomorrow and wanted to know if we could host him for a few days." He picked off more cat hair with a frown. "I told 'im I'd check with you, but it shouldn't be a problem."

"So, what brings Mister Dan, the drama magnet, to our neck of the woods? I thought he's still in Europe working for that travel company or whatever. What happened to that?" Todd felt his heart skip a beat. "Don't tell me he got fired? Is he—?"

"Relax," Jerry cut him off. "He's fine. He's coming out here for his nephew's graduation. You know him. He forgot to let us know. Or anyone else for that matter." He fussed with his hair.

"God, what a mess. I still can't believe Dan was in the Air Force." Todd shook his head. "I guess his messy, last minute, snarkiness is part of his charm and why we love him."

Getting off the sofa, Todd studied the yard and then looked up at the blue sky and white, puffy clouds lazily floating by. "The yard looks good," Todd said as Jerry flopped onto the couch and picked up his tablet. "Hey, don't be sitting on the couch all dirty like that!"

Jerry raised his eyebrows. "Whatever, Mister Fussy." He stretched his arms over his head, still holding the tablet. "Anyway, he needs a place to stay and wanted to crash here instead of with his family. It should only be a week or so, but with Dan, who knows?"

"Ah, well, that's cool. Why didn't he send you a text or something? After all, he lives on his smartphone, like someone else I know."

"Bite me," Jerry jabbed back with a bright smile. "I wanted to check in with the office. And I'm not nearly as bad as someone I know, Mister Man." Jerry poked Todd in the stomach.

Todd offered an innocent smile and knocked Jerry's feet off the sofa so he could sit.

"So, do we know the details yet, or is he gonna text us the flight info?" Todd rested his arm on the back of the couch.

Jerry closed the tablet and rested his head on the back of the couch brushing up against Todd's hand. As he looked up at the ceiling, he released a heavy sigh. "Nah, he's gonna text us either tonight or tomorrow morning. It was a quick call." He lifted his head and turned to Todd with narrowed eyes. "By the way, you didn't close your email this morning, Mister Man. When I went to check my messages, I noticed you had a message from your brother, still unopened. You should respond to it, or better yet, delete it?"

"I know, I know. I saw it when I was doing the checkbook." Todd grimaced. "I'll deal with it later. Just...not now. I don't want to pay attention to Brad's shit. I'm still pissed over the fight."

"Come on, Todd." Jerry's lips pinched together. "I mean, you've been nothing but moody and cranky since you got it. Why don't you confront him on his conservative garbage? We're married and there's nothing he can say or do to change that. Honey, I love you, but we don't need his drama."

"I know." Todd scanned the room, not wanting to meet Jerry's eyes.

*Dammit, Jerry. Brad hurt me and I don't want him to hurt me anymore. Hurt us anymore. He's my brother and I love him and it kills me that he hates me and that he hates the idea of us.*

"Your folks finally came around, and who's more narrow-minded and old-fashioned than them? He might be working with a couple of gay engineers or scientists and coming around. You do *comprende* how much us gays love our space stuff?"

It had taken a year after they got married, but his mother had started to call them, and now things with his parents were almost back to normal—strange and awkward, but better than nothing.

"Maybe, it's work-related and Brad wants to give us a heads-up about something at cool over at NASA. They could have found a true Earth-type planet." Jerry waggled his fingers in front of his face moving his head side to side. "You know; it might be something important."

Todd couldn't stop the grimace from hitting his face.

*Or maybe it's more of his conservative religious shit that he shares with the world. How can my brother hate me and us so much?*

"I mean, if it was that important, I suppose he'd call?" Jerry said.

Taking a breath, Todd tried to keep civil before responding. "Jerry, can we just not talk about it? I said I'd deal with it, okay?" Todd's face was getting warm.

*I love you but you're pissing me off. You know not to push.*

"Plus," Todd continued, "if it were truly important, Mom would've called, and I'm sure if it was space-related, we would've found out on the TV or the net." He huffed. "I talked to Mom last week and everyone was fine. So it's something I couldn't care less about. Probably religious stuff on us going to hell. You should see what he posts on Facebook." Todd saw Jerry's face. "Yes, I check his Facebook page. So what?"

Jerry's head shook as he raised a hand to his mouth, undoubtedly to cover a smirk.

Sighing, Todd took a moment to pull himself together. "Sweetie, I know you're curious. I am too, but Brad only talks shit. So what could he possibly have to say?" He sighed and rubbed his hands over his face, playing with his goatee. "It's been years—and not a peep; the only news I get is through Mom, and that is limited because she doesn't want to get involved." He waved off the conversation with a motion of his hand.

"All right," Jerry stood and bent over, shifting his back until a pop echoed through the room. "So much better." He slipped his shoes back on.

Todd heard the words that were unsaid: you're hiding again, you're avoiding, you should deal with it head-on. It was the same conversation they always had when Jerry thought Todd wasn't facing something. What made it worse was not only did it come from a place of love, but Todd recognized that Jerry was correct.

Jerry smiled that wonderful smile of his and stuck out a hand. "So, how about you come out and help me with the rest of the yard? Then maybe I'll let you scrub my back in the shower and perhaps do a few other things."

Grinning, Todd took his hand and pulled himself off the couch. He gave him a soft kiss on the lips. "Promises, promises. Let me go pee, and I'll be right there."

Jerry ran his hand along the side of Todd's face and his smile deepened. "Can you imagine Brad and Dan in the same room?"

"Oh God, that would break the snark-o-meter for sure." Todd laughed. "That would be a disaster. I'm not sure the world could survive the two of them together."

# Three: Family Reunion

TURNING HIS GAZE out the bathroom window, he could see the golden foothills just beyond the neighbor's yard. Today was perfect. A few clouds floated softly by on a nice breeze. The wind always helped freshen the air. He loved that clean summer scent.

On his way out of the bathroom, a knock came from the front door. "Ah man," he said as he headed to answer it.

His head shook side to side as he took a deep breath and opened the door. It was like looking in a mirror. The same blond hair and hazel eyes. The man was a little shorter and had a dimple in his chin, but otherwise, they had nearly identical features. Both looking more like their father than their mother. People always said they could pass for twins, even though Brad's voice was deeper, and he was two years older. Unable to move from shock, his eyes narrowed.

"Hey, Toddy."

Hearing the voice snapped him out of it. "What the hell are you doing here?" Todd demanded, raising his voice more than he wanted.

All the anger and hurt from the last several years rushed back. His head filled with the images of their last altercation. Brad condemning him and Jerry. Brad standing there pounding a pointed finger on Todd's chest. Their father had to pull Brad away, and Jerry had to keep Todd from fighting back. Todd ended up with bruises on his chest. It was the last time the whole family had been together.

Without hesitation, his fist made contact with his brother's face, sending a sharp pain up Todd's arm and ringing in his ears.

Brad faltered back. "Shit, Todd, you feel better now?" He came up holding his jaw.

"No! Not yet!" He went to strike Brad again.

This time, Brad blocked and grabbed his fist, not letting go. "I admit I had it coming, but one is all you get."

Todd struggled to get free, but Brad held him.

"I'm glad you never learned your follow-through. One more hit, and I'd have a broken nose." He tightened his grip on Todd's hand. "May I come in?" Brad forced his way through the door, closing it behind him with his foot.

"What the hell do you want?" Todd spat as Brad led him to the living room. "Let me go, you ass."

Brad pushed Todd onto the couch. "Relax, all right? I'm not here to cause trouble." He scanned the room and sat in one of the side chairs.

During the scuffle, Todd didn't notice how bad Brad looked. He had dark circles under his eyes, his face was unshaven, and his hair was a mess.

*Something's wrong.*

Todd was leery, but his tone softened. "What's wrong? Why the hell are you here? And why do you look like shit?" His voice was raised. He took a breath to relax.

Brad rubbed his jaw then ran his hand through his hair. "Listen, Todd. I need to talk to you and Jerry." His eyes scanned around the room and then out the front window. "Where's Jerry? Is he here? I saw two cars so he must be here, right?"

"Why do you care?" Todd examined the bloody cut on his knuckle and pulled himself together. "Yeah, he's out back." His fist throbbed from the punch and Brad's death grip. His brother always had strong hands. Probably from the pocket pool he played when he was younger.

Todd shook his hand as he stood and crossed to the window next to the fireplace, where Jerry was raking up the leaves from the grass.

*Of course he didn't hear anything; it's like he's not even here.*

"Jerry, come in here," he barked.

"What? I'm in the middle of doing the leaves." Jerry stopped. "Come on, I thought you were on your way to help me? What, does someone need help washing their hands after their potty break?"

Not believing that his lousy brother was sitting in their living room, Todd didn't want to deal with this. And now Jerry was trying to be funny. He didn't know, but still. "Get your ass in here, will ya? Brad's here, and he wants to talk to us."

"Wait. What? Are you kidding me? Are you—?"

"Just get in here," Todd cut him off. "And get some ice from the kitchen." He closed his eyes. Trying to sound civil, he forced a smile. "Please." He closed the window and went to sit again. "Okay, Jerry's coming. Now, what do you want?"

"Hold up, Toddy. Jerry needs to listen to this as well." Brad continued to nurse his lip and jaw. The cut wasn't very deep, but still, there would be a nasty scab afterward.

Todd studied Brad.

His jeans, polo shirt, and shoes were nothing out of the ordinary, except they looked like he had been wearing them for a couple of days. Smelled like it too. Brad appeared exhausted. Todd started kneading his sore hand, his anger turning to worry. Brad was many things, but never unkempt or unshaven. His stomach sank as Jerry came into the room.

"What do you want..." Jerry glanced at Todd and held up the bag of peas wrapped up in a towel.

Todd pointed to Brad.

Jerry nodded and handed them over to Brad.

"Peas?" Todd said, and Jerry shrugged.

"Thanks." Brad put the makeshift ice pack on his lip.

Jerry took a seat next to Todd on the couch and reached for Todd's hand. Brad's touch always made stressful situations better.

"Well, we're both here, and you have our attention." Todd glared and hissed. "So what the fuck is going on?"

Brad rolled the frozen peas from lip to jaw and then back again. "I hope you don't kiss Mom with that mouth," he teased, with a crooked smile. Apparently, he was trying to add humor but failed. Brad let out an awkward sigh and turned to the two of them. "Right...well...okay, here's the deal. First, I want to say that you're my baby brother, and I love you. I'm sorry for everything. I never should of let things get as bad as they did. I know I've been a royal pain in the ass, and you don't deserve it. Neither of you did, and I'm sorry." Brad turned his gaze to the floor. "Jerry, I never even gave you a chance, and that was wrong of me—"

"Oh, what-the-fuck-ever!" Todd snapped. "If this is why you're here, forget it. You can fuck off and leave. Go back to your perfect little family, and your perfect little world that doesn't include any gay people."

Todd stood and started for the door, but Jerry grabbed his arm, preventing him from moving. "Honey, sit down and listen to your brother. He's trying to apologize!"

*Fine, but only for you.*

Todd scanned from Jerry to Brad. He quietly returned to his seat. Bianca jumped up and began to paw at his lap. She was making a comfy nest to curl up on.

"Thank you, Jerry—"

"Just stop." Jerry glared at Brad. "Look, you jerk. You come to our house after all these years. After all the garbage you said about us and getting into a fight with Todd. A fight you started. Not to mention the family drama you caused after that." He rubbed the armrest of the couch. "You've had a stick up your butt for years. Don't assume for one minute I'm on your side. I'm not." He glanced between the brothers. His voice softened as his shoulders relaxed. "I mean..." He sighed. "You deserve to say your peace without interruption. Now get on with it."

Brad nodded at Todd and indicated Jerry. "Is he always like this?"

Todd gave an annoyed frown as he fumed.

"Well, he's a tough S-O-B, that's for sure. No wonder you love him." Brad adjusted the bag of peas on his lip.

Todd shook his head, choosing not to respond. "You were apologizing for being a complete ass..." His vision went hazy and his heart beat faster.

*It makes sense now. Brad sending the email and then showing up here, him apologizing, and the way he looks. How serious and calm he is. Why didn't Mom say anything? She mustn't have known.*

Todd shifted and turned to Jerry, then back to Brad; his mind working a mile per minute. He thought they must be the first ones to be told.

*Poor Lori and the kids. What are they gonna do? Sure, Lori works, but it isn't enough to support the three of them here in San Jose.*

Before Todd could stop himself, he yelped out, "Oh my God, you're dying! That's why you're here. You're sick, and you've come to make peace. How can this be happening? Brad, I'm so sorry. What happened? How long do you have?" His eyes started to fill with tears.

"Todd, take a breath. You're all over the place." Jerry squeezed his hand.

He tried to breathe. "I can't believe this. You're an ass, but you don't deserve this—"

"Toddy, I'm not sick," Brad interrupted. "Do you hear me? I'm not sick and I'm not dying. God, what a freaking drama queen." He glanced over his shoulder out the front window, then focused back to them.

"Hey watch it! Don't talk to him like that. You did just show up out of nowhere."

"Sorry." Jerry held up his free hand.

"Plus, I'm the only one who can say that." Jerry let out a tight chuckle.

"Screw you both," Todd snapped. "This isn't funny. It's all part of the package. Anyway, what was I supposed to think? You come here all nice and apologetic. So who *is* dying?" Tears began to form in his eyes.

"Oh, for the love of... I'm sorry, okay? Listen, I'm not sick or dying. Lori isn't sick, and Kevin and Michelle are fine. Now, can I please finish without interruptions?"

*He's acting like he did when we talked about bad news as teenagers. What's going on?*

He felt Jerry put his hand on his shoulder and give it a squeeze. "Fine, go on," Todd said.

Jerry, out of habit, reached for the Kleenex on the coffee table and handed it to Todd. He took it and wiped at his eyes.

Brad changed the position of the now dripping bag of peas and damp towel on his lip. "Listen, I still have to go talk to Mom and Dad. There's a lot that has to be done before Monday."

Brad's eyes bounced back and forth between them and the clock on the wall. "I'm sorry for everything I've said and done, above all else your marriage and the fight. I should never have acted that way." He checked the window again. He spoke faster. "Look, I couldn't keep this from you guys. It made me realize what a dumbass I've been. It put things in perspective. Anyway, please, you need to be prepared even if there's barely any time."

Todd and Jerry shared an awkward glance.

"What the hell are you talking about? Time? What time? What's going on, Bradley? Prepare for what?"

*It's like being at work when someone needs to file a grievance. They never make sense at first and bounce around. It's annoying as hell.*

Todd frowned.

Jerry sat forward on the couch with both hands resting on his legs. "Come on, Brad, what's going on? Are you trying to sound insane? Or are *you* the real drama queen?"

Jerry grinned. "Nice one."

Brad ignored them. "Listen. Toddy, you and Jerry need to get things together. Something big is gonna happen. Hell, the whole fucking world is gonna change. I'm not convinced that they'll be able to keep a lid on things much longer.

"They?" Todd asked. "They who?"

Brad ignored the question. "I'm living proof of that. They've been so busy I took off and came here." He spoke with a greater sense of urgency. "Let me ask you this. Isn't it odd that three weeks ago the president said our troops would be in the Middle East for an unspecified amount of time?" He paused but didn't wait for a response.

"Now, look at the military." Brad leaned in. "They're pulling back troops to the States. Calling it 'troop rotations' and rewards for the hard work and sacrifices they've made. What about us pulling our troops from Europe and Asia?" He pointed in the general direction of the study. "Not all of them; that would be too much, I guess, and there would be too many questions. I'm sure they're trying keep it quiet." He stopped. "You've noticed, right?" he pleaded. "It started happening last week. Everyone's seen it, but nobody cares. Well, nobody who matters, anyway. Why?"

Todd shrugged, unimpressed by Brad's ramblings. Todd petted Bianca, who was resting contently unfazed by the whole affair. Much like Jerry, Bianca was a comfort to him. Her presence made him feel safe.

Todd's voice sounded more like he was reading from a teleprompter than actually speaking casually. "Of course, we have. I, well, we watch FOX News, CNN, and all of that. All the politicians and military advisors are saying the troops are doing better than planned." He shifted. "That the training, or whatever, was going well, and they wanted to give more of our troops leave. Even get them back home to their families. Not to mention the costs; they are doing this to help save the country money."

Brad shook his head, while Jerry nodded in agreement.

"In fact," Todd continued, "everyone at work is thrilled, well, except for Varick; he's worried about our government contracts. He pulled me into the office and wanted me to start examining our staffing numbers in case we have to make cuts. Considering our year, I doubt that will be an issue."

Jerry nudged him.

"Right," Todd focused. "Anyway, people at work are actually giving the president a bit of a break. Hell, even our dumbass Senator English has said a few nice things, and the Secretary of State, Martha Webster, has been everywhere towing the government line. Saying how good we're doing."

*He didn't like her, she always seemed too fake.*

Brad adjusted the peas, and his chin dropped.

"Brad, this is a good thing," Todd said. "Hell, both parties have been supportive. So what's the big deal?"

"Dammit, Todd! That's just it," Brad snapped. Bianca twitched her tail at Brad as he started talking louder. "No one is bad-mouthing the president, and the whole tone in Washington has changed, at least from what I've witnessed." He ran his free hand over the stubble on his face. "They've tabled their bickering, and they've been working together on a variety of domestic issues. And most of it has been behind closed doors, so people aren't aware of what's happening. It's like what Mom would do before people came to the house. Clean up what you can, and put away or hide what you can't."

"Brad, do you honestly think President Zachary would act secretively?" Todd crossed his arms in front of his chest. "He's supporting the troops while trying to get the cost of the military under control. That's all." He uncrossed his arms. "He's a good man. Doing what it takes to keep the military strong, and the economy from tanking, even if that makes him unpopular." He glanced over to Jerry and added, "Even if he doesn't like us gays. Anyway, what do you think is going on? You're rambling like a nut."

Lately, something did seem different now that Brad mentioned it. It was like everyone in the government was taking Prozac and singing Kumbaya. Troops were coming home faster and people were supporting the president. Yes, some of the media had said things, and there had been a few strange mentions on the net; however, they were mostly ignored. Wasn't it normal? Wasn't this type of background noise always going on?

"Todd, listen." Brad glanced over his shoulder before continuing, "Hell, they're getting so busy, they didn't even question me when I left my office. There isn't anything else I can do anyway, so they were kinda glad to see me go, I guess. The only reason I'm involved is because I was talking to the guys on the International Space Station. They were the first to hear from the ships."

Todd and Jerry stared at each other. Jerry sank back into the couch. Todd moved forward as the cat jumped off, giving him a dirty look. "Ships?" They asked in unison.

Brad crossed his arms and continued speaking fast, the damp towel and bag of peas now resting on his lap. "I don't have all the details. But there will be an announcement Monday night by President Zachary. It hasn't been publicized yet, and once he speaks, people are gonna freak out." Brad leaned closer to Todd. "You and Jerry need to make sure you have food, water, and everything you need for a couple of days. God, when this hits, people are gonna panic."

Jerry went to speak, but Todd grabbed his hand out of fear, and to keep him from interrupting. Jerry crossed and uncrossed his legs. Once his feet were on the ground again the heel of his foot started to tap on the floor as his leg shook.

"The military," Brad continued, "from what I can put together, are back to help keep the peace. The military came in and locked us down after we reported the news to our boss at NASA. They kept a bunch of men and officers there watching us. We couldn't even change or get fresh clothes. They locked us up tight. Anyway, they're staging in and around large metropolitan areas. Including the Bay Area. They can deploy in an hour, possibly two. At least, that's what the officers were saying. Those bastards weren't even following their own orders; some of them were making calls to their families, warning them, but not saying why. It's been nuts."

Brad took a slow breath and forced a smile. "Just call in sick on Monday. Stay here, go to Costco. Get what you need for a week, perhaps longer. The estimate is that it'll take a couple of days for people to settle and for the country's assets to be secured." Brad collapsed back on the chair, watching for their reactions.

"Brad, what the hell are you talking about?" Todd asked. "Did I hit you that hard? You're starting to freak me out. You sound crazy." He leaned in. "And since when are you buddy-buddy with military officers who've got this kind of access?"

Reaching out, placing a hand on Brad's leg, and watching him, Todd's gaze softened. "Are things okay at work?" He turned to Jerry and then back to Brad. "Is it possible you're having a nervous breakdown?"

"Todd, I'm fine. I'm not having a breakdown. Listen, I get that it sounds scary. Hell, I'm freaking out, but I don't anticipate there's anything to be afraid of. I promise." Brad took a couple of breaths to try to relax. "This is real. Listen, focus on how you feel at this moment. Imagine everyone else when they get this news. You know how people are. Hell, you work in human resources; you deal with irrational people on a daily basis. Now amplify it by adding aliens." Brad took the towel from his lap and moved it to his still red mouth and jaw. "The religious nuts will go to town, I'm sure, not to mention the potential of new hate groups popping up. Todd, the military will have the situation under control, but you need to be prepared."

Jerry shook his head, and Todd wasn't sure where to focus as Brad continued, "Todd, we aren't alone. They're out there right now. They're in different types of ships. At least, that's what the guys on ISS said. They're aliens—real live people from another planet." Brad's words fell from his mouth, and the more he spoke, the more his body tensed.

Jerry had pursed lips and a furrowed brow. Todd sighed. Jerry wasn't buying into any of this, but Todd wasn't so sure. There were a lot of odd things that had happened over the past week. Most importantly, Brad talked right to him, not dogging him. His body was open and every movement he took matched what he was saying.

*Oh my God. Is this possible? Brad can't lie. Not like this. I could tell.*

"Brad, I want you—"

"To what, Todd?" Brad stopped him. "I know how I sound. They closed all communication with the space station and sealed the observatories that can see them. I don't know if any of the other countries know yet. But they must. I tried to contact a counterpart of mine in the UK—he works for the European Space Agency. He said they had a terrorist scare, and they were evacuated. It's been a week. Why wouldn't they let them back in? A terrorist scare that takes a full week to sort out? Tell me that doesn't mean something. And that's not all! There are some of the independent observatories that have mysteriously gone silent."

Jerry shifted on the couch. "Come on, it's nothing. I mean, I'm sure it's not—"

"Are you?" Todd interrupted, "Are you sure about anything right now? Because, Jerry, I'm not."

"When the military came in, I was able to talk to Lori, but I couldn't say anything. I had to make up a story so she wouldn't worry. Toddy, I had a fucking MP standing next to me when I talked to her." Brad raked his hands through his hair. "Anyway, everyone at the office was put under house arrest, like me. But today they let us go. Well, they didn't stop us when we left."

"I finally got to see my family, and I convinced Lori. Thank God. I'm sure it was only because she loves me and because I've been gone all week. I haven't even showered yet." Brad leaned back in the chair. "I sent her off to the store before I came here. You can call her or text her to prove I'm not nuts. Hell, try texting anyone on my work contact list. Good luck reaching them. Toddy, things are gonna change. I hope it's gonna be amazing."

Jerry's head shook.

"Brad, are you on drugs?" Todd tried to find another answer for this. It was too outrageous to be real, even with the strange things they heard on the news. And he did read of the sudden shutdown of the Mauna Kea Observatory for maintenance. Still, the little voice in the back of his head told him to believe his brother.

*Could we be that blind?*

Todd's fingers tingled. He was squeezing Jerry's hand a little tighter than he intended. Jerry moved his hand, giving it a quick shake. "Come on, Brad, do you honestly think the government could keep this quiet? It's not possible. The internet. Social media. Trust me, it would get out."

"The government's been able to keep this quiet because it's happened so quickly, and the ships are still too far off." Brad stopped a moment before speaking. "Todd, do you believe me?"

"What about the internet?" Jerry demanded. "People can use their telescopes and take photos. Post them online. What about that?"

"And would you believe them? How many fake UFO reports are on the net? All the false video. No one pays attention to that stuff," Brad said. "Anyway, the ships are too far off for photographs snapped on your phone."

All Todd's education and training told him Brad wasn't lying. He heard the concern and the sincerity in his voice. No matter how crazy it sounded, Brad was telling the truth. As far-fetched as it sounded.

Todd glanced at Jerry, knowing he, too, had been having trouble digesting the whole story.

Jerry rubbed his eyes. "Brad, this is a lot to swallow. I mean, granted, there have been crazy things going on, but that's nothing new. What do you expect us to say? Do you want us to accept this without question? You haven't spoken to Todd in years, and now you're here with this story."

"I'm convinced," Todd said softly.

"Oh, come on!" Jerry turned to him. "You can't be serious?"

"Jerry," Todd started, "Brad is many things, asshole included. But he wouldn't make up something like this. He was always honest, and a big tattletale, getting me into trouble whenever I did something wrong."

"Hey!" Brad barked.

"I'm sorry," Jerry said. "Todd. Come on, he's joking...this...this can't be real. Your brother is—"

"You don't know me." Brad took a deep breath. "I don't expect you to buy this, but it's the truth. God knows it's the truth."

Jerry rubbed his face as he leaned back. "I get you want to apologize and make things better, but this story can't be real. This is crazy talk. Come on, it can't be."

"Okay, Brad, I believe you." Todd wished Jerry knew his brother like he did, or thought he did. "Jerry, he's my brother. I'm asking you to trust him. If not for him, then please do it for me. And Bradley, if it's some joke..." He fell silent.

The worry all over Jerry's face made Todd's heart sink. What could Todd do? This was his brother, and his gut told him it was the truth. He could make Jerry understand. He had to at least try. "What else do we need to do?"

# Four: Last-Minute Reservations

NODDING, MIRTOFF TURNED toward Danu. They had been reviewing her schedule and the coming event for hours. There was much to plan for, and she was worried. They were worried. The whole of the Nentraee civilization was relying on this going well.

*And I still have to deal with General Gahumed and her proposal.*

Danu's head tilted as he focused on the meeting details. His hand lifted from the datapad, and he brushed a piece of hair back over his ear. He was a handsome enough Altraee male and represented his clan well; his black hair and bright green eyes always seemed to bring a smile to everyone's face—even hers. But right now, this was a distraction. She had to pay attention to her duties, not to an attractive member of her staff.

"Madam Speaker." Danu checked his datapad. "The leaders of Earth want to move the schedule up by one of their days. They're trying to get in front of rumors."

"Of course," Mirtoff said. Security was at the top of the list. Everything they'd seen in Earth media over the last several months warned them that these humans didn't value life the same way the Nentraee did. There was no telling what would happen when their arrival was announced. She would need to be more guarded than she had hoped. If they had another option, a better option than this world, she would take it. But the ships were getting old, and her people were restless—they had been in space for too long.

They needed this.

She went through the revised schedule and updated human timeline. "It appears the changed timeline won't affect our preparations. It is their announcement and our introduction to their people. I still want us to take our later dealings with them as slowly as possible. I don't want to rush into anything." Mirtoff shifted in her chair. "At least not until enough time has passed, allowing the Earthlings to understand the situation and grow accustomed to our new shared reality."

Tapping her fingers, she changed the information on her device to the venue. She had hoped to have the first meeting with the humans in the new diplomatic ship Mi'ko had constructed; however, they wouldn't be able to accommodate the number of people to be included.

*We wasted resources building the ship and now it sits.*

She swiped the image of the diplomatic ship out of her view.

*With luck, it'll be useful once our two peoples become accustomed to each other.*

"Very well." Mirtoff put the datapad down. "I expect you to ensure the details are worked out before we go." The cool of her desk chilled her hands as she rested them. "I don't want to go in showing force, but I want to be prepared if need be. Please make sure General Yee Awon is in contact with both our shuttle and our people on the ground."

Danu made notes.

"That said, I want to keep my personal escort small: no more than two guards," Mirtoff concluded.

Danu's eyes were wide and his typically full lips thinned into a firm line. "What of the humans' most recent schedule change?" His face didn't reflect the worry in his voice.

"At this point, it's up to the Earthlings on how to address our first introduction." She reached over to the docking port on her desk, pulled out a fresh datapad, and tapped. "We've had to trust them so far. Unlike General Gahumed, I see no reason to not continue along this course of action. Our stream has been calm so let us continue in good faith that it will remain so. I don't want to be like Gahumed who only trusts her clan, and even then, not all of them."

Danu nodded his agreement.

"Plus, if I left the planning to her, we would meet them armed, showing force, and not try to trade for resources."

"Which is why you're our Speaker, not her." Danu finished his notes.

*He is too generous with his praise.*

Mirtoff turned to gaze out the office window, their worn-out ships and Earth off in the distance. She saw Danu glance at her in the reflection.

With a soft sigh, Danu left the office as Mi'ko walked through the door. The two males couldn't be any more different. Danu was young and had the physique of a Head Security Aide; his clothes showed his toned and muscular form. Mi'ko could have been Danu's father. He had the body of an older man who spent a great deal of time behind a desk and got little physical exercise. His suit was loose, to hide the bulges and softness of his body. They offered each other a polite bow as they passed. The door closed between them.

Mi'ko came more into the reflection, reminding her of the day he brought news of the humans. Today, they had a new set of worries. He poured a cold cup of tuma. The edges of her mouth softened. He didn't like the sweet and spicy taste of the drink. He was pouring it for her.

*He knows me well.*

"Where's Faa?" Mi'ko saw the empty couch.

"He doesn't handle my stress well. So he elected to stay with my brother and niece until this introduction is over. The poor thing." She turned from the window.

"I know you're worried. There's a great deal at risk." Mi'ko handed her the cooled cup.

The scent filled her lungs with that familiar tingle she enjoyed. She took a sip. "Wouldn't you be?"

He took a seat.

She sipped her tuma, then said, "As General Gahumed has been pointing out for months now, the humans are barbaric." Mirtoff shook her head. "They kill each other and think nothing of it. Even their entertainment shows violence and disregard for life. How they've managed not to destroy themselves up to this point is amazing. We've not seen anything like it." She put down the cup. "Even now, they fight, and we can do nothing. They have the societal plagues our world had before the Clan War." She huffed. "It pains me, but for once, I agree with General Gahumed. We should limit our contact. Scientific and diplomatic contact to start."

Mi'ko nodded.

"They're capable of many great things, but the fighting..." She sighed. "I don't understand them."

"It's not our home. They are far from perfect. They must learn, like our people. We were not always peaceful."

"We almost destroyed ourselves back then." She pursed her lips. "I know we've been over this many times before, but I'm worried. What if us showing up causes the least open-minded of them to do something drastic? We could prompt them to have their own Clan War."

Mirtoff skimmed the various reports on her desk—everything they had gathered on Earth and the humans, much of it from their UN organization. An attempt by Earth to form a global government: United Nations. From what they had learned, it was not an overly useful organization. *If it were up to me, I would abolish it.* Her eyes closed. That wasn't her decision; it wasn't her home.

She sipped her drink, cooling her nerves. "What if I'm the Speaker General that allows our race to die off because of these beings? Because I fought to trust them and work with them. Then a single human decides to end it and ends us as well."

"Mirtoff, there's hope. Not all of the information we've gathered is pessimistic. They've accomplished a great deal. They went from learning to fly and then to space in under seventy years. It took us almost double that time. As a society, they help each other when there is a local disaster. Even in their poorest areas, they've improved life expectancy. Humans are able to cure several terrible diseases. They have much to be proud of. This is the safest and wealthiest time in their history."

She rested her hands on the desk. "You believe in them?"

"I still have concerns, of course," Mi'ko said. "They seem to protest over many trivial matters. Even in their most stable regions, citizens fight with law enforcement and riot, and they seem very sensitive, easy to offend and not allowing for an open exchange of differing opinions." He glanced up at her. "But, I believe in their potential."

Mirtoff received reports from some of the most powerful domains on the planet. Each culture was different. "There are two hundred and three countries on Earth, and most of them compete with each other in one way or the other. The ones that don't fight only pretend to be friendly. People are starving in some areas of their world, and in others, they seem to consume all there is to eat. It's shameful; they could feed all their people. The ability is there now, and yet they choose not to." She rubbed her temples. "Maybe we should pass them up and move on. There are other resource-rich systems and worlds. Even Faa has lost his excitement, the poor little one. The more I learn of them, the more I'm unsure of my choice."

Mi'ko met her gaze. "Madam Speaker Mirtoff, I've never known you to make a bad decision." He paused and reached up to fix his tieback and address the lopsided bow. "We picked these humans because their level of development is almost in line with ours. We have found that not only do they value technology, but we also share some of the same precious metals and jewels. They are more advanced in some areas and less in others. This gives us a way into Earth's markets, should they approve. And more importantly, from a biological point of view, we are similar."

His lips hinted at a grin. "The potential to trade and learn from each other is great when the bridge is equal distance. Don't you agree?"

Mirtoff sensed the lines on her face softening.

"They have space capabilities," Mi'ko continued. "An orbiting platform, and they've been to their own satellite. There are human probes on the planet they call Mars and elsewhere in their solar system."

Mi'ko rested his hands on her table. "No other beings we've encountered have been this developed. I believe this to be the best option. Everyone is getting excited to meet and interact with them." Mi'ko stood up and bowed in support. "You've done well, and the choice to be here is done in the best interests of both the Nentraee and the humans. I'm sure J'Veesa would not have led us here otherwise."

"You've always had a level head, Mi'ko." Mirtoff rubbed the back of her neck. "I can see why Laina was joined to you and allowed you to raise her children. Thank you."

Picking up one of her datapads, Mirtoff pulled up a file. "We've identified upward of seven thousand languages on this world. Who has heard of such a thing? It's impossible to learn them all," she said in amazement. "We should focus on their main languages: Chinese, Spanish, and English."

"Remarkable, but to be fair, I'm more interested in learning about their technology." Mi'ko scanned the office. "They have unique organic and synthetic polymers. These are things I've never heard of or seen before. Think of the benefits to our people with what we could trade and acquire. We have a chance to change our economy and grow in prosperity."

"Ever the industrialist, Mi'ko." Mirtoff picked up her cup of tuma and finished it.

Mi'ko's crooked tieback was loose again. He reached to fix it. "I'm afraid so, Madam Speaker."

Shifting through the datapads on her desk—food, military, weather, culture, family, religion, biology, others—she pulled one out. "There are many technology centers on their planet with a few highly advanced areas. The United States of America's western boundary is a large hub for scientific and industrial development, according to these reports."

Mi'ko nodded his agreement. "As is much of the United States." He took the offered datapad. "They seem to be the politically dominant country, for good and bad," he said, then added, "There are others who, I believe, are as dominant—Russia, China, Japan, India and many of the countries in what they refer to as Europe." His eyes twinkled and the lines on his face seemed to vanish. "I've had Weaqu and GanCee busy with research. I want to know everything about their superior optics, advanced biometrics, and their uses of these new polymers. Who knows what other areas of technology they have that we have not researched; it's fascinating."

The longer Mi'ko spoke, the more relaxed Mirtoff became. Hearing his excitement and his optimism was catchy, and she was grateful for it. "I should have figured as much." The edges of her lips turned up and her eyes opened wider. "How many languages have you learned, Mi'ko?"

He offered her a smile as an answer but said nothing else. She would let him keep his secret. "Where do you plan on focusing?"

"We'll contact their centers of technology, of course, but I want to start in the United States. There is an area called Silicon Valley—an intriguing place with its research and development. It reminds me of my home city of OoNowa on Benzee. I'll start there."

Mirtoff's cheeks raised in a warm smile as she turned to the window. Earth waited off in the distance.

# Five: The Plan

JERRY COULD ROLL his eyes all he wanted. It didn't matter what Jerry thought right now. Brad had regained Todd's trust.

"Monday, stay home. Don't go to work." Brad rubbed his hands on his legs. "Mom and Dad will stay with Lori and me. Just for a few days. Jerry, it would be a good idea to check in with your family, because once this hits, the phone lines are gonna be jammed."

Jerry only offered a curt nod.

"I don't think you should tell them anything, but make sure they have what they need," Brad offered.

"Don't worry." Jerry crossed his arms in front of his chest. "I won't be sharing this info with anyone."

"If the phones don't go crazy, I'll give you a call on Monday. We can see how things go from there."

"I hate to bring this to your attention, Todd, but what are we going to do with Dan?" Jerry asked. "He'll be here tomorrow. What are we supposed to tell him?" His voice shifted higher and squeaked. "Ah...sorry, Dan. Aliens are coming. We have to stay home, or they'll eat our brains."

"Who's Dan?" Brad asked.

"He's a friend of ours," Todd explained. "He wants to stay with us a few days."

"Ah, well that shouldn't be a big deal." Brad checked the clock on the wall. "Listen, I've got to head to the folks' house. Toddy, tell me you'll stay home on Monday. You too, Jerry, just to be safe, please. I want to make sure my baby brother and his family are safe."

Jerry sighed. "Fine."

"We'll stay home on Monday." Todd's jaw was set in determination. "All three of us will stay home."

Jerry remained quiet, keeping his arms crossed in front of his chest.

Brad stood with Todd.

"By the way, what was in the email you sent me?" Todd asked.

Brad sniffed as his cheeks lifted into an awkward smile, "Oh, that. I knew you didn't read it, judging by how surprised you were to see me." He paused, "You realize you need to work on not holding a grudge, little brother."

"Pot. Hi. This is kettle." Todd glared at him.

"Anyway, dick, perhaps you should try addressing things head-on. Like I am now." His face changed into their mother's favorite expression—the one she used when he had gotten in trouble for eating the dried dog food as a kid.

Todd's chin dropped as he glanced at the hardwood floor.

"All it said was 'I owe you an apology. Something big is happening, and I need to talk to you. I'll come see you as soon as I can.'"

"So, basically, a cryptic, annoying note that would've pissed me off. Got it." Todd tried to hide his embarrassment with a grin.

With a half smile on his lips, Jerry nodded. "Look, Brad, I don't want Todd to get hurt. This better not be some trick or something. He deserves better than that. Especially from his family and you. He's trusting you but—"

"I know," Brad interrupted him calmly.

"Jerry, I realize this is hard for you," Todd said. "Please, just do this for me. Please."

The room was silent.

"God, I'm sorry. I can never recover that lost time, and I feel like shit for it. Not again. Never again." Brad enveloped Todd in a hug. His arms tightened almost painfully. "I love you so much, Toddy."

"I love you, too, Bradley, but you're on probation. I don't want to hear any dumb crap anymore."

"Not anymore." Brad held up his hands. "I was so stupid, and all my bigotry did was strain our relationship. I realize that now."

"I'm sorry about your jaw and lip." Todd rubbed his goatee-covered chin as if he had a sympathetic pain there. He took the thawed peas and damp, reddish-stained towel from his brother. "Did you want more ice or something?"

"Nah, I'm good." Brad rubbed his jaw. "Lori isn't gonna be pleased, but I'm pretty sure she'll get over it."

"You're one hell of a guy." Brad turned to Jerry. "I didn't see it before. I guess, I pictured you as one of those overly dramatic drag queens." Jerry's eyebrows raised and Brad shrugged. "I was an ass. Anyway, you must be special to have captured my baby brother's heart. I'm sorry. I should've been a bigger man, and treated you—" He paused, shame in his voice. "—as you deserved."

Jerry opened his mouth to speak, but Brad held up his hand, stopping him. "I understand I've asked a lot of you, not only to forgive me, but also to trust me and my crazy story. I hope you'll do both. There really is an alien fleet out there, and I think it's gonna change everything. I'm not crazy." He grinned mischievously. "Well, maybe a bit. I'll let you figure that out on your own."

"I guess bad humor runs in the family." Jerry's expression lightened toward Brad, and he stuck out his hand to shake.

Brad pulled him in for a hug. Jerry's body stiffened for a moment, then relaxed.

As Brad left, the locked clicked, securing the door. Todd focused on where his brother had just stood, his thoughts bouncing around his head like a ball in a pinball machine.

"Todd?" Jerry said.

Todd faced Jerry and they headed back to the living room in silence. Picking up the remote, Jerry unmuted the TV and flipped through the channels. There were no special reports.

"Thank you for doing this, for believing him." Todd snuggled closer to Jerry on the couch, resting his head on his shoulder.

Putting down the remote, Jerry moved his shoulder, so Todd sat up, "Come on, so what's the plan...Toddy?" His eyes narrowed. "I mean, really. What're we supposed to do? Hole up in the house and wait for...what? Assuming this isn't a big joke on the two of us."

"It's hard." Todd straightened up. "You don't know him, but Brad isn't lying or making this up. I suggest we do what he advised. I filled up my car, so I don't need gas. How's your car?"

"Come on," Jerry scowled. "You work for a high-tech company in human resources. You don't have a PhD in lying-ology. I mean, it's unbelievable. Honey, I love you, and I'm happy he apologized, but it can't be real."

Todd didn't want to push Jerry too hard. His aggravation would blow over. "We don't need to go to Costco—we have most of the things we'd need already. I'll drive to the store and pick up some fresh fruit and veggies." He glanced over at Jerry. "We needed to do that anyway with Dan coming. I'll go to the bank and get cash."

Jerry shook his head.

"None of this is gonna hurt us. If nothing happens, then at the very least my brother and I made up. And that makes everything else worth it."

"Fine." Jerry crossed his arms. "But this better not be some mean trick. You know, scare the fags. Especially after that drag queen remark. I've never even worn makeup."

Todd raked his teeth over his lower lip, catching bits of his goatee. "Dan hasn't called yet. My guess is we'll get a call tomorrow to pick him up. Is there anything else from the store I should get?"

"No." Jerry let out a sigh. "Well, taking Monday off could be a good idea. We'll get to spend more time with Dan." He raised an eyebrow at Todd. "I'll go get gas for my car. I'll take care of the bank, so we still have money to pay our bills. You can go to the store. I'm only doing this to make you happy." He headed to the study.

"Thank you."

Emerging with keys in hand, Jerry said, "When I get back, I'm going to finish the backyard, and you have some plants to water."

"I'll take care of the plants." Todd stopped Jerry before he got to the door. "What if this is real? Why now? What do they want? Could they be friendly? If it was something bad, wouldn't they attack us already? What do we do if they attack?"

"I've got no idea." Jerry's penetrating blue eyes bore into Todd. "And right now I can't consider what this means. I was planning on calling Mom tonight anyway, since Dan will be here, and we'll end up being busy with him." He gave Todd a peck on the cheek and was out the door, heading to his car, before Todd could question him further.

Todd stood alone in the living room and scanned the space, suddenly feeling vulnerable. With the front windows open, he heard Jerry's car start and pull away. The TV was still going. The conversation had shifted toward the stock market and business news. "Well, if it was the end of the world, they wouldn't be talking about the market now would they?"

Bianca walked from the study to behind the entertainment system, heading off to a cubby she liked to hide in and take naps. He frowned. Would this be like the movies, where the aliens came to conquer and enslave people? Would they be dead in three days? Or would they come to help? What would they be like? More importantly, would the government be able to keep people from going nuts?

Checking his watch, noting the time was 2:14 p.m., Todd sighed. "Well, in forty-eight hours, I'll get to find out. Isn't that right, Miss Kitty?" He glanced to where Bianca was hiding behind the TV console. So what if he sounded crazy? Lots of people talked to their pets, even if they weren't right there.

*It's not like they talk back.*

Locking the front door, Todd inhaled the smell of fresh cut grass then headed to his Jeep.

"Hey Todd, how's it going?"

After jumping out of his skin, Todd turned to see Steve, his neighbor, with his daughter nestled in his arms.

*I never remember her name. Amy? Sandra?*

He shook his head.

*It doesn't matter.*

He smiled and waved. "I'm good, Steve. How're you?" He tried his best to slow his breathing, and he wiped the sweat from his brow.

Steve let out a laugh as he shifted the baby from one arm to the other, "Oh we're good. Sorry to startle you. We're heading to the park to enjoy this sun."

Todd glanced up at the sky. "No worries. I was in another place." He focused his attention back on Steve. "Yep, it's a terrific day. It's why we live here, right?"

Steve mimicked Todd, checking out the sky. "You got that right." He lowered his eyes back to Todd. "Hey, you hear about the earthquake up at Mt. Hamilton?"

"Earthquake? No, why?"

"Yep. Didn't feel a thing here, but I guess it messed up the observatory's lens. They had to close the whole place for repairs," Steve said.

"I didn't hear that. When did it happen?"

"Couple days ago, I guess. I couldn't find anything on the USGS site, or on the news, but who knows? Technology, right?" Steve chuckled. "Well, I've got to get going. Sophie can only stand being held like this for so long. Say hi to Jerry for me." He shifted his daughter as he put her into the stroller.

"Take care, Steve. Bye, Sophie." He waved as Steve and his daughter walked down the street.

*Earthquake, my ass. They needed justification to close the observatory.*

He frowned as he listened to Steve hum "The Farmer in the Dell" as he pushed his daughter, unaware of what was coming.

Todd took in the neighborhood, watching the people going about their business: Mowing lawns, working on cars, playing with their kids, and for a second, he thought he should warn them. But what if Brad was wrong or going crazy? There could have been an earthquake. *It's possible.* He rubbed his goatee. After getting into the car, he turned on the radio to distract himself from his thoughts. "Hungry Eyes" filled the car. Soon, he was tapping his thumbs to the beat.

# Six: Shopping

TODD DRUMMED HIS fingers on the wheel as he drove to the store. Todd forced himself to sing along with the radio, ignoring the people who were out and about in the neighborhood. *Are there normally this many people out on Saturday?* He gave up on the song. The only beat he heard was the thumping of his heart.

At the corner, he noticed the Tamale Lady. She came to the neighborhood every few days with an old pushcart and red-lid cooler. He had always wanted to try one of her tamales but kept putting it off. It seemed trivial, but he had put off too many things too often in life already.

"There might not be any more tomorrows," Todd muttered. He went to reach for his wallet but stopped. It was just out of his reach. He pulled over to the side of the road, gave his horn a quick honk to get the woman's attention, and then leaned over to pick up his wallet.

Turning down the radio as she approached, he waited. She smiled as she hauled her cart over to him.

*How different her life must be.*

She sold food to the neighborhood while he worked in a comfortable office with a view of the mountains. He couldn't imagine having to work in a hot kitchen only to then pound the pavement for half the day under the blazing sun.

"How much?" His face relaxed as he watched her.

"Two dollars," she replied with a heavy Mexican accent.

"What kinds do you have?" He raised his voice as if to make his English more understandable and pointed at the tamales.

She thought for a moment and said, "Pork, beef, and cheese." The upbeat tone of her voice was friendly. She had deep-brown eyes with perfect eyebrows and shoulder-length brown hair. Her toothy, white smile contrasted with the deep olive tones of her skin.

*She's kind of pretty for her age.*

"Two pork and two cheese, please." He took a ten out, handed it to her, and he accepted the food. She went to give him change, but he stopped her with a wave of his hand. "Nope, that's for you. Thank you."

"*Gracias,*" she answered with her big bright grin. "Have a nice day." She started to push her cart back to the sidewalk.

As he rolled up his window, he heard her call out again, "Tamales."

*Well, something for supper.*

He got to the intersection preparing to turn left. Before he turned, two military trucks passed, heading in the direction of the observatory.

"What the hell?" he said, his heart skipping a beat.

He was surprised by the vacant spaces in the parking lot of the supermarket. The whole shopping complex seemed almost deserted. No one was honking or stopping suddenly when someone else backed out of a parking space. There weren't even shopping carts scattered around the lot.

It was a Saturday afternoon, and there were hardly any shoppers. Where was the person from the deli out barbecuing chicken and steaks? Or the groups of Girl Scouts selling cookies. No one was in the drive-through at the coffee place. Something wasn't right.

*Shouldn't it be busier?*

He checked the clock on the dashboard. His palms started to sweat and his heart sank. "No." He shook the thought from his mind. He needed to stop his mental torment. He thought of Jerry and tried to channel his husband's strength and composure.

*Where are you when I need you?*

He huffed.

*Why can't I be more like him?*

Todd nabbed a cart from an empty parking spot and put his empty shopping bags in it. Moving toward the store, he passed a woman who had her son in tow. He smiled at her and the little boy. The mother seemed distracted with her cell phone at her ear while digging in her purse, trying to find what Todd assumed were her keys, while her son played with a stuffed toy. The little boy beamed and waved at him.

"Hi!" he said, holding up his purple dragon. "I'm Roger, and this is Rufus."

"Hello." Todd caught the woman's eyes.

*Should I warn her? Would she think I'm insane? Probably. This whole thing is nuts. But what if it's real?*

She shifted and nodded at Todd as she pulled out her keys.

"Don't bother the man, Roger." She moved them over to her car.

"Bye!" Roger called out.

"Bye." Todd waved at the little boy. The boy had big, bright green eyes and dark hair with a tiny curl that fell on his forehead. *Cute kid.*

Todd made a mental list of all the things he wanted. Generally, he would go to the store needing a gallon of milk and end up coming home with four or five bags filled with different groceries they couldn't live without. He walked over to bins full of fresh, bright vegetables, glistening with dew from the sprinkler system. *There is so much here.* He didn't want to overdo. He filled his cart with broccoli caps, red potatoes, onions, apples, and strawberries.

While gazing at the bananas, it struck him this might be his last trip to the supermarket. If the aliens invaded, they would destroy the food distribution centers, water supplies, and the larger cities, including San Jose. That would be strategic planning on their part.

*How easy would it be for them to wipe us out? They're in space. How do you fight back against that?*

Trying to relax, he held onto the bag of bananas with shaking hands. "Okay, cool it! Relax," he whispered.

*You know it might not even be real. You're here to get what you need for Dan's visit. Look at all the people here in the store. Relax.*

He focused on the bananas and his breathing, forcing his hands to stop trembling. Nothing else was there. Just Todd, the bananas, and his breathing. The bananas faded, replaced by images of every alien disaster movie he had ever seen.

What hope would they have against an advanced alien race? None, and he knew it. Sweat poured from his forehead, and his heart banged in his chest. He focused on the bananas, but the other images filled his head. In and Out. He struggled to force himself to breathe. He wished his husband was here.

"Honey, are you okay?" a soft female voice asked. "You're as white as a ghost. Do you want me to call for some help?"

The voice pulled Todd back. He snapped out of it and saw an older woman and man examining him with worried expressions.

"No, I'm fine... I'm just a little lightheaded. Thank you." He grinned at them. "Just a headache." Their eyebrows grew closer together and their lips stretched thin with worry. He wanted to scream at them "Run! Get what you can! Leave! Go to the mountains! Hide!" Tell them everything Brad had told him. But to what end?

The woman turned toward her husband and then back at Todd. "Are you sure, dearie?" Her husband watched Todd as she spoke.

"Do you want water or something?" the older man asked. The kindness on his face helped to soothe the worry in his mind.

Finally, Todd forced himself to relax. His heart slowed its pace. "No, I'm good. Just a sudden sharp pain; it'll pass."

"If you say so, dearie," the older woman said, then reached out and patted his hand on the cart.

Relaxing his face, he wiped at his forehead. "Thank you, both."

Watching them walk off, he waved. "Yes, thank you," he whispered to himself. "You almost had a big lump of a man crying on the floor in the fetal position." He dropped the bananas into his cart. He didn't want to fall to pieces, at least not here in public. If the aliens were here to invade or attack, they would have already done so. Wouldn't they?

Todd finished his shopping. But before leaving, he remembered he needed ice.

He paid and got everything safely loaded into his car. He sat in the driver's seat, taking several deep breaths to calm down. He pushed away the thoughts of what would happen if there was an attack. Not being able to get to family or friends, probably separated from each other and dying alone. *Enough.* He took another deep breath. He didn't want to be a mess when he got home. It was embarrassing enough having the elderly couple see him fall apart.

Starting back home, he passed several more military trucks heading in the direction of the observatory. "What the hell?" he mumbled as they passed.

*The two from earlier. But this isn't normal. This isn't right. God, Brad's right. It's happening. What are we gonna do?*

When he got home and pulled into the driveway, he saw Jerry's car. The tension in his shoulders unwound immediately.

*Thank Christ.*

Jerry was home. His rock, his center was there. The man he had chosen to share the rest of his life with. Jerry wouldn't let him freak out. Jerry would keep him safe through this.

*What would I do without him?*

# Seven: Confrontation

MIRTOFF TAPPED HER fingers on the desk. She was heading to the Rádo to give Gahumed news on her human relocation plan that she would not be happy to hear.

*Gahumed's plan would cause a war with the humans and that was something none of them wanted.*

She inhaled. Gahumed had no problem suggesting taking advantage of a lesser species like she wanted to do before. Mirtoff could not allow that. Not with the humans of Earth; thank J'Veesa, all but Vi-Kamu and Gahumed agreed with her. Still, it wasn't going to make this task any less difficult, considering their history. Vi-Kamu didn't require a personal visit from her, but out of respect, Mirtoff was forcing herself to go and see Gahumed in person.

Mirtoff peered out the window. Seeing the Rádo with its heavy armaments and fighters coming and going from the three launch bays was magnificent. This ship, like the other military vessels, was ready at all times to ensure the safety of the civilian population and protect the fleet.

The Rádo was also the headquarters for the Nentraee Military. It was a modified Kĩ-Class Battle Cruiser that housed the General Command Offices. Should there ever be a conflict, this was where the generals and commanders would get their orders. It held seven-thousand military personnel and housed their special fleet of stealth ten-person actionships, the most deadly military craft they had.

*I hope to never need them.*

Mirtoff passed several uniformed personnel performing system checks and running drills. It was good to see as she made her way to General Gahumed's office. She didn't come to the Rádo very often, and when she did, it was mostly for inspections and morale.

Reaching the command offices, she approached the young female at the reception station.

"Madam Speaker, welcome to the Rádo." The female officer stood and bowed.

"Thank you."

"You honor us with your presence. I'll let the general know you're here." The officer returned to her seat and started tapping on her terminal.

Mirtoff examined the reception area; unlike the civilian ships, this place had a claustrophobic feel. It was built for function, nothing more. She remembered when the ship was under construction at the Candra Shipyards. They barely had the drives working prior to the evacuation. It took five additional years to complete, but the end result was worth it.

"Madam Speaker. You can go in." The officer bowed again.

Mirtoff bowed in return and proceeded into the general's office.

The office wasn't nearly as formal and polished as hers or the vice speaker's, but it was bigger.

*Probably needed to be this large for Gahumed's girth. Or perhaps her ego.*

Various monitors mounted on the walls ran status reports for ship-to-fleet control. This one office could manage the majority of the task force. The monitors displayed only the Nentraee Government Seal. The design comprised of seven gold patterns, each a symbol for one of the clans.

A bank of windows on the back wall showed a view of the internal command center. A large workstation loomed nearby, as did chairs and the conference table that could hold all the generals comfortably for any type of meeting. In this large space, the colors were drab.

*I'm not a soldier. I could never work in a place like this. There needs to be plants or color. Something.*

"Madam Speaker." Gahumed offered a curt bow as she stood from her desk. She was a big woman, born for the military, with broad shoulders and a tall frame. Mirtoff was always impressed with how the general managed to keep her brown hair in such snug braids and an even tighter bun.

"General Gahumed. You run a remarkable ship. You should be proud."

"I'm honored to have such a post within our government." She tapped her workstation. "Dála, please, bring in two chilled cups of tuma." She turned to Mirtoff. "You enjoy tuma, correct?"

"Of course."

Gahumed pointed to the conference table. "Please, come. Let us sit."

Taking a seat at the table, Mirtoff waited for Gahumed to join her. "I assume you're here to talk about my suggested plan for dealing with these humans?" Gahumed almost hissed out the word 'humans.'

"I am." Mirtoff pulled out her datapad and loaded the information, then swiped it over to the largest of the monitors on the wall. The image started with the Earth rotating. Once it hit the area of the planet she wanted, she zoomed in on a small island continent. The image moved in closer to a smaller island mass off the island continent's coast. "Your proposal to occupy the area known to the humans as New Zealand is dangerous."

"I don't agree." Gahumed rested her hands on the table. "I picked that area with defense in mind. It's remote. The land mass is small enough, and we can easily control the surrounding space. They have a limited population of four point six million that can be relocated to Uztralia—"

"I believe they call it Australia," Mirtoff interrupted.

"Regardless, they share a similar language and background. I don't see an issue." Gahumed brought up demographic information of her own. "New Zealand can be made to become sustainable for our needs and allow us business options with the humans."

"A forced relocation won't work." Mirtoff's ears started to swell and warm up.

*Relax. Don't let this plan anger you.*

Mirtoff took a breath. "How will that help us build a positive enough relationship with them so we can conduct trade?"

"We could offer them helium-3 for the territory," Gahumed countered.

"And what if the Australians don't want four point six million new humans?"

"Why not?" Gahumed smirked. "They have the land mass, and from the reports, the two territories have good relations."

"The issue, as I understand it, is none of Earth's governments are willing to give up their territory to us—"

"Madam Speaker," Gahumed interrupted, "they are a barbaric species that fight among themselves for land all the time."

"And how would we be any different?"

"It's not the same thing," Gahumed said.

*It's exactly the same thing. You don't want to see it. You're a hypocrite.*

"We can't trust them." Gahumed swiped her hands over her datapad. "They won't work with us in peace and certainly we can't trust them to be truthful with their motives. Despite what you and the vice speaker may think. We can easily go there and use our military to take over the area. Then we move the humans and make reparations." She picked up her datapad. "Denes and my staff have run the scenario based on the information we've gathered. The losses were negligible." She swiped the data up to the monitor.

"Yes, General Gahumed, I'm sure the work of your son is admirable and perfect." She rubbed the tips of her ears. "Just like him—"

"Are you mocking the abilities of my son? He is a fine male with a brilliant military mind. He is the type of male that every Nentraee of his gender should strive to be." Her full lips pulled into a stiff line, and her ears started turning an angry shade of blue.

"Of course, General Gahumed, he's the perfect male. Unlike all others. We are all aware of this fact." Mirtoff forced her gaze not to move from the general's. How poor Denes lived with the pressure for perfection was impressive.

*It's possible, on that fact alone, he may actually be perfect.*

"I don't appreciate your tone, and as a full member of the Speaker's House, I would expect better." Gahumed didn't bother to hide the tips of her ears.

*This isn't going well.*

"My apologies." Mirtoff offered a stiff bow. "You want to go to war with the humans for territory? That is not the way of J'Veesa."

"Don't assume to understand J'Veesa's will. Your people don't have the relationship with J'Veesa that mine do." Gahumed's ears flared.

Mirtoff kept quiet.

*Your people. My people. What is the difference? J'Veesa sees us equally.*

Gahumed swiped information to the largest monitor. Battle statistics filled the screen. "I don't consider it a war, more of a forced relocation. We'll be fine."

"And if they decide to involve other countries?" Mirtoff rested her datapad on the table. "Then what? It'll be the Clan Wars all over again. Haven't—" She stopped and her chin dropped to her chest.

*We've been through that once on our world. How can we force that on another?*

"It'll be nothing like the Clan Wars." Gahumed sat taller in the seat. "Once, these humans see our military might, they won't challenge us. They would lose even if they used their strongest military deterrents. It would be nothing like the slaughter that your clan caused back then."

Mirtoff's eyes shot up. "The Za'entra? They were fighting back your clan because they had no choice. Your clan and the Martween and U'Zraee clans were slaughtering them. It was only because of their numbers that they were able to endure. How can you say—"

"I speak the truth." Gahumed slammed her hands on the table, causing it to shake. "You and your clan have always blamed us for that war. We never started it—"

The soft chirp of the door interrupted them. They both turned as Dála entered, holding a tray with two cups on it. She quietly placed a cup in front of each of them and left the room.

"I'm sorry, General Gahumed." Mirtoff stood, the tips of her ears on fire. "I appreciate your proposal. However, I came to inform you that your suggested plan for New Zealand has been rejected. We will not risk war with the humans to gain territory." She glanced at the tuma and then back to Gahumed. "I appreciate the offer of the cup of tuma. However, I'm afraid I can't stay."

"This is a mistake, Mirtoff." Gahumed stood. "You'll see when they resist the arm of peace that you and others in the Speaker's House extend to them. My idea is the only one that can guarantee the safety of our people."

"No, General. I would sooner leave this planet than go in and slaughter them." Mirtoff headed out of the office, her hands in tight fists.

*There is a peaceful solution. I need to find it and keep the military generals from forcing us into an armed confrontation. I won't be the first speaker general to go to war with an alien race.*

# Eight: Hints of Things to Come

TODD FROWNED. HE wasn't pleased by Jerry's teasing.

"I can't believe you freaked out at the store like that." Jerry shook his head. "I mean, I'm glad you're all right and made it home. But, honey, you can be such a..." He paused. "Well, a drama queen. You get yourself so worked up. I'm surprised they didn't call 911." He put the last of the ice in the freezer.

"That's what you're focusing on?" Todd crossed his arms.

Jerry faced Todd. "I love you. I do. And I accept you for your quirks just like you accept me, but Todd, it's going to be fine. Nothing is going to happen. Brad probably misunderstood, or it's stress."

"What about what Steve said? What about the military trucks heading up to Mount Hamilton? Not one group of trucks but two? Jerry, this is real. Something big is going on."

Jerry was silent for longer than what Todd hoped for. He finally spoke, but his voice was gentle. "Fine, but there's nothing we can do. I mean, it's out of our control. We've done what we can." Jerry unpacked the last of the grocery bags putting the bananas away. "We still don't have all the facts, and I'm still not buying the whole alien story. Sorry."

"Unbelievable." Todd slumped.

"Oh, now stop. I'm not picking on you. You overreact all the time." He wrapped his arms around Todd and kissed his cheek. "I love you so much, but I'd hate to depend on you in an emergency," he admitted with a light-hearted smile. "I could see you fall to pieces. Needing to be rescued by a big, strong fireman. He'd have to throw that big, sexy ass of yours over his shoulder, carrying you to safety. All the while, you'd be kicking and screaming."

Todd didn't respond. He continued frowning.

"What? Don't glare at me; it's true. This is why we're together. We complement each other. You're the sensitive one and I'm the pain-in-the-ass realist. Plus, you like firemen. Who doesn't?"

"Whatever." Todd pushed Jerry off, taking a few steps away and stopping with his hands on his hips.

Jerry pointed to Todd.

"Oh, shut up." Todd lowered his hands. He decided it was best to change the subject before he got angry, "So, what did your folks say?"

Jerry jumped up on the counter, holding out his arms.

*If you think I'm gonna come over there and lean against you, you can forget it.*

"I didn't tell them, because I didn't need to. Mom and my aunt spent the whole day shopping. I figured they'd be fine, assuming this is even real."

Todd kept his mouth shut.

"I mean, can you imagine their reaction?" Jerry said. "They'd think I went nuts. Anyway, it was best for them not to know." His mouth formed a gentle smile. "Sweetie, they have everything they need; it'll be fine. My mom is always prepared with her canning and huge Costco-sized bags of flour and all that. Plus, my aunt has her 'Mormon bunker' filled with everything they could possibly need for a year."

Sadly, Jerry was right; telling them would be a nightmare no one needed. Todd hated when Jerry was right. It wasn't natural. It was that stupid practical realistic side that he both loved and hated at the same time.

"Did you at least make sure your aunt and uncle would be around on Monday?" Todd rested against the opposite counter.

Jerry hopped down from where he was sitting. He put his hands around Todd's waist. "Yes, dear. They're going to be around. In fact, it's kinda funny, because the cousin's lunch was canceled." Jerry paused. "Anyway, the four of them are still planning on lunch together and watching some new video that my cousin put together."

Todd embraced him and met his gaze.

"They'll be together all day. Does that make you happy?"

Todd felt Jerry's breath on his face. "Yes, yes it does."

Jerry gave him a kiss.

"Well, we've gotten our to-dos complete." Todd released Jerry. Why don't I go finish with the stuff in the yard—"

"I just put the tools away," Todd interrupted, his voice dragging.

"Oh boohoo."

Todd had to force himself not to smile.

*He's trying to get me to focus on other things so I don't freak out again.*

Heading to the back door, he stopped and then slipped on his shoes. Jerry added, "That'll give you a chance to figure out what you're going to cook to go along with the tamales." He raised his eyebrows. "Unless that's all we're planning on eating tonight."

"Fine. I'll figure something out." He rubbed the back of his neck as the patio door closed.

DINNER WAS QUIET. Todd had expanded on the Mexican theme and made tacos to go with the tamales. He dropped his napkin onto the plate. "All right, those tamales were good." He patted his belly. "We should've tried them sooner."

"Well, now we know, and your tacos were the perfect complement." Jerry stretched a bit before he got up and collected the plates. "Come on, let's get this put away and cleaned up."

They were busy with cleanup, not paying attention to the television, until they recognized what sounded like a special bulletin. Getting into the living room, they fell silent watching the TV. Reporters jockeyed for attention from the press secretary in the White House briefing room.

"If they're going to make an announcement, isn't it usual for the press secretary to tell us what the topic is?" one of the reporters questioned, her voice raised so she could be understood. "Particularly one called without advance notice."

"The president informed me about the address an hour ago," Press Secretary Frank Chen said to a visibly annoyed member of the press. "The president will address the nation and Congress tomorrow night at eight eastern time."

Jumping on the end of his sentence, a female reporter shouted, "Does this have to do with the troop movements in Europe and Asia?"

"Yes, President Zachary will be addressing the troop rotations and provide an update on military movements," Chen answered. "Next question, please."

Todd turned to Jerry who was focused on the television. He would have thought he was a statue if it wasn't for his breathing.

"What about FEMA?" A female reporter yelled at the press secretary to get his attention. "FEMA has been reported outside of Hartsfield-Jackson Atlanta International Airport, Los Angeles International, and Chicago O'Hare. They report they are conducting practice disaster emergency responses, but reports say they look like they are staging for something."

Chen's face brightened with a smile. "FEMA conducts regular joint exercises with city and state officials all the time. Those are the three busiest airports in the country. It only makes sense for FEMA to practice disaster response with them on occasion to ensure we are prepared. Next question."

"Will the president—" A male reporter leaped out of his seat to be heard over the other reporters shouting for attention. "—address the reports of the UN peacekeepers going in and sealing the Roque de Los Muchachos Observatory on the Canary Islands? We've been told that the White House made the request. Is that true?"

"I have no information on that," Chen answered sharply. He nodded to an aide, "Last question." He pointed to another reporter.

The older reporter stood. "We've heard reports that President Zachary has been meeting privately with several leaders in Europe. He's also met with the Japanese Prime Minister, the Prime Minister of Australia, and the Chinese Premier. Is he going to be announcing a shift in our strategy toward China?"

"As you know, the president meets with world leaders on a regular basis—"

"All in the last week?" the older reporter interrupted.

"As I said, the president meets with world leaders on a regular basis. He is not announcing any shifts in policy toward our friends in China. Now, if you'll excuse me, I have nothing more to share." With that, Mr. Chen left the podium and headed off stage.

Jerry bit his lower lip and Todd shifted back and forth on his feet.

The camera returned to Tonya Smith. "For those of you joining us, late-breaking news from the White House. President Zachary has announced that he will be addressing the nation tomorrow night at eight eastern. As we get more details, we'll bring them to you. Now back to *The Lineup* with Kimberly Guilfoyle."

Jerry crossed his arms. "Huh. Your brother might not be crazy or lying." Jerry's face was pale, and his eyes were wide. "I'm not sure what's happening, but I'm glad we got stuff for the house." He reached for Todd's hand as they continued watching the TV.

# Nine: Dan's Arrival

TODD STARED OUT the open front window, allowing the breeze to brush over his face. The room was quiet except for the occasional car driving by and the neighbors across the street in their front yard playing with their dog.

After the announcement, Todd and Jerry had searched for additional information online, but found none. They turned the TV and laptop off.

*What was the point?*

They already had more information than the media, or most other people for that matter. Absentmindedly, Todd got up, forcing Bianca to leap from his lap, where she had been snoozing comfortably, and headed to the toilet.

The house phone rang and Jerry answered.

Todd listened from the bathroom. "Hello." Jerry sounded vacant, unlike his usual, chipper self.

"Oh, hi, Brad. How're you?"

There was a pause.

"Yes, we caught the broadcast."

Another pause.

"Yep, we took care of that... No, he's in the bathroom..."

Todd turned the corner and headed back into the living room. Jerry shifted the phone in his hand. "We're set. What about you? Do you really think everything will be all right? I talked to my folks already, but should I call them again?" He mouthed Brad with his palm against the headset.

Todd returned to his spot on the sofa.

"All right… Yes, we're fine… Of course, I don't think you're lying. Well, not anymore. I mean we still have to find out what the president has to say, but…" Jerry didn't finish his thought. "Did you want to talk to your brother?"

Todd sat up and reached out his hand.

"Really? Yes, he washed his hands… I heard the sink…" Jerry rolled his eyes. "Okay, that sounds good. Tell everyone there we said hello. Be safe…all right?" Jerry shook his head at Todd. "Okay… So, call us if you need anything. Bye." "Your brother's interesting." Jerry raked his hand through his hair. "I'm not sure which he was happier about—that we got everything done, or that I no longer considered him crazy. Oh, and he sent us both friend requests and wanted to make sure we respond."

Todd smirked.

"He'll call in a few days," Jerry said. "They were getting the kids settled, and your folks organized. Anyway, it sounded as if they had a busy afternoon."

Todd imagined his dad trying to justify to Brad why bringing his guns would be a good idea, while Lori stood, her arms crossed, resolutely telling their father "no." Assuming Lori won the argument, it couldn't have been easy.

Hearing a familiar chirp, Jerry held up his cell to see a friend request from Brad. He tapped a few buttons on his smartphone.

"Pretty weird, right?" Todd said. "I hope this is gonna change our relationship with my family. Assuming everything's all right."

Resting his head on Todd's shoulder, Jerry mumbled, "It'll be all right. Everything'll be okay. We're going to be all right."

TODD HURRIED ALONG the devastated street, his clothes torn and burned. Around him, a thick blanket of gray filled the air with a putrid smell of rot. He recognized the overturned cart and the woman's hand grasping out at him.

What happened?

He was at the store.

There was panic. People grabbed and fought over everything in reach. People argued over cans of soup and packages of chips. Pure anarchy. There was so little left when he arrived.

It was every man for himself.

He remembered spotting the bodies of an old couple next to the now emptied-out produce area. They hadn't stood a chance in the panic. All around him, hysteria, a frenzy that he'd taken part in. He didn't recognize faces or know names. He remembered stepping over the body of a child. Holding what? Something purple. A woman dead next to him. Her purse's spewed contents of cellphone, keys, wallet, and change around her. He tried to get what he needed before...before what? He couldn't remember.

Rushing down the street, Todd no longer comprehended where he was. Finally, he found a familiar house through the endless sheets of gray. Everything burned: trees, cars, homes, and people. All gray, everything covered in an unholy layer of ash.

Slowly, he made his way home. As he walked, he glanced at what remained of a stroller with a burned body kneeling before it protecting a baby. He steadied himself and hurried over to the remains, reaching out his hand in terror.

*God in heaven.*

His stomach lurched as he fell back, tears streaking his face. It was Steve holding his infant daughter, failing to protect her. Failing to save her. They were dead, everyone dead, all dead. He was distraught as a haze fell over his mind.

He tried to cry out for help but found he had no voice. His throat scorched and voice obliterated. Gone. Was it the rancid smoke around him, or was it the reality of what had happened? Either way, no sounds slipped off his tongue. A deafening quiet surrounded him. A menacing emptiness mocked him with everything he had once held dear. There were no planes, no cars, no dogs, nothing. All gone. Whatever happened long since finished.

Running past the crumbling world and into the remains of his front entry, Todd gasped at the devastation. He didn't know where else to go.

The burned remains of his once comfortable home taunted him. Home was supposed to be safe. He was supposed to walk through the door and feel happy. He called out Jerry's name. His voice faltered. The harder he tried the more ear-piercing the silence became.

Todd rushed to what had once been their living room, he searched desperately for Jerry. How could he not be here? When he went to the store, Jerry was still there, but that had been—how long had it been? He couldn't remember. When he ran to the den, he found it, too, was in ruins. The large window had blown out, and the heavy curtains were shredded, laying on the floor. Where had Jerry gone? Wrecked room after wrecked room, and there was no sign of Jerry. The house abandoned, except for the layer of gray.

Slowly, it sank in. The aliens hadn't come in peace. They'd destroyed it all and killed everyone. There was nothing left. He was alone. Finally, he moved to the back door and looked through the shattered window.

A figure hovered over something small in the yard. The figure was covered in filth and torn clothing. Jerry. It had to be. If there was a God, the man there in the yard would be Jerry.

Todd could survive anything, even this, as long as he had Jerry.

He ran to Jerry and reached out to touch his shoulder. His husband turned and gave him a sickening, bloody smile. Todd stopped dead in his tracks, his soul ripped from his body.

Jerry chewed on something, something small, his mouth covered in bright-red blood and white fur. Todd recognized the first thing devoid of the color gray—Bianca's white fur. Todd heard the words "Mmm, kitty stew." Jerry's features were splattered in white fur and blood.

Jolted awake, Todd struggled for breath as he stifled a scream.

*Only a nightmare.*

The bed, the dresser, the night tables, and the pictures on the wall were as they should be. Everything seemed in order. Nothing was in ruins. No layers of gray, no horrid smells. The house was fine, and they were safe in bed.

Todd took several deep breaths, but they didn't calm his pounding heart. He got up, shuffled to the nightstand, and hit a button on his iPod. The room filled with sounds of soft rain and sounds of the ocean. It cleared his mind and relaxed his tightened muscles. He climbed back into bed, shivering from the chill in the air. Jerry turned over, exhaling softly. Todd pushed past the terrible images in his mind. After what seemed like hours, he drifted off to sleep.

As the morning crawled out from the darkness, the buzz of the phone snatched Todd from his sleep. Blinking several times he frowned and glared into his pillow; he had spent much of the night, after his nightmare, tossing and turning.

He reached blindly, fumbling for the buzzing phone.

Through a groggy haze, Jerry said, "If that's your brother, I'm gonna kill him." He rolled over and put a pillow over his head to block out the ringing.

Tapping his phone, which made the buzzing stop, he spoke. "Hello."

"Hey! What's up?" A friendly and loud, masculine voice said on the other end of the phone. At this moment, the voice needed to go away. Todd had fallen asleep a few hours ago, and he didn't want to hear a gregarious voice.

"Morning, Dan. How're you?" He sat up, jealous of Jerry, who refused to come out of the covers. "What time is it?" He rubbed his eyes trying to wake up.

"What the hell kind of greeting is that? Were you and Jerry up all night having nasty, hot sex? 'Cause, child, you sound like shit."

*Oh, joy, Snarky Dan is alive and well. Grr.*

After a pause, Dan added, "It's eleven. Barely morning at all, ho."

Todd checked the clock—10:00 a.m. *Ugh.*

"I'll be in San Jo' around two p.m. your time. You better be done molesting each other by then so you can come get me. I'll be on Delta flight 1742." Dan paused. "Did you write that down? You better be writing this 'cause I don't want you to lose me."

"Yes, Dan," Todd grumbled. "I got it."

"Whatever, ho. Listen, get Jerry's pecker out of your hand and write this down. Delta flight 1742 at two p.m.," insisted Dan.

Todd growled, fumbling for a minute, still not fully awake. He grabbed a piece of paper and a pen. "Two p.m. San Jose Airport, 1742. Got it. See you then."

"Talk to you in a while. Byeeee." Dan's tone was bouncier now. "Thanks for hosting me. Kisses."

"See ya then. Bye." Todd clicked the phone off and dropped it on the bedside table next to the note. He collapsed back onto the bed, throwing his arm over his face.

"What did Dan have to say?" Jerry asked sleepily as he rolled over to talk to Todd.

"Nothing. Gave us the flight info." Todd closed his eyes for a few minutes, and almost fell back to sleep. After the nightmare, the idea of the warm water sounded good to him. "I'm gonna take a shower."

"Have fun. I'll be right here when you get done." Jerry closed his eyes, drifting back to sleep.

Getting up, Todd pulled off his pajamas and hung them up in the walk-in closet. He padded his way to the bathroom. As he took a look in the mirror, he was greeted by the dark circles under his eyes, his messed-up hair, and scruffy face—not to mention the paunch he was starting to get around the middle.

*Wonderful.* He sneered as he jumped into the shower.

The shower's warm water hit his body, erasing the memory of the nightmare. He felt life rush back into him. With each spit of water, the fear and stress washed away.

Still warm from the shower, he slowly pulled himself together. He saw Jerry lying in bed watching the ceiling. "I'm gonna make some breakfast?"

"Fine by me." Jerry puckered his lips making kissing noises. Smiling, Todd crossed to his side of the bed and leaned in to kiss him.

He closed the bedroom door and made his way to the living room, Todd stopped as he saw the TV. He thought for a few moments and decided to tempt fate. He grabbed the remote from the coffee table and turned on the TV.

*Please be normal. Please be normal.*

To his relief, it was filled with regular news. There were no signs of invasion; everything seemed ordinary.

*Should I warn my friends? I could text Kati and give her a heads-up; saves me from having to explain everything. No. She'll call the cops and have me committed.* He shook his head. *Or she'd say I was full of shit and tell me to go fuck myself.*

SAN JOSE INTERNATIONAL Airport was not what one would expect for the center of technology and innovation. It had two terminals, and it only handled smaller planes. None of the double-decker planes landed there.

As Jerry and Todd drove into the one-way, traffic-controlled roundabout, people rushed around, heading to one destination or another. Couples kissed each other goodbye and hello, pulled bags from cars, and put them onto curbs. One family had Mickey ears. Clearly on vacation. Porters stood ready to help if needed.

*It's what you would expect on a normal Sunday.*

"You know, I'm not sure if I'm sold on the whole metal and glass bubble thing," Jerry commented. "I mean, it's nice that there are so many people here." He glanced at the newer metal and glass section of the airport.

"Huh, what?" Todd snapped out of his daze, focusing on Jerry through his sunglasses.

"I said, 'It's nice to see so many people here.' It's good for the economy." Jerry shook his head, annoyed.

"Yep. I suppose. Slow down. We don't want to miss him," Todd said as they approached the terminal.

"Oh, please! How can anyone miss Dan? He's probably got on a florescent caftan and an oversized white sun hat."

"He's not that outrageous." Todd shook his head at the image.

"If you say so." Jerry pointed to the curb in front of the baggage claim area. "There he is."

Standing with his suitcase, Dan was dressed in black jeans and a bright blue polo shirt. He towered over several of the people around him. There were still remnants of his time in the military with how he stood. The strong shoulders and the ridged stance reflected his once-perfect body. But since he left the Air Force, his focus changed from a regimented life to one of fun, food, booze, men, and maybe too many of his mother's tamales.

As they pulled up, Todd thought Dan looked pleasant enough; his face was handsome, and he still had a solid shape to him. Jerry jumped out. "Hey you messy-ass-ho, how you?" he asked as they hugged.

"Oh, the flight. I'm a mess." Dan opened the back door, tossed the suitcase in with ease, and threw himself onto the seat.

Jerry and Todd shared a glance.

"Child, there was nothing but a bunch of stupid-ass lesbians on the flight. They were a bunch of nasty bitches."

"God. Dan. Really." Jerry glared at him through the rear-view mirror.

"Whatever. If I could've gotten out and walked, I would have. What happened to all the menz? It was awful." Dan huffed and puffed.

"So you're still a lesbian-hating fag, I see." Todd held back a chuckle. "You need to get over your hatred of women and maybe tone down the whole lesbian thing. Someday you're going to get punched for it."

"Or worse." Jerry added.

"Ho, please. I don't hate women. I love them. I adore them. They are wonderful for straight men and they are a big part of why we're here. People need to get over this politically correct shit. We've gotten way too serious." Dan rolled his eyes. "This one woman on the flight was just nasty to everyone, and she really pissed me off." He huffed.

"There were no cute boys on the flight?" Jerry smirked as he glanced in the rearview mirror.

Dan fussed about, pulling lotion and ChapStick out of his pack. "No! What kind of nasty ass flight has no cute boy flight attendants? Oh, but girl, there were these hot FEMA and military boys at the airport."

"What?" Todd peered over his shoulder.

"Oh, some drill shit. Denver was a mess. I swear, if I didn't know any better, I'd say the military was up to something." He tried to catch his reflection in the rearview mirror as he fixed his hair.

Jerry reached out and put a hand on Todd's leg, giving it a squeeze.

"Oh, come on, Dan." Todd's grin hurt his cheeks. "There must have been a couple of cute guys for you to drool over."

Dan pulled a brush, going to work right away on his hair. "Jerry, love, shift the mirror. I can't see myself." He continued to tilt his head so that he had a better view of himself.

"Driving here. More important than your face or hair," he said.

"How rude." Dan stopped preening and focused on Todd. "Well, there was one. Oh my God, he was fine!" He took a breath, fanning himself, and continued, "He wanted me. He said hello and asked me to move out of my seat. Then, he got in and sat right next to me! Can you imagine? He was in love with me."

"Of course he was," Todd said as they drove out of the airport and headed home.

# Ten: The President's Address

TODD AND JERRY cleaned up after dinner, while Dan leaned against the counter watching. Every few seconds Jerry checked the clock on the kitchen wall. He had been doing so since they sat to eat.

"The president should be on in a few minutes," Jerry said. "Let's get this finished and go watch."

"Wow! Since when are you interested in political stuff? I thought after the debacle of the last election you swore off it."

"I did but, you know, this could be important," Jerry said.

"Doubtful. Unless there is something you know that you aren't sharing?" Dan crossed his arms and his gaze narrowed.

Todd met Jerry's stare as he bit at his lower lip catching bits of his goatee.

"Ah...I mean...well."

Dan laughed and relaxed. "Oh you are too easy." And he continued chuckling. "Seriously though, you never cared about these things before. Is there some hot menz you want to see? Don't tell me you have a thing for that *pendejo* in the White House. Ick."

Jerry dried his hands on the towel, hanging it back up on the oven door. He stood there a moment longer than what Todd would have expected.

"God! Is Todd finally rubbing off on you?" Dan took a sip of wine. "Bringing you over to the political dark side?"

Jerry kept quiet and headed into the living room.

"If it was something to do with a new tech gadget, I get it, but politics? Oh did you see the live stream from Apple? I think they are slipping. Ah well. So the news? Yuck!" Dan waved his hand as if he was swatting at flies.

Todd moved back as Dan rushed past him. Dan stood in front of Jerry and grabbed his head with both hands as he stared.

"Who are you? And what have you done with Jerry?" Dan's gaze ran over Jerry's face. Then he placed his free hand on Jerry's forehead. "Do I have to make you turn and cough?"

"Not so fast, *chica*." Todd finished off his water before putting the glass in the sink. "That hand had better not move any lower than his shoulders, or I might cut it off."

Dan turned, lifting his hands in the air as if at gunpoint.

Jerry pursed his lips and shrugged past Dan. "Anyway! I want to listen to what he has to say. And I pay attention to the news, buddy boy. Considering what they said about the troops in the press conference, I don't want to miss it. It might be important. And I might be interested in that."

"I guess." Dan sat in one of the side chairs. "I was talking to this hot boy at the hotel yesterday, and we were joking that it might be some kind of scandal. You know how these political types act so innocent until you catch them doing an intern or find them on the internet half naked with their sad little dong out. Then they try to cover it up. Maybe, he got caught with his hand in an intern's pants. Now that would be worth seeing."

"And we would've known already." Jerry shook his head. "Nah, it's something else."

"Okay, ladies," Todd sat on the sofa and tried to get comfortable. "Let's watch and see what the president has to say." He tried not to show how worried he was; part of him wanted to listen to the address and the other part wanted to go back to his game world. It was either going to be the end of humankind or a new beginning for them all. His hands started to sweat, and his stomach lurched. He took a breath and reached up to scratch his goatee.

Jerry clicked on the TV. "Wasn't this on the Food Network before dinner?"

The Food Network logo was on the bottom of the screen, but the TV was playing the news.

"Okay. That's weird." Dan's eyes got large and his smile flattened.

Jerry flipped through the stations, and it was the same thing. All the channels were showing news, even the Disney Channel. He turned up the volume as the announcer began speaking. "President Zachary sure has everyone up in arms today. Members of both the Senate and the House of Representatives have been flying in to make it to the address. In under five minutes, the president will be addressing the nation. And for the first time since nine-eleven, it will be broadcast on every station."

Playing with the end of the armrest on the couch, picking at a string, Todd replayed the last twenty-four hours. His thoughts drifted to his family, the stupid fights, and all that wasted time. He focused on how stubborn he had been, and for what? All he wanted was to repair the relationship with them. And thanks to Brad, they were on their way.

Todd took Jerry's hand and swallowed heavily, remembering how lucky he was to have Jerry. His face softened, and his heart steadied.

"Ladies and gentlemen, the president of the United States of America."

The Sergeant at Arms snapped Todd out of his thoughts. People clapped and cheered as President Zachary walked up to the podium. Normally, he would stop and take his time shaking hands. Tonight, he pushed through. Reaching the podium faster than normal, the president started to speak, quieting the group.

"Thank you all. Mister Speaker, Vice President Fillmore, members of Congress, members of the Supreme Court, and diplomatic corps and my fellow citizens. Today, I stand before you, not as the president of the United States, but as a man from one planet in one small solar system, a tiny speck of a much larger universe. Filled with wonders both great and small. For centuries, man has searched the skies wondering if we're alone in the universe. Or are we the only outpost of life in this galaxy?"

The president paused.

"That answer has finally come. Ladies and gentlemen, we are not alone." He stopped and peered into the camera. The lines on his forehead relaxed, providing the kind of comfort only a man in his office could.

Todd and Jerry shared a glance, then turned to Dan. His eyes were large and his expression blank. The color slowly drained from his face. Dan's hands started to shake, causing him to hold his wine glass with both hands so it didn't fall. Jerry's hand tightened around Todd's as they continued to watch the presidential address.

"Scientists on the International Space Station discovered the unexpected—several alien ships of varying configurations. Within a few hours of this discovery, the lead ship contacted the space station. After discussions within the United Nations Security Council, every scientific mind familiar with this type of scenario was contacted. The purpose of which was to formalize a response. This was not a single national endeavor, but a worldwide initiative.

"Our nation has been in constant contact with our allies and friends from around the world as well as with our guests. All nations approved a motion that no information would be released to the public before now.

"I want to emphasize three things: first, from what we've learned, these aliens mean us no harm. Let me say that again. They are here for peaceful purposes and peace alone. Second, the United States of America and our allies, along with the UN Security Council, have worked together with our guests. Lastly, as part of our good neighbor policy, I've been in contact with both the prime minister of Canada and the president of Mexico to offer our support, logistically or militarily, and assistance to secure their territories should the need arise.

"Acting in our nation's best interest, and after consulting with other world leaders, I made the decision to bring much of our military home to keep the peace and help enforce local laws. As of this moment, by executive order, I am suspending the Posse Comitatus Act. We are not declaring a state of emergency, nor will we do so.

"As a precaution, effective tonight and for the next forty-eight hours, there will be a national curfew of nine p.m. In addition, by executive order, all financial institutions will be closed, including the New York Stock Exchange. These actions are being duplicated around the world. This is for forty-eight hours and forty-eight hours only. Any future actions will be implemented, as needed, with the full approval of the Senate and the House. It is vital at this sensitive time we remain calm and go about our normal lives.

"Regarding our guests: they are called the Nentraee and are a humanoid race. Their leader has requested to meet with the full assembly of the UN tomorrow at noon. The address will be in English, with simultaneous broadcasts in all other major languages worldwide. As I address you tonight, all current materials on the visitors are being sent to local television stations and posted on government websites.

"My fellow Americans, we are on the brink of a new frontier. These are exciting times, and my only hope is that, as a race, we pull together and show our guests what it means to be human. We can learn much from each other.

"Before history is written in books, it is written in courage. Like mankind before us, we will show that courage, and so we will move forward—optimistic about our world, faithful to its future, and confident of the experiences to come.

"May God bless America."

The president's posture was strong in front of a flabbergasted audience. Finally, there was robust applause as he left the room among mumbled conversations of those in attendance. The cameras panned around to the House chamber, and the network cut back to a stunned-looking newscaster. She turned off-camera, muttered something, and then turned back. After she regained her composure, she spoke, "Ladies and gentlemen...uh...we have heard the single most important speech in our history. The lifelong question of intelligent life on other worlds has been answered. There will be an ongoing dialogue between the aliens and our world leaders tomorrow. We...um...we're going to break, and when we come back, we'll go over the information sent to us from the National Security Office." The TV went to a commercial break.

Dan, Jerry, and Todd looked at each other.

"Holy shit!" Dan yelped. He finished off his wine in one gulp.

"Okay, so what does this mean?" Todd squeezed Jerry's hand, which was damp.

Pinching the bridge of his nose, Dan said, "Well, it means I need to get drunk. Where's the booze?" He got up and headed off to the kitchen.

"I guess Brad wasn't lying. He was a day off, but he wasn't lying." Jerry's face was pale, and his eyes grew large, and droplets of perspiration started to bead on his forehead.

Todd bit at his goatee again and ran his hand through his hair. He had nothing to say. Everything Brad said was real; there was no avoiding this.

"I should call my folks." Jerry grabbed the phone off the coffee table and headed into the study.

Todd sat alone. Outside were distant noises.

*I don't hear anything odd. No screaming. No car wrecks. No gunfire.*

He went to pet Bianca on his lap when he realized she wasn't there. He wondered if she had sensed what was coming and took to hiding.

From the kitchen, Dan called out, "What do you guys want?" Silence. After sounds of wrestling, Dan added, "Ah, never mind; you'll get what you get."

Rocking back and forth, Todd stared at the TV. There were more important things to focus on. What would this mean to the people of the world? What did these creatures look like? Would they appear human, be some lizard-type creature, or something completely unknown?

Walking back into the room, Jerry set the phone on the table, his face paler than before he left.

"I...I can't get through. The cell phone and the regular phone are both busy. Maybe I should text them?" Jerry wiped his hands on his pants, collapsed on the sofa, and started a text. "I guess everyone's calling family and friends. I'm glad I talked to my folks already."

Breaking from his trance, Todd picked up his laptop and opened up the internet browser. He clicked on his Facebook page. "It's running really slow. Everyone must be online too." He started to type a message but stopped clicking. He frowned. "And now nothing. Dammit!"

He tried again, but this time he got the message: "Due to current demands on our system, we are unable to load the page you are requesting. Please try again later." He clicked over to Twitter and received a similar message. Then he checked the other social media sites he could think of, with no positive results. "So much for technology." He scowled and closed the laptop, putting it back on the coffee table.

Walking back in with three drinks balanced in one hand and a bottle of spiced rum in the other, Dan held the glasses out to Jerry and Todd. He held up his glass and showed a nervous grin. "Well, to what comes next. Cheers!" He downed his full glass and poured another before either Todd or Jerry took sips. He put his glass on the coffee table and wiped his mouth with the back of his hand. "I should try to call my mom; she's probably freaking out."

"Don't bother," Jerry said. "I tried, and the phone lines are busy. Even my text messages aren't being sent yet." He tossed the cell phone back on the coffee table.

"Todd tried his Facebook page, and it crashed. Everything was gone. I guess the social media sites and the cell networks couldn't handle the volume." Jerry's jaw relaxed. "I'm sure they'll be fine. We'll have to wait. I might try later tonight when things settle down."

Dan thumped back in his chair. "I'll text my mom and my sister anyway. It'll go through at some point, and they'll know I'm all right." He picked up his cell and tapped out a text.

The commercial ended and they turned toward the TV. The newscaster came back, with a bright, fake smile on her face, appearing composed.

"Wow!" Dan said. "The show must go on."

"Welcome back. For those joining us, moments ago, President Zachary finished his address to the nation. We have the information from the National Security Office and we can tell you that a race of humanoids known as the Nentraee—I'm hoping I am pronouncing that correctly—" The newscaster let out a strangled chuckle. "—from the planet Benzee, have made contact with our planet. The report says their home world is forty-three light years from us. Tomorrow, the speaker general of the Nentraee people will address the United Nations General Assembly."

The newscaster switched camera angles as the screen split. Information on the Nentraee filled the other half of the screen as she spoke. "There are three hundred eighty-eight total ships of different sizes and types. They will be coming into orbit during the next ten to twelve hours. The largest ships will be able to be seen by the naked eye.

"As stated by President Zachary, effective nine tonight, a national curfew will be in effect. That is in a little under an hour for those of us on the East Coast. The curfew will occur between nine p.m. and nine a.m. for the next forty-eight hours. We are being advised that Army National Guard troops are mobilized to keep our cities safe. Also, we are being advised that police, fire, public works, and life-safety workers are being asked to report to work."

The newscaster relaxed. Todd saw her take on a more professional posture with each consecutive word.

"All forms of nonessential travel will be discontinued tonight at ten and will not resume until after the forty-eight-hour cooling-off period. FEMA has been activated and is currently setting up temporary shelters for any travelers stranded. We are hearing from our bureaus around the world that similar precautions are being put in place in several countries."

The announcer continued, "The Posse Comitatus Act, which many of you may know prohibits federal military personnel and units of the United States Army National Guard from acting in a law enforcement capacity within the United States, has been suspended. With its suspension, our armed forces will be working with local law enforcement throughout the country to maintain law and order and help administer the forty-eight-hour cooling-off period.

"Once again, ladies and gentlemen, if you are on the East Coast, the curfew will take effect in under an hour. If you are on the streets, head home. If you work in fire, police, public works, or life safety, you are requested to report to work immediately and await further instruction."

"How did they plan this so quickly?" Jerry asked.

"It's not that difficult." Dan didn't take his eyes off the TV. "They have this shit planned out."

"Shh," Todd hissed.

"We're getting word from phone companies around the country and globally, reporting a collapse of their systems; both cell phones and landlines have been affected." The announcer was back on. "A spokesman for AT&T informed us they are working on the problems and hope to have the phone lines up within the next couple of hours. Cell companies and even social media sites are reporting similar problems. Please be patient."

"Tell us something we don't know," Todd said.

Jerry and Dan nodded.

"Information being sent by the speaker general of the Nentraee will be broadcast tomorrow at noon eastern. Directly after that, the president will again address the nation from the Oval Office. Stay tuned for news from around the globe. We go now to—"

Jerry picked up the remote and turned off the TV.

Todd raised his eyebrows.

"I think, that's enough of that." Jerry was pale but sounded composed. "We won't know more until tomorrow. They're going to rehash the same facts till then."

With the TV off, Todd could hear what transpired outside—a big bang and then a car peeling out down the street. Then some yelling.

*So it begins.*

Another loud bang came from outside. Jerry shuddered and Dan jumped. He checked out the front window and saw his neighbors rushing to their car. "Well, Nathen and Claire are getting ready to leave." Todd turned to Jerry. "I wonder where they're gonna go."

Dan took another sip of his drink, which he had refreshed. He rolled the glass between his hands. "Not far, if I know the military." He leaned back. "My guess is they have most major cities closed. They'll be sending people home."

Jerry and Todd shared a look.

"Even though the curfew doesn't begin till nine p.m., it doesn't mean they won't start closing the highways, airports, and train stations. If they are stopping the trains and planes, they'll need that time to make sure that people return home, or if not, they will keep folks where they are. Which would explain why FEMA is involved. They'll use the airports and train stations as temporary shelters." He chuckled. "Our military may be many things, but people can't call them inefficient. Hours before that address, everything went into action. I guess that would explain why there was a military transport sitting at the airport yesterday. Christ, I'm lucky I got here yesterday. That would have sucked hardcore being stuck at the airport."

"What do you think is going to happen?" Jerry asked.

"Well, just what the president says." Dan shrugged. "They'll shut us up tight. With air traffic stopped, the Air Force will be patrolling our skies. They'll put everyone on alert and watch for some crazy country, like North Korea or Iran, or who knows to do something stupid."

"They'll focus on protecting our assets; food, water, sanitation, medical, transportation, all that stuff," Dan said. "The way the president addressed us, it appears they're not worried the aliens are hostile, but it wouldn't surprise me if you don't see the vice president for a while. They'll have her nice and secure, just to see how this plays out. They will move the president to various secure locations. He won't be in one place too long." Dan shrugged. "That's my guess."

Todd wanted more and he leaned a bit closer to Dan.

Staring at his glass, Dan continued, "I doubt we'll have to worry about these Nentraee. If they were hostile, they would have attacked us already. We don't have any way to fight an attack from space. Well, at least not that I know of. It's possible the CIA or the NSA does. Perhaps NASA. Anyway, nukes take time and there is always the issue of them not working or working too well."

Dan paused.

"My guess is they're friendlies and want something. Probably to trade." Dan polished off his third drink and put the empty glass down. His mouth lifted and his eyes sparkled. "I guess I won't be going to the beach to cruise the boys tomorrow." He sat back deeper in the chair. "That sucks! They're keeping me from my menz. How rude."

A knock at the front door caused the three to jump.

Todd answered the door, seeing his neighbor standing on his porch. "Hey, Nathen, are you okay?" he asked. Nathen was pale and sweaty. "Is everyone all right? We saw you guys take off. What happened?"

Nathen shook his head and ran a hand over his face to try to remove the sweat. "I just thought...we thought..." Nathen took a shallow breath. "I wanted to let you know that they won't let us leave. They're sending people home. We thought..."

Nathen took another shallow breath and continued, "We thought we'd head to our house in the mountains. Before the curfew." Nathen shook his head. "But...Todd...man, the radio says they've already closed the freeways. They closed every damn freeway. I don't get it. So, we tried to go up Mt. Hamilton Road, but the military had it closed, too, turning people around. It's insane! They wouldn't fucking let us leave. Todd, man, they even pointed their guns at a few people, maybe worried they would challenge them." Nathen glanced over his shoulder to his house. "I thought you should know in case you try to leave. I can't believe this. This is America. They can't do this..." Nathen trailed off, shaking his head.

Nathen and his family were good people. Hell, all the people in the neighborhood were nice. There was another car accelerating down the street; both Todd and Nathen watched it speed by.

Todd was mentally and emotionally drained. Still he tried to brighten his expression. "Nathen, it's cool. We decided to stay here. Don't worry. These aliens, Nentraee, or whatever, aren't here to hurt us." He paused.

*Wow, is that what I was like yesterday? Poor Jerry.*

"It'll be fine. Listen, I talked to my brother; he works for NASA, and he said we have nothing to worry about." He put his hand on Nathen's shoulder. "Look, why don't you and Claire come over and hang out? You're more than welcome. We would love the company, you know, while we try to wait this whole thing out." He peeked over to Jerry and Dan, who both nodded.

Nathen shook his head, clearly not hearing all Todd said. Certain words must have struck a chord because Nathen started talking fast. "The phones are working again. We tried texting but got nothing back and our internet isn't starting up. Is it working?" he asked, with a nervous smile. "We couldn't get through to anyone. When did they start working? I've gotta let Claire know. Thanks, Todd." Nathen rushed back to his house.

Todd forgot the phones had been out. Maybe the phones could have been working intermediately. How else could he have spoken with Brad? *Crap! How could I be so careless?*

He returned to the sofa. "He's a mess."

Jerry nodded.

"Considering the things going on, he seems pretty good," Dan said. "Good job trying to calm him down with the phone thing. You know they still aren't working, but it'll give him something to focus on." He glanced up at Todd. "I've got to say I'm impressed with how well you're handling this. It's like you knew this was coming."

Todd chuckled nervously.

Rubbing his forehead, Jerry turned. "Dan, would the military fire on civilians?"

"It's possible," Dan said. "If they had to. That's what they've been trained to do, but they would use their guns more to scare people. Fire over their heads. Our guys are trained well and aren't the gun nuts and baby killers the libs try to make them out to be." He took a shaky breath. "I guess the next forty-eight hours will tell." He glanced at their drinks. "Who's ready for another round? I'm pouring."

# Eleven: Welcome

STANDING IN THE shower, feeling the hot spray of water falling down the sides of his face, Todd was preoccupied with thoughts of the aliens.

Sure, the media reports said they were a dual sex humanoid species, but what did that mean? Were the released photos of the Nentraee accurate? Would they have different races like humans? What was their culture? Why were they here? Why did they pick Earth? Were these the same aliens that had been visiting the planet for decades? Taking people and experimenting on them? And if they weren't, then did that mean there were even more aliens? Did those aliens exist, or did people make false claims?

He found it hard to focus. Still, he tried to enjoy the relaxation of the hot water as it hit him.

*I need to wake up.*

He yawned and finally picked up his razor. It was so much easier to shave his goatee in the shower. How could anyone shave without running water hitting their face and the steam? It made such a difference. He shaved around his goatee, making sure its lines were straight and neat.

"Todd, it's almost time," Jerry called out. "The address will start in a few minutes. You better hurry up."

"I'll be right there." Todd turned off the showerhead and grabbed a towel. "I need to get dressed unless you want me to come out there naked."

"No thanks, girl!" Dan shouted. "I'm sure the aliens aren't ready to see that yet. And, child, neither am I."

"Bitch!" shouted Todd.

Once dressed, he walked into the living room and sat on the sofa. "See—plenty of time."

Jerry ran his hand through Todd's damp hair. He held out his wet fingers, letting the droplets fall on Todd's chest. Then Jerry wiped what didn't drip off onto Todd's pants. "While you were in the shower, Kati called," Jerry said. "She wanted to make sure we were okay, seeing as you're a drama queen and all. You know, make sure you weren't hiding under the bed."

Todd shook his head harder than needed so that he would get Jerry wet.

"Hey! Jerk." Jerry pulled up a pillow to try to block the water but was too slow. "Anyway, she said there were only a few people at your workplace, so they closed up and headed home. I guess the boss man didn't even show."

"Good."

"She said the roads were pretty empty and most places seemed closed. Anyway, she got ahold of her brother in New York, and he told her it was quiet there too and security was tight. I mean, even tighter than after nine-eleven. Anyway, I told her you'd call later."

"Crap!" Todd said. "I didn't even think to call her. Man, she's gonna kick my ass."

Dan said, "Yep, you're toast. But don't worry, I'll come to your funeral. I've got this sexy as hell, little black number that will drive the menz crazy."

Jerry rested his hand on Todd's leg. "She's fine. A little shaken but good. Friends of hers came over last night, and they watched the news together."

"Good. I'm glad she wasn't alone." Todd scratched his goatee. "I should've called her. Hell, I didn't even check in with my gaming group. I'm sure they're okay, but I should've at least tried, well not last night, but this morning now that things are working again. I'll post some messages and let folks know we're fine. I was focused on us, and I didn't even think of our friends." He reached for his laptop.

"Bitch, please get off the cross," Dan said. "Someone needs the wood. Don't worry, they're all fine. It's not like anyone called you. Plus, as your oldest and dearest friend, I can assure you, if I wasn't already here you wouldn't have been a big priority for me either. That's how we are. That's how everyone is. In times of extreme stress, we can only typically focus on what's in front of us."

"Seriously, you wouldn't have even tried to contact us?" Jerry said. "And I've known you for how long?"

"Long enough to know not to answer that question." Dan waggled his eyebrows. "Honey, everyone was freaking out and they probably still are. It's not that they don't care, they're in shock." He reached out and patted Todd's leg. "It's like after nine-eleven. People were glued to their TV's worrying what was going to happen next. And yes, I would call and check in with you guys at some point, but not right away. It doesn't mean I don't love you." He batted his eyelashes. "Anyway, just pretend you weren't able to get through. Don't admit to it. Duh." He beamed and winked at Todd. "Well, that's what I would do. Of course, I've grown fond of my balls. Now zip it. They're getting ready to start."

Todd left his laptop where it was and glanced at the television as the anchor talked about reactions from around the world. Images of different locations flashed on the split screen as the newscaster continued.

The Pope held a special mass at the Vatican as tens of thousands of people poured into Saint Peter's Square; it was the largest gathering in modern memory. There were so many faithful, that the Swiss Guard called in the Italian military to provide additional crowd control.

The image changed. It showed Prague; the people there had panicked and rioted in the streets. Several large fires had been started with reports of mass casualties. It took local police and the military several hours to get things under control, not only in the city but the surrounding area as well.

Reports from Brisbane showed broken windows and small fires in the downtown area. Looters left broken out windows on several stores. There was minor panic, but the local police had it under control. An evening overshot showed the city quiet in anticipation of what the visitors had to say.

Next came a picture of the North Korean flag. The news anchor adjusted in their seat. "It has been reported by the South Korean News Agency and American Armed Forces at the demilitarized zone that troop movements along the border with North Korea have stopped. Current reports say that the North has pulled its military back and left only a few soldiers to protect the border."

"Doesn't surprise me," said Dan.

The screen changed once more, pulling up images from the Middle East. The anchor turned and spoke to a different camera. "Reactions from Cairo to Tehran have been silent. Our correspondent in Cairo reports that once the announcement was made all violence stopped. Most of the population gathered at local mosques.

"In Saudi Arabia, the roads leading to Mecca and Medina are filled with pilgrims. After both Israel and

Palestine authorities issued their statements, all hostilities ceased."

As the time for the address drew closer, the anchorperson appeared again to speak. This was live. The other pieces were replays from earlier.

"Ladies and gentlemen, we are moments away from the Nentraee delegation's arrival at the General Assembly Hall. This will be our first look at this new species. We are—" The newsperson stopped and turned. "Yes, the speaker general is on her way. With that, we go to the General Assembly Hall at the UN."

The UN Secretary General Duck-Hwan Park stood behind his green marble desk with the president of the General Assembly and the Undersecretary General Assembly Affairs and Conference Services. Behind him was the UN emblem on a gold background. "Ladies and gentleman of the Assembly, my fellow Terrans, I would like to introduce Speaker General Mirtoff Esmi of the Nentraee people."

The crowd of delegates stood and applauded. The doors to the hall opened and through them came what appeared to be a tall female flanked by two attendants. They moved to the lectern as applause thundered.

Todd leaned forward and studied the woman, fascinated. She and the other aliens seemed tall but not so tall that they stood out. As reported, the aliens were, in fact, humanoid in appearance; two eyes, a nose, a mouth, and two ears.

She wore a beautiful, purple cloak, embroidered in gold and silver with different symbols on it, each as elaborate as the next. From what Todd noticed as the camera zoomed in, it seemed Middle Eastern in style or even African.

*That's kind of interesting. I guess it makes sense. Two arms, two legs, one head, what other fashion options could there be?*

The material had a heaviness to it. The fabric moved like the leaves of a tree on a windy day. Under it, he noted, she was in what appeared to be a functional human suit. Todd wasn't sure how to describe the color. It was a light cream color below, but the top was as white as snow.

The camera focused on the Speaker General and the world saw her face. Her skin was smooth and a fetching tan tone that offset her auburn hair perfectly. She had pronounced pointed ears. Her eyes were a rich, dark brown. The bridge of her nose didn't stop at where her eyebrows would be if she had any but continued up her forehead into her hairline. The alien's hairline seemed farther back, revealing a large forehead that seemed to have gentle ridges and dimples in it. It wasn't unattractive, but it sure wasn't human. Her hair was done up in an elaborate braided bun. Her features were darker than her guards', but they shared the strong forehead, the continuation of the nose, and pronounced ears. Todd thought the Speaker General was by far the most attractive.

Her attendants wore a different type of outfit from her under their red cloaks. They also had embroidered symbols on them, different from the Speaker General's.

"You think those Nentraee with her are like guards or something?" Todd asked.

"Duh. Ya think?" Dan said.

"No weapons?" Jerry asked, turning to Dan.

"Don't count on it," said Dan, his eyes not leaving the TV. "They have them concealed, I'm sure. Probably under their dress robes. There is no way they would let their leader come here unprotected. Assuming this is their actual leader, it's possible they are sending someone in her place. It's not like we would know. Honestly, I'm surprised there aren't more people with her. Making me suspect that this isn't actually their speaker general."

The speaker general stood at the matching lectern with a smaller version of the UN seal on it. The lectern was in front of the desk for the UN Secretary-General. Her posture was ramrod straight and her shoulders level. She scanned the assembly hall with an air of confidence. Todd suspected she might be covering up her own nervousness. An apprehension everyone on Earth was suffering, possibly even more than anyone up there in those ships.

"Good afternoon, representatives of Earth," the speaker general said.

Musical qualities to her voice gave her an almost singsong accent. It wasn't a soft female voice; it was stronger than what he was used to.

"Thank you for allowing me to address you. As the UN Secretary General said, I am Mirtoff Esmi, the speaker general and leader of the Nentraee people. It is a great honor for me to stand before you today."

There was applause that forced her to stop and wait before she continued.

"I shall speak to why we have come to Earth. We are here during a time of great need. Our home world, Benzee, was destroyed years ago by an astrological event. Before our planet's destruction, we put all of our resources into saving as many of our people as possible. This was not an easy task. I am saddened to say out of the four hundred million citizens of our world, we only rescued a little over two million. We had to leave most of our people to perish in the devastation."

The camera watched as she scanned the room. Her pain and humility were palpable. This wasn't easy for her. It couldn't be easy for any of them. Mirtoff's shoulders dropped and her eyes softened.

"The last of our civilization, our culture, and our home are on our ships that now circle your world. We have spent many years searching for a planet to call home. Eleven months ago, we received a signal from Earth. We followed that signal here. We did not know what to expect when we found you. Your signals were random. Your messages strange to us. Most seemed disturbingly violent."

This caused the room to stir. There were hushed comments in the background. She stopped for a moment and watched the reactions from the room. Her face shifted with a second of uncertainty before she continued. It wasn't something she should have said, but she couldn't take it back now.

"As we moved closer, we were not positive we would find anyone alive, based purely on what we saw on those recorded messages. We do not judge. It is a shared history for both of us. We, too, have a history of violence with our own people. A violence that almost destroyed us. You can imagine our great pleasure when we found you alive and your world intact. We did not expect to find as advanced a civilization as you have here. It pleases us greatly." She bowed.

"That's odd," Jerry said.

"During our travel to your world, I asked my scientific advisors to study Earth and your communications. For the last several months, we have studied your many cultures and learned several of your dominant languages. We are ashamed to say, we have not learned them all. For that, I apologize."

She surveyed the room, gauging the reactions of the audience. It was interesting to see her pause and take in the people around her. But she seemed so determined and guarded.

"After study and observation, we found we have much we can offer you in trade, and much that you can offer us. Our hope is to share our technology and all we have learned of science, space, and medicine. In exchange, we ask you to allow us to share your world peacefully. I have spoken with your world's leading governing body regarding our offer."

She stopped, and this time she spoke to the camera. This portion was directed at the people of Earth. Even her demeanor seemed to change. Her eyes closed slightly, and her head tilted to the right. The ends of her lips lifted into what was easily recognizable as a smile.

"We have much to share and to learn from each other. The Nentraee come to you in need and in the hope of building a future of friendship. We understand we ask for a great deal and do not expect an answer immediately. Our only hope is you will consider our offer. You have diverse cultures, like our own, and we hope we can share ours with you. I thank you for allowing me to speak."

She bowed, and then she turned and walked to the door, her guards with her. The Assembly applauded, coming to their feet again. The camera panned to various delegates, still standing and applauding.

Back on the screen, the announcer spoke. "That was our first introduction to the Nentraee leader and her people. I understand we're going to a short break. The president will address the nation from the Oval Office when we return."

It was the beginning of a new world. For the first time since Brad came with the news, Todd felt excited and hopeful all the way to his core.

Jerry broke the silence. "All right, they come in peace..."

*Did Jerry actually say that?*

Todd stifled his grin by pretending to yawn.

"And need our help. I mean, it sounds weird and vague, but okay." He turned to Todd and Dan. "How is this going to work? I mean, where will they live? All this did was raise more questions than answers. Are we biologically compatible? What if they have diseases that are as common to them as the cold is to us? But instead of the sniffles, it kills us. Or vice versa?" He rubbed his mouth with his hand. "I mean, this is too strange."

"I figure that's what the president will tell us," Todd chimed in. "We'll probably treat them like everyone else. You want to come to this country, then you have to immigrate here. Or, they might give them the moon to settle. I'm sure it won't be quick. Yes, they did study us, but that doesn't mean we won't need to do our homework on them, right?"

Todd rubbed his hands together, suddenly antsy. "They sure are different. What do you think Dan?"

"Well, it's strange." Dan's face was expressionless. "Obviously unprecedented, for sure. I guess they could have easily launched an attack and taken us over if they wanted since they've been studying us. I hope they get we're not one big, happy planetary family." His bottom lip moved side to side along with his jaw.

"I don't know what they're going to do," Dan said. "Her address was too vague for my taste. And the comments on how brutal we are, it sounded preachy—and you saw the reaction in the General Assembly Hall. That didn't go over well." Shaking his head, he took a breath. "Anyway, there's nowhere for them to settle and create their own society. They would have to adapt into ours, and I don't know how well that would work." Dan glanced back at the TV as the president was preparing to speak.

All three men sat and listened to the president and his plan for the Nentraee. How all options would be explored. He wanted to reassure the country that no decisions had been made.

Todd stopped listening. Was this by chance? Was it possible that God was stepping in and saying, "Okay, kids. Stop acting like fools and stop bickering. There are real problems, and you need to focus. Learn from these Nentraee."

"I wonder how many backroom deals will be made over the next couple of weeks," Jerry said. "I mean, forget the internet or bio-anything; these guys are the next big ticket. They have military and technological advances every country on the planet will go after. I'm not sure the Nentraee realize what they are getting into with us. Perhaps they should've bypassed us altogether." His eyes had no sparkle in them as he glanced at the floor.

His comment pulled Todd from his own thoughts.

"Come on, hon." Todd patted Jerry's leg. "This is a great opportunity. They seem peaceful. I hope this'll be the wake-up call we need as a whole to move past our differences. Maybe we'll stop the fighting and killing."

Jerry didn't say anything. He was quiet and there was almost an aura of sadness around him.

Todd shook Jerry's leg to try to get his attention. "Plus, you know you want to get your hands on their space toys."

Dan joined in, "Think of their gadgets. It'd be cool to see one of those ships and meet the people. Did you hear the speaker general of the UN? 'Terrans' he called us. 'Terrans' like something right out of Star Trek." He grinned and added, "Oh, and child, did you see that hot little security boy with the black hair and green eyes? Well, I think he was a guy." Dan leaned back, a quizzical look took over his face as his eyes shifted back and forth. "No, it had to be a guy, my naughty bits were tingly." He laughed. "I wouldn't mind checking out his undercover weapon. Yum and *E*."

"Yeah, seeing the ships and the technology would be pretty cool," Jerry admitted.

Todd took Jerry's hand and kissed it, raising his eyebrows. "I'm sure it'll be fine. What could go wrong?"

# Twelve: Rethinking Ideas

MIRTOFF FINISHED HER speech, and the room erupted in hand clapping. She expected this. She had been briefed by both human cultural advisors and her own team on what to expect and what certain human reactions meant. It was surprisingly alien, but comforting in a different way from the quiet bows of her people.

With a few polite bows of her head, she left the assembly hall. Danu and Tun'ae had insisted that once her address was finished, they'd move her back to the shuttle and onto the speaker's ship, forgoing the offered human reception. It was a security procedure she did not wish to fight; she had seen the reports on how violent humans could be.

As she was whisked away, she focused on what she had seen during her address. Several of the human's faces were polite, as anticipated, but what struck her the most was the uncertainty of not only the people in the assembly hall, but the human security and media. They seemed leery of her. Would the humans of Earth react this way to all her people—untrusting, scared, and uncertain?

*Maybe it's to be expected. We're new to them. Would we act much differently?*

"Madam Speaker, we should continue moving." Danu peeked around the area.

Not realizing she had stopped, she resumed her brisk pace.

The offers for a reception to welcome her people to Earth had been refused. It was too soon. The humans needed time to adjust and reflect. There would always be time for gatherings and celebrations once the humans accepted them. At least that was what the Speaker's House had originally planned. But now, perhaps, that was not the correct response, considering the sheer number of invites to meet with the various heads of state.

Her lips pursed. One must always give others time to reflect, so one could grasp new knowledge and ensure there would be no misunderstanding.

Once inside the limousine provided by the government of the United States to take her away from the eyes of the humans gathered to see them, she breathed a heavy sigh of relief.

"That went well, Madam Speaker." Danu adjusted his dress robes under him as he tried to get comfortable, and his head hit the roof of the vehicle each time he moved. "These vehicles are not built for comfort."

"These vehicles are built for humans, not us." Tun'ae shifted how he was sitting as well.

"I'm uncertain we handled this first engagement correctly," Mirtoff said. "They seemed fearful."

"That reaffirms our stance." Danu shifted again in his seat. "A reception would be inappropriate. They need time to reflect on your words. Once they do, we can build trust, and fears will lessen. They've been given a lot of information. Remember, Madam Speaker, we've had many months to prepare while they have not. For most of them, yesterday was the first time they heard of us."

There was a soft chirp.

He pulled out his datapad. "Ah, my report."

Tapping her fingers on her leg, she said, "I'm not sure we should have declined our invitation to the proposed social function. Human culture is different from our own. We're relying on our own past cultural dealings from pre-Clan War to interact with them. Everything we've seen and learned, to date, shows these creatures as social beings. They use community affairs as a time for relationship building. Even gatherings that are about facts and details or reflection and study have some form of social element. Sharing of a meal being the most common."

"Madam Speaker, you did well and should be pleased." Danu bowed his head to her before returning to his datapad.

"How did the broadcast go?" Mirtoff stared out the window, trying to move her thoughts forward. "Did everything work as we promised?" she asked of Tun'ae, her second aide.

Tun'ae pulled out his datapad and moved his hand over the device, calling up the requested information. "Everything appears to be in order. We were able to bounce the broadcast both off their satellites and our ships. We translated your address easily enough. It should've been seamless, with a minimal delay."

"Thank you, Tun'ae." Mirtoff continued glancing out the window for distraction and noticed the humans rushing beneath the tall buildings. "It's similar to the way our world once was. Don't you agree? It's amazing how some things are consistent in this universe."

*Maybe Speaker Rosta was right. The speech might have been too curt.*

"Tun'ae, I want to monitor their broadcasts." Mirtoff wished she had a cold cup of tuma. "After the announcement of our arrival yesterday and the resulting acts of violence around the planet, I want to make sure we are not taken by surprise again." She faced her aide. "These humans are unpredictable; they don't even understand themselves. The places they thought would be violence-free were not, and the locations they said had the highest chance of violence did not."

Tun'ae nodded, working his datapad.

*What else are we wrong about?*

She stared through the glass at the driver, dressed in a dark suit and dark glasses. The look contrasted his hairless head and mouth and chin hair. "President Richard Zachary spoke highly of this driver. He's one of the president's own security detail."

Danu shifted and stretched out his legs. "That's what we've been told. I suggest we continue to speak in our language. They won't respect us if we are too open. Plus, we gave them more details on our circumstances today than we should, making us look needy and weak." He scanned the passenger section of the limousine. "They could have listening devices."

Danu was a suspicious male by nature, making him one of the best security aides.

*Did we give the humans any information they couldn't figure out on their own?*

To her, it seemed vague and generic; lacking. However, it was what the Speaker's House wanted, chiefly General Gahumed.

She twisted her head, causing the braids to get caught between her shoulder and the seat back. The members of the Speaker's House didn't see the humans' reaction as she did. "I think...yes, we need to be more open with them." She checked the vehicle's console next to her seat. She pushed a button and the window next to her started to lower. She frowned and pushed the button again and it started to rise. She picked another button and the screen between the driver and her delegation began to lower. "Starting now."

The chauffeur glanced over his shoulder, then turned back to his driving, adjusting the mirror so he could see the speaker general and she could see him. "Madam Speaker, is there a problem? Do you or your aides need something?"

"I wanted to have dialogue with you, if I may. I understand you are only our cha fer..." Mirtoff pursed her lips.

*That's not the right word.*

"Our driver."

The man was quiet. She continued, "Do you have a mate? What of children? I myself do not, but I have a brother and one niece. I am curious at how you will feel on this. Can you share your thoughts? You are not a leader, but I am interested."

Both Danu and Tun'ae spoke in their own tongue. "Madam Speaker," Tun'ae said.

"This is not appropriate. Please," Danu pleaded and almost reached out for her.

His hand retreated. She quieted them both with a wave of her hand, squashing any further comments.

The human sat with his back and shoulders perfectly level. Both of his hands were on the vehicle's steering mechanism, and he stared straight ahead. The hair above his eyes raised, and his lips pinched tighter.

*Some of the human males are so hairy.*

Then he met her gaze in the rearview mirror with a polite, but firm, expression on his face. "I'm sorry, Madam Speaker. I'm not authorized to comment on the current situation."

Mirtoff took a breath. Of course, she couldn't fault him; it was an answer that one of her aides would give. He was trained military, after all. What had she hoped would happen? Security was the same, another universal consistency, although an unfortunate one.

"You are a good soldier, Mister Nicholson. I can appreciate that. I hope you and your people understand that we are not an enemy."

He adjusted the mirror again and continued to drive in silence.

Protocol. She was surrounded by it. When would she meet a being that wasn't part of the governmental bureaucracy?

*What would become of us for it?*

"Thank you for hearing me, Mister Nicholson." She tapped her fingers on the armrest. "I shall speak fondly of you to the brother and the niece. I hope you will do the same." She raised the window between them.

She shook her head and turned to her aides. "That river met it's end faster than I would have hoped." She reached fussing with the braids in her bun. "They don't trust us. This is going to be a problem."

"You cannot know that from this one human male," Danu said. "Now please, don't worry, Madam Speaker. You have a busy schedule for the next few weeks. It'll take time for us to trust each other. Trust is earned, not given. Remember this is new. We need to present them with the opportunity to review and study."

She didn't respond. She put herself in the human's place. How would her world have reacted during the Clan Wars? Would they have stopped infighting and helped them? Or, attacked them out of fear? Her biggest question and worry—would humans allow them to live here in peace?

Watching the buildings pass by she turned and glanced at her aides, both working, ensuring that everything was still secure at the transport. The vehicle made its way to the private hanger. They crossed the security gate. The press was still there, waiting for them.

"Well, at least their media is free. That says something of them," Mirtoff said.

Danu lifted off the seat and adjusted the position his feet were in. "Well, some of them have free press," he said, turning back to his datapad. "Speaking of the media, your next speech is ready. Our media corps will be waiting for you when we get back to the ship."

She wanted a nice chilled mug of tuma. "Our media is going to have many questions."

"Of course, that is their nature." Tun'ae crossed his feet in front of him, unintentionally kicking Danu in the shin. "Apologies, Danu. This vehicle is extremely compact."

Danu bowed.

Tun'ae continued, "Luckily, we've had time to prepare. It will not be on the humans, but an update on what we plan to do."

The driver pulled into a private hanger and then stopped the car. Getting out of the vehicle, he moved over to the door and opened it. First out was Tun'ae.

Mirtoff ducked her head and stepped out of the vehicle, followed by Danu.

The driver stood motionless and stiff.

"Mister Nicholson, I will meet with President Zachary tomorrow. I will thank him for your services. Personally, I wish to thank you again for hearing me." Mirtoff offered a polite bow and headed toward her ship with both aides flanking her.

The hanger had been cleared for the Nentraee's use. The speaker general's ship stood ready to depart. The Nentraee Guards stood watchful and at the ready with their weapons drawn.

The shuttle was similar in size to several of the human airships that she noted off in the distance. However, the shuttle's design had smoother lines and a more organic finish with no bumps or cracks in the hull. Her shoulders relaxed as she walked up the stairs, the familiar surroundings a welcome site. Once inside, she retreated to her cabin.

Placing her hand in front of the sensor by the door behind her in her private cabin, she closed herself off from the rest of her team. The space was comfortable, but basic, with several chairs and a desk with a monitor on top. Several other monitors were placed around the cabin. On the back wall of the room was the emblem of their home world and their people. The design was comprised of seven gold symbols, one for each of the clans, and in the middle the crest of the speaker general.

The crest changed for each speaker general, and Mirtoff's was graceful in gold and silver. It reflected the two things most dear to her: intelligence and peace. The symbols were intertwined, showing that each depended on the other. They reminded her of home and of her mother. Her mother would tell her and her two siblings that it was only through intelligence that peace could be achieved; that was how the Clan Wars finally came to an end. Her mother would remind them that the war started because of the actions of some reckless Nentraee.

Mirtoff undid her dress cloak's clasp and draped it over one of the chairs. She dusted off a piece of lint from her suit coat and headed over to her desk, where a cool cup of tuma waited for her. She picked it up, took a sip, and sat, positioning the monitor for a better view. "Open a line 10-5B-PT7."

"Madam Speaker, excellent address. And the humans appeared pleased with it," said Mi'ko. His bright aqua eyes sparkled, making him appear years younger.

"You can thank Danu and the Speaker's House for the words. My only part was slight edits and delivery. The credit is theirs." She tried not to sound sour. "But I thank you, Mi'ko. It went as well as could be expected."

"Our media has been monitoring the situation on Earth and the speech, of course. They are anxious for your address later today."

She said nothing and took a sip.

"Mirtoff, is something burdening you?"

"I want to make changes to our future dealings." She put down the tuma. "I'm worried that we're doing this incorrectly. The humans are incredibly social. Nothing like us. We need to present a more social aspect of our personality to them."

"We have followed the procedures you and the House approved of, Madam Speaker. We have done nothing wrong."

"True. However, what we approved might be a problem; we're dealing with them as if we're dealing with our own kind from long ago. They're not like us, and we need to take that into account. I know this has not been approved by the Speaker's House, but as vice speaker, I would like your support."

She relaxed her hands and neck. She hadn't realized how tense she was. "I would like to make a translated version of my address to our people available to the human media. I want to show the humans as much openness as we can. There will be questions and uncertainty on all sides. I want to have an 'Earth Network' where our people can view their media if they choose. I want to consider going to some of these receptions we've been asked to attend. Not all of them. We should pick carefully."

Mi'ko ran a hand over his mouth, and he pulled at his bottom lip.

Outside, the windows to the cabin showed the skyline of New York City. She hadn't noticed the takeoff.

"Of course, Mirtoff," said Mi'ko. "Do you consider it necessary? The human governments have been open and helpful."

"Yes, I know." Mirtoff picked up her tuma and took another sip, enjoying the cool, sweet and spicy flavor. It relaxed her. "I'm not worried about the governments. I'm more worried about the people. My suggestion is that we don't agree to everything, but a tightly controlled list of events that will help to cut off any unknown tensions."

Mi'ko leaned back in his chair and pulled his hand away from his chin. "If you deem this is proper, I'll support you no matter what. Now, please excuse me. You have given me many tasks."

She bowed. "Of course, Mister Vice Speaker."

"I'll see you back on the ship, Madam Speaker." Mi'ko bowed in return.

The screen went blank, and then back to the emblem. Mirtoff tapped her fingers on the desk for a moment. "Open a line 10-5B-OU5."

After a moment the screen filled with the image of her brother. "Mirtoff." Ecra came to the monitor. The smile on his face caused his cheeks to lift. "We didn't expect to hear from you today. It brings me joy. Suloff, come say hello to your auntie and bring Faa," he said over his shoulder.

"I assume you've seen the broadcast?" Her tone was businesslike. It wasn't easy for her to switch modes so suddenly. Some, like Mi'ko, were masters at it. She never thought herself so rigid, but many did.

His eyes narrowed and a frown slipped across his face. "Of course. Why?"

"Hello, Provider." Faa pushed his face in the screen. "Faa been good. Faa had scratches." His head tilted and one of his ears flopped over. "Provider come soon? Faa miss Provider."

Her whole expression warmed. Faa had a way to brighten her heart. "I'm glad you've been good, little one. I'll see you soon. I miss you, as well." Seeing Faa's bright green eyes and how they twinkled filled her with the warmth of home. The effect caused her to sit taller and lean in. She wanted to reach out and stroke his soft fur and feel his warmth under her touch.

"Come, Faa," Suloff said from off screen. "You did a good job, auntie. The humans aren't nearly as ugly or hairy as I thought."

Ecra frowned at her.

Pretending to stifle a yawn Mirtoff covered the grin on her face with her hand. She bowed to her niece. "Thank you, Suloff." She turned her attention back to Ecra. "I would like to spend time with you tonight when I return. May I join you and Suloff for a meal?"

"Of course," Ecra said. "You know you're always welcome. I'll get the evening meal ready, and we can talk then. It'll be good to see you."

"Very good." Mirtoff's spirits rose as the weight of both worlds were slowly lessening. "It'll be good to spend time with you as well. I'm looking forward to it."

"As do I, sister. See you soon." Ecra bowed. The screen turned black and filled with the Nentraee symbol.

*Family. I need to spend time with my family and relax. So much has happened, and I need the time away.*

Finishing her drink, Mirtoff savored the last of the cool spice and stood. She walked to the window, watching the ship move through Earth's early afternoon sky.

"This is new for all of us," Mirtoff told herself. She leaned her head back, putting her hands to her sides and offered a small prayer for all of them. "Please, J'Veesa, guide me and help me to make the right choices for my people."

# Thirteen: At the Office

TODD COULD FINALLY relax. His head wasn't pounding, and the back of his neck didn't feel like a giant knot. The events of the last few days were behind them and life was starting to return to normal; the curfew was lifted, and people returned to work. With little incident, President Zachary decided the forty-eight-hour cooling off period had been effective, and no other restrictions were necessary. As predicted, the stock market suffered the largest two-day drop on record but rebounded as the world settled and collectively decided humankind could live with the realization aliens existed.

Talk turned to where the aliens should go and how they would adapt. All *Terrans*, as people were starting to refer to themselves jokingly, talked about was how different the Nentraee appeared and how mysterious they seemed.

The media provided updates and mentioned different countries signing agreements with the aliens. Reports aired of religious groups protesting against the arrival and claiming the Nentraee were here for nefarious reasons. Protesters shouted Earth was for humans only. Religious zealots claimed that if God wanted the Nentraee here, he would have mentioned them in the Bible.

As he looked around the CRiNE conference room, Todd wondered how it made the aliens feel.

*Was this why they were being so standoffish?*

He pulled a chair off the stack and placed it. He was setting up for the all-staff meeting Varick wanted to have.

"What do you think, Kati?" Todd asked.

She didn't respond, so he kept talking. "My brother said they're gonna visit San Jose. He doesn't have the details, and he's been busy with keeping things calm. Their space technology is more advanced than ours. Duh. They may even have stuff like terraforming and artificial gravity. Cool, right?" Todd glanced up at her.

Kati refused to answer. Her head was slightly tilted, and her lips were sealed together; she was still upset, and it showed on her normally very pretty face.

"Oh, come on, don't glare at me like that." Todd frowned and lined up the chair he'd just put down with the row of chairs in front of him in an attempt to keep the chairs even.

"I can't believe you didn't call me. You didn't even try to warn me." She crossed her arms in front of her cashmere blazer, forcing her chest to pop out a little more. "You're lucky I don't cut off your balls and add them to my collection. I called you once the phone lines were back to normal, right? I didn't forget you." Kati adjusted her silk shirt, picked up a chair from the stack, and dropped it next to the one Todd had just left. "You're lucky I'm helping you at all, ass."

Crossing over to her with a big, dopey smile on his face, Todd said, "C'mon Kati, you wouldn't have believed me if I told you. It was crazy. With Brad showing up and dropping this bomb on us what was I supposed to do? My head was somewhere else. Plus, Jerry didn't even believe him. He thought we were both nuts. There was no way I was gonna risk telling you. Who knows what you would've done?" He lowered his head and stared at her. "I told you that in confidence, so don't go off and share that bit of info. I didn't even tell Dan."

He got closer to her and lowered his voice. "You're still my favorite bitch here," he teased.

"You better watch your tongue, Mister HR Manager." She pushed him back, waving a finger back and forth. "If people hear you talk like that, I won't be the only one getting in trouble for inappropriate language in the workplace."

Todd pursed his lips.

Despite her expensive outfits and soft feminine exterior, Katherine had the mouth of a trucker. Todd had to tell her often to soften her language because some staff found her too foulmouthed and irreverent. Personally, he enjoyed her honest non-PC nature. It was the same with Dan. They had no problem telling people what they thought. If someone didn't like it, they would tell them where to stick it too.

She picked a piece of white cat hair from his dress shirt. "Seriously?" She held the hair up so he could see it. She dropped it, and it floated away.

"What can I say?" Todd scratched his goatee. "Bianca purposely puts her cat hair everywhere. If I'm wearing black, it's like the kiss of death!"

"You should have your house boy—"

"Who?"

"Dan." Kati shook her head. "Anyway, you should have him scrubbing your house, and maybe get him a French maid outfit. It'd be super cute," she said. "How long's he going to stay this time?"

"I don't know. With the Nentraee here and his mother completely freaking out over them, what could we do? So, we told him he could stay with us as long as he needs; plus I can't, in all good conscience, make him sleep on the couch at his sister's place, and there is no way he would survive staying with his mother." He shrugged.

"Ah, you and Jerry are such good friends."

"I guess so," he said.

"You 'guess so'? Well, I'd be charging his ass rent at the very least."

"Nah, we're fine. We have the space, and he's no trouble. Plus, he does help around the house and all that. Honestly, isn't that what friends do for each other?"

"Maybe I need to suck up to you more just to keep you around."

"Har har." He dusted his shirt. "Anyway, we're finished here, and it's almost lunch. What say I let you buy me lunch to make up for things?" Todd pushed out his lower lip in his best pouty face, making it quiver, watching her through big, open eyes.

"Oh, fine. How can I stay mad at such a pretty little gay boy?" Kati quipped. She walked up to him and smacked his face with affection.

"Ouch." He raised a hand to his cheek. The smack was harder than it should have been, and Todd knew it. Kati wouldn't forget, and she'd make sure he wouldn't either.

"Where'd you want to go?" she asked.

Todd rubbed his cheek as they left the conference room.

"Let's go to the Poor House? We haven't been there in a while."

"Sure, that sounds good. Let me get my stuff. I'll meet you in the lobby."

Todd and Kati spent their lunch eating and talking about the Nentraee like everyone else in the restaurant. Getting back to the office, Todd parked his Jeep, and he and Kati got out of the cool car. Peeking around the parking lot as the waves of heat reflected off the asphalt, a small drop of sweat ran down Todd's cheek.

"Jesus." Kati huffed, waving her hand by her face.

They hurried to the office building to get back into the chilled air. Finally, he opened the lobby door and welcomed the rush of the cool breeze from the building's air conditioning. He shuddered as he went through the second set of glass doors and saw Varick standing at the reception desk, dropping off an overnight envelope.

"Ah! Todd, come to my office, please?" Varick commanded.

Todd always smiled when he heard his boss's German accent.

"Sure, Varick. What's up?"

Kati walked through the interior lobby doors and headed back to the offices. "I'll talk to you later, Todd."

Varick ushered Todd into his office. Once they were in and Varick's office door shut, Varick went behind his desk and sat. Todd took in the sight of his boss reclining in his chair. He was an imposing bull of a man whose brows were always wrinkled in a serious expression.

*The man had never met a joke.*

Todd raised a hand in front of his face, pretended to yawn, and hid his amusement.

"What's going on?" Todd sat. Experience had taught him the only time Varick wished to see him was when there was a problem. Their work relationship was built on trust, respect, and noninterference, which afforded Todd latitude. He braced himself for bad news.

Varick's face transformed into what appeared to be a painful expression.

It was so off-putting that Todd had to catch himself from yelping.

*Holy crap, it's a smile. No, it's a sneer-grin.*

"All is well." Varick's words almost sounded like the German "alles ist gut." Todd couldn't tell anymore. "I was granted a meeting with one of those things." He was still sneer-grinning from ear to ear. "We did it! Well, I did it." He sorted through his notes on his desk. "Mi'ko Soemu. He heads their Business and Technology Information Ministry. He's their vice speaker, as well. Mister Soemu will be heading up their efforts to integrate our technologies."

Somehow the sneer-grin grew bigger on Varick's face. "It would appear they are very interested in our expertise. They like our biometric algorithm and the robustness of our hardware. We were on their short list of companies."

"Outstanding." Todd smiled, and his head nodded with excitement.

"I'm sure it helped that we have several government contracts. Our form of biometric scanners are new to them, as is our software." Varick beamed.

It was unbelievable; this was great news. Todd knew how important this would be for CRiNE and for Varick. And to see Varick this animated over anything was enough to make Todd chuckle. "That's great."

"I want you there." Varick's face became serious.

"Wait? What?" Todd forced himself to relax, letting it soak in. "But why do you want me there?" He shifted in his seat. "Not that I don't want to meet them. I would love to, but why me?"

"You're the only one in the company who has a degree in psychology and knows how to deal with people properly." The sneer-grin was starting to come back. "Grant and Lorena will be there, as well."

Todd was ready to speak, but Varick raised a hand, stopping him.

"These alien things are new to us. I want your help understanding them. The government-provided information says having someone who can offer this sort of support is good. They can give us a list of contractors, but I don't want to pay for that. We can't afford the cost. You're good enough." Varick folded his hands on his desk. "Basically, I want you to be my Counselor Troi from Star Trek for our first contact." He let out a single laugh.

Todd's heart started pounding, and his forehead started to sweat.

*I can't believe this. This is amazing. I mean, holy shit! I get to meet the aliens.*

After several minutes of silence, Varick leaned forward. "Are you okay?"

Todd nodded, remaining quiet, his head finally quieting. He processed Varick's words.

"Todd?"

Todd shook his head. "Um...all right, I can do that. I can be at the meeting for you. A government official might be better, but if it helps the company." He stopped and studied Varick. "One suggestion, you might not want to refer to them as *things*."

Varick's mouth twitched. "Good point. See? The perfect Counselor Troi."

*Har har. I hope he's not expecting me to wear the outfit.*

He didn't mind the Counselor Troi jokes. Varick had discovered he liked Star Trek by accident during his first interview, and they bonded over it at once.

"So, when's the meeting?" Todd asked, getting up.

"It's set for Thursday, the twelfth of July. That gives you time to go over the information the government sent us on how to deal with those... I mean...the Nentraee. They'll meet us here at the office, and we'll put them through the whole dog and horse show."

Varick still had problems with American colloquialisms, but Todd caught his meaning.

"I don't have the details yet, but I'll have Jim provide you with them," Varick said, writing something on one of his notepads. "Another thing—there'll be a welcome party downtown that night at the Fairmont. I expect you to be there as well. Bring Jerry. I'm sure he'd like to attend."

"They agreed to a reception? Wow!" Todd walked to the door. "That should be fun."

"I'm sure it'll be good for everyone," Varick said. "See you at the staff meeting."

Todd left the office. How great was this? He caught himself in a skip-hop and made his way to Kati's office. He had to tell someone. Now he would have to pull up the information on the aliens and study. He was sure there would be a lot he would have to learn. If the government was sending information, then there would be more online as well. It was going to be an education, and somehow, he was pretty sure Varick wouldn't be giving him any more money to do it either. The man was as cheap as he was stoic.

Todd poked his head into Kati's office. "You got a minute?"

Kati held her hand up—she was on the phone. "Listen, you dipshit. Get me my brochures by Friday, or I'll have your balls as earrings and your dick as a pendant. Do I make myself clear?" She hung up the phone and smiled at him.

"Buttercup, how can I help you?" she asked, typing something onto the keyboard.

"Ouch." Todd shook his head, trying to get Kati's vivid imagery out of his mind. "Was that really necessary? I mean the poor guy."

"That 'poor guy' has been dicking around with our order for a month. He's been throwing every excuse at me in the book, and when we met face to face, all he did was stare at my boobs. So...yum...you bet he deserved it." She glanced up at Todd. "What did Big V want?"

"Oh, right. Varick's got a meeting with the Nentraee. They're gonna come here to the office." Todd's voice became animated, faster than normal. "And he wants me in on it. Can you believe it? How cool, right?"

Kati stood, knocking her chair back so hard it made a loud bang. "Holy Shit! That's great! They're coming to the office? Wow."

Todd talked over her. "I mean, there is so much we don't know about them, and now I get to sit in a meeting with them? He wants me there. Did I tell you that? So I can make sure he doesn't screw up. Say something dumb, you know? I wonder what they're gonna be like? I hope they're nice. God, I hope the meeting's not boring. Crap, what if Varick makes a dumb joke? Oh God, what if I make a dumb joke?"

"Breathe." Kati snapped her fingers at him.

Todd inhaled catching whiffs of Kati's floral perfume and hints of smoke from lunch. He hoped it would help him relax, but it wasn't helping; he was too excited.

"There's some dinner welcome event. I get to go to that too." Todd was still racing through his words. "I can bring Jerry. How cool, right? We get to meet them in person!"

"Slow down there, big boy." Kati frowned, glancing at her fingernails. "I'll only get to meet them in passing, I suppose. It'll depend on what Grant wants, the rat bastard. Maybe, I can sweet-talk my way in?"

Todd nodded, but they both knew there was no way it would happen. Grant was the VP of Marketing and Sales, and he would never allow Kati to attend. It wasn't her area.

"Do you suppose Varick or Grant will say anything at the meeting today?" she asked.

"I guess. He's excited about it. I can't imagine him not telling everyone." Todd checked his watch. "Speaking of which, I need to get my butt in gear and finish. Talk to you later."

"See ya," Kati called out.

He went back to his office and tried to focus on preparing for the meeting. He moved his replica Star Trek phaser on his bookcase so he could get at his employee benefits binder. Flipping through the pages, he started to bob along to Scott Williams's "Parson's Farewell" playing on his iPod.

Scattered around his desk and on the rest of the shelves were little toys people had given him over the years. It was all in an effort to make his office as unthreatening as possible. Right next to his desk phone was a photo of him and Jerry from their trip to London. They were standing next to one of the guards at Buckingham Palace. It was true they never smiled, but at least they got a photo with him. They had joked about patting the guard's butt right before the photo, but he was armed, and they didn't want to get shot.

Todd's heart was finally getting back to normal.

*Aliens. I'm going to meet the aliens.*

He still couldn't believe this. He glanced out the office window at the foothills. It was hazy, but the mist hadn't covered them entirely. They were golden and speckled with trees.

*It's beautiful.*

Todd sorted through his emails. "It must be a slow day. Only twenty new messages," he said to his tiny office.

Scanning the list for one name in particular, Todd found Jerry's name and clicked on it:

Nothing happening here. I'm setting up a couple of new computers. I'll be in and out. Hope you had a good lunch. Is Katherine talking to you, or are you still in trouble? Do you still have your balls? Talk to you later.

Todd hit reply and typed:

*OH MY GOD! I found out Varick got a meeting with the Nentraee. Can you believe it? How cool, right? Anyway, I get to sit in on it. Sounds like a great opportunity. It'll be cool to meet them, best part is that we—this means you too!—get to attend a welcome dinner event afterward. And, yes, you'll have to wear a suit. This month is going to be busy. Lots to prep for.*

# Fourteen: How Open is Open?

THE OTHER SIX members of the Speaker's House watched her, each representing their respective clans. The meeting went as well as Mirtoff had anticipated. They were gathered in her office around the conference table. Thank J'Veesa that Mi'ko had convinced them to meet privately and not in the Council Chamber. It allowed for a franker conversation.

Slamming her hands on the conference table, Gahumed La-Enn scowled at Mirtoff. "You intentionally agreed to accept these welcome events and receptions before even speaking with us. We agreed—"

"No, General Gahumed," Mirtoff interrupted. "You and the other generals decided that we would not attend the human receptions, and everyone, including me, went along with it. You weren't at the United Nations. You haven't been in the meetings." She forced her voice to stay level ignoring the burning ear tips of the generals. "These beings aren't like us. Social gatherings mean a great deal to them. They celebrate many things: historical events, political gatherings, physical contests, great battles, and religious ceremonies, to name a few. This is important to them, and we didn't take that into account. Operating from our perspective won't work."

"Are you implying, Madam Speaker, that you were intimidated into both making the speech and not attending the welcome after the address at the human United Nations?" General Vi-Kamu Fanion asked.

"That's not what I'm saying. I'm not some pre-emisaration child who was upset by not being included in some game." Mirtoff pushed a braid of hair off her shoulder, trying to keep her voice calm. "We did the best we could with the information we had. But I was there. I saw them. I've spoken with many of the humans since, and I'm suggesting we attend some of these events."

Since her first official address, Mirtoff had grown more and more uneasy of their initial decision of a more isolated approach.

Syde Badrah, the youngest member of the Speaker's House, spoke. "Well, I, for one, am pleased with the new opportunity. I'll volunteer to attend as many of these events as you'd like, Madam Speaker. They have amazing customs I would like to learn more of. Their young have these events where they drink a liquid—beer—that makes them lose their senses, get physically sick, and pass out. That is just one. They have other events where—"

"Thank you, Speaker Syde. I believe we understand," Gahumed cut him off.

Mirtoff frowned. Gahumed did this to Syde all the time. The way Ghumed's ears flared when Syde spoke showed such contempt for him. Yes, he could be overly eager, but he was an official member of the Speaker's House who represented his clan well. Gahumed always pointed out his shortcomings. No male was perfect in Gahumed's eyes. No male except her son, Denes. He was a flawless soldier and a strong male. He was never afraid to speak his mind. Gahumed was proud of him, and in her eyes, Denes was infallible.

*J'Veesa forbid something ever happen to him. Who knows what she would do?*

Syde fell silent.

Rosta Gonu bowed toward Syde. "General Gahumed, it'll give us the opportunity to understand them in a setting where they are comfortable, not for us—"

"And what of security? What of the safety of our people?" General Yee Awon kneaded his hands.

"It'll be a mix of both human and Nentraee security," the edges of Mi'ko's mouth went flat. "Yes, we'll be cautious. General Yee, your people are well-trained, and I'm sure we won't have any problems."

"The humans have not been happy with our unwillingness to socialize with them, 'to get to know them better,' as they say," Mirtoff said. If the members of the Speaker's House had experienced what she had, they would understand. "We've given them time to reflect on the new information we've provided, but I'm afraid they still perceive us poorly. I'm trying to change that."

"I simply won't agree to these foolish human receptions." Gahumed massaged her ears. "It's too risky. We have no idea what these creatures will do."

Mirtoff had called this meeting with the hope of having a consensus, but Gahumed fought her at every corner. She was the speaker general, and the decision was made. "I don't seek your agreement, nor do I need it. When we left our world, additional powers were granted to the speaker general to proceed with first-contact situations as she deems appropriate. I'm exercising those powers now. This meeting is a courtesy to inform you"—she glared right at Gahumed—"what I plan to do."

Gahumed's eyes grew large, and her ears flushed anew. "You power-grabbing, filthy little *Ĩ-ta!*"

Every muscle in Mirtoff's neck tensed.

Mi'ko slammed his datapad on the table and stood, his ears an angry blueish hue and double in size. "You will not use that disgusting word in my presence ever again, Gahumed La-Enn. Do I make myself clear?" His voice was calm, but his words were not. He met her gaze as she shifted in her chair, licking her lips.

Neither Mi'ko nor Gahumed backed down.

"Gahumed, please, that was out of line," Vi-Kamu Fanion said in a tone barely over a whisper.

Mirtoff knew Fanion was normally Gahumed's strongest ally, but Gahumed had crossed a line.

Fanion said, "Speaker General Esmi, I would like to apologize for my colleague."

"I believe your colleague, the Speaker of the Clan Dentraee, General Gahumed La-Enn, can speak for herself." Each word Mirtoff said bit at the air. "And she has made her opinions perfectly clear." Her hands started to tremble, so she placed them on her lap out of sight of the others.

*I will not show Gahumed or any of them weakness.*

"As vice speaker," Mi'ko said, "I've already volunteered to attend the first reception. It will be in the city they call San Jose. I'll appear with my aides, and I would like to invite a delegation from our House of the People to join; they'll be in the area for meetings," he said, with a firm nod. "Are there any additional objections?"

Gahumed glowered at Mi'ko but said nothing.

*She's not continuing. Is that possible?*

Gahumed's face was tight as she spoke, "If I may, I would like to apologize for what I said, and I will not block this plan. I've stated that I don't agree. If the speaker general and the vice speaker are this strongly in favor, then I shall not object."

"I have no objections," said Speaker Syde. "I would like to include a few staff as well, if you don't mind." He beamed at Mirtoff and then at Mi'ko but avoided General Gahumed.

"No objections from me," Speaker Rosts added.

"If this is what the speaker general deems is in the best interest of our people, then I support it as well," Vi-Kamu said.

"As do I," Yee agreed.

Mirtoff let out a brief sigh of relief.

*A hard-fought battle. Still, I'm not sure if it is thanks to my sound arguments or to Gahumed's outburst. Either way, I'm grateful.*

MIRTORFF'S OFFICE WAS quiet. The only noise came from the hum of the ship, and the anxious trembling of her leg. She reflected on the meeting with the Speaker's House and how quickly Gahumed stopped; was it possible Gahumed was planning something, or was she being paranoid?

"How many of these things have you agreed to?" Danu ran his fingers over the datapad.

As she scratched Faa's head gently, her heart slowed, and she relaxed. Faa was such a tiny thing. She learned from Tun'ae that humans had similar companion animals. After her meeting, she was foregoing her normal cup of tuma because it was making her more edgy than she wanted. "We need to show them openness, and if that means I must sit with all their media, then I'll do it." She turned to Danu meeting his hopeful gaze. "The one you should worry for is the vice speaker. He has to attend the first reception. It will set precedent for all the others to come."

"Of course, Madam Speaker. Still, I would be remiss to point out I worry that it's too much. They have hundreds of reporters and media outlets worldwide, and if all you do is grant interviews, then how will anything get done?"

She smiled at him.

*It's his duty to remind me that I'm but a single individual. There is only so much I'm capable of, and right now, he believes the river I navigate will swallow me up. He's such a worrier. Still, he's probably right.*

Faa murmured under Mirtoff's touch, "So good, Provider. Faa love," he purred in his high voice, his soft, gray fur getting messed up by her touch.

Mirtoff and Danu grinned. Cádo had a way of bringing calm and joy to everyone around them. It was their simple way, and their happiness rubbed off on people.

"Okay, little one, go to your couch." Mirtoff sat up and straightened the top of her suit.

Faa glanced up at her with a hint of a sulk on his face but did as he was told.

"Danu, it's important to all of us that we make this work. The Speaker's House has given their support, as has the House of the People."

*Reluctantly.*

Danu carried worry in his eyes. Most males were worriers. Perhaps it was that part of their nature that helped them be good fathers. "It is also why we've agreed to this first reception with more to come, I hope."

Danu put his files down on the highly polished surface, then turned to her, his full lips pinched closed. "Of course, Madam Speaker."

"Danu, please don't be so disappointed in me," Mirtoff said. "And please don't worry so much. I realize I'm asking a great deal of you and your staff." Her face softened, meeting his bright green eyes. "Please understand how important this is. They are a new species. Even with our months of study and preparation, they have surprised us at almost every turn."

"Very well." He studied her carefully. "However, I ask that you share more of these duties with not only the vice speaker but some of the other members of the Speaker's House. Spread these interviews and meetings around. Don't try to do all the work yourself."

"We have no diplomatic corps, so who do you suggest?" Mirtoff asked. "General Gahumed La-Enn would be counterproductive. Or perhaps General Vi-Kamu Fanion? Her thoughts run deep, but her ability to share them..." She shook her head at the idea. "Unless you're talking military strategy, General Vi-Kamu Fanion would not represent us well, at least not yet." She sighed. "None of the generals that have seats within the Speaker's House are able or willing to do such a thing. They are hard enough to deal with on matters of state. Asking them to partake in interviews—no, I cannot ask such a thing. It would be bad for all involved."

"All right, what of Speaker Syde Badrah or Speaker Rosta Gonu? Both are well spoken and adored by not only their clans but all the Nentraee," he suggested. "They could be prepped and properly scripted. It would give the humans additional faces of our people and clans. It might help, and it might be good for them—give them experience with the humans."

Mirtoff was becoming distracted trying to focus on their conversation but wanting the day to be over. She wanted to push from her mind what Gahumed had called her. Her thoughts turned to the taste of a chilled cup of tuma. She had discovered the humans had a drink similar to tuma called *coffee*. She had yet to try it, but the humans seemed to love it.

"Madam Speaker," Danu said.

Mirtoff focused again on Danu and the conversation. It was true that Speaker Syde Badrah and Speaker Rosta Gonu were well-liked among her people, and they had both expressed interest in human contact. Her concern was that Rosta was not known to be the most logical and tended to speak too freely, sometimes causing trouble where none was needed. Syde was a good male, an enthusiastic male, but not a strong male. He would easily back off if pushed.

*Syde could speak regarding health and education, and Rosta could talk to their agriculture advances and other matters of the Nentraee's interior. It may work if done correctly.*

"Very well," Mirtoff said. "Danu, please see that both Speaker Syde Badrah and Speaker Rosta Gonu are included in these interviews with the human media. Focus on their areas of expertise." She watched him with the slightest of grins. "Since this is your idea, I'll leave it up to you to work with their staff and ensure that we're not appearing foolish or too open."

Danu bowed, hiding his own smile, but Mirtoff caught it.

*He really has a beautiful smile.*

"Of course, Madam Speaker. I'll have the changes sent to them, and I'll arrange meetings with their staff."

"Excellent." Mirtoff stood up and stretched. "What other matters do we have to go over tonight?"

"Nothing that can't wait until tomorrow. I don't want to keep you from your family," Danu stood and made his way to the door. "Have a good night, Madam Speaker." He glanced over to the cádo who was curled up on the sofa. "Good night to you, little Faa."

Faa lifted his head, and his tail swished softly on the sofa. "Goodbye," he said happily, his big eyes following Danu as he left the office. "Is it time, Provider? Is it time to see Ecra and Suloff?" He jumped off the couch and bounded over to her.

"Yes, little one." Mirtoff smiled. "Now come. We don't want to keep Ecra and Suloff waiting. I hope he has a nice, cold cup of tuma waiting for me."

MIRTOFF AND FAA reached the living quarters of her brother and niece. As a part of the Speaker's family, they were given larger quarters than most, in a special area of the speaker general's ship. The area was secure, so she was able to move freely without the need for security which was nice, but if she was honest, she didn't mind having Danu around. When she was in this part of the ship, she felt the most like her old self. She didn't have worries or cares. She was a normal Nentraee with a normal life. Even Faa picked up on her mood shifts when she was with her family.

The door chirped as it opened, and she was met by the warm smile of her beloved brother. "Mirtoff," he greeted her with a tender touch of his hand to her cheek.

She reached up to his hand and held it there, enjoying the warmth and the familial touch. "Hello, brother." She touched his cheek in a similar fashion.

Faa laughed, bouncing through the door, squeezing past both of them. "Suloff, come scratch back. Faa here, time for scratchies." He giggled as he scampered off.

Both Ecra and Mirtoff smiled.

"He is such a dear one." Ecra watched Faa rush off.

"I'm blessed by J'Veesa's love to have him." Mirtoff entered the apartment, smelling the spiced meats and vegetables. "Is that...?" Her face filled with joy. "Does this mean Ra'pia will join us tonight?"

"No, not tonight. She has to work late." Ecra walked to the kitchen. "And yes, my sister, that's *OmLanga*. I made it special for us." His grin divided his mouth in two. "Just like father used to make back home."

The quarters Ecra shared with his daughter were cozy and well lived in. They were nothing like the small quarters they'd once had on the agricultural ship. The pale-yellow walls with warm brown tones of the furniture reflected hints of their home and clan. Even the windows that opened onto one of the ship's many gardens were designed to be like those they once had in their family home on Benzee. Next to the windows was a door leading to a small balcony, where they could sit. Bright light filled the space with warmth.

"I haven't had that in so long. How did you arrange it?" Mirtoff followed the smells that filled her with memories of family and love.

"I have my ways." He turned back to the meal prep. "Working on the agricultural ships has its benefits." His head tilted, viewing her over his shoulder. "Do you remember us sneaking in while father was busy helping Ta'nan with school work? You would help me up onto the counter to taste it." He laughed. "You would get us into so much trouble."

"I have no recollection of such things." Mirtoff grinned. "What I remember is you constantly begging Ta' and me to include you. 'Toffy, I want to come. Toffy, where are you going? Toffy, if you don't let me come, I'll tell mother.' That's what I remember, brother."

As he twisted away from her, his tieback was exposed. She reached out and yanked the tie, which held his long brown hair in place, out and snickered.

"Not funny, sister," Ecra nabbed the tieback and fixed his hair.

She knew he hated when she messed with his hair, but she had done it ever since they were children. "I miss them."

"Not a day goes by I don't remember our family," Ecra said. "Having to say goodbye, knowing there was nothing to be done. The military there to make sure we left. It was awful."

Reaching up, she loosened the braids of her hair, allowing them to fall to the small of her back. "Everything I do now is to honor our family. I want this to work. Ecra, this needs to work. Our people need a home. They need ground under their feet. We can't risk any more lives."

He stretched out and touched her cheek. "You're my sister, and I realize everything you do honors our family and our clan. I know they would be proud of you. Not because you are speaker general, but because of all you do for our people. Everyone respects you."

"Not everyone, brother." She frowned, recalling the awful things General Gahumed had said to her.

*Who used such language these days? Weren't they beyond that now?*

She pushed the thoughts from her mind.

"Aunt Mirtoff!" Suloff came out from her room, Faa in her arms, his tail happily swishing back and forth.

"I see you've made Faa very happy, Suloff." She walked over to her niece, touching her cheek with care. "Faa, you're too big. You need to let Suloff put you on the floor."

Faa worked his muzzle into a pout. "Faa happy. Faa not too big."

"It's okay, Auntie." Suloff held Faa rubbing the top of his head. "He's not that heavy...yet."

Faa nuzzled into Suloff's arm. "Faa comfy."

"Who am I to argue with the two of you?" Mirtoff rustled the top of Faa's head.

Ecra held out a glass of e'xin for Mirtoff. "Come sit. Let the worries of the day be gone from here."

Sipping the e'xin, savoring the richness, she smiled with relief. "Very nice. Is this new from the agro ships?"

"Yes, I'm very pleased. We're hoping to be able to double production in the coming months. Now that we've reached Earth, getting more resources would be helpful." His brows raised with hope.

She took another sip of the warm liquid. It would be nice to be able to give her people more luxuries such as this, but it was best not to make promises she was in no place to keep. "Send your request to Speaker Rosta and her staff. You realize I can't play favorites in these matters."

"I know, I know, but you can't fault me for trying," Ecra said. "Do you remember mother coming home and father greeting her with a glass every night? She would have the one e'xin. Do you remember?"

"Of course. But I remember a little one, no bigger than Faa, occasionally knocking the glass over when he rushed to greet her," Mirtoff mused. So many images of the past filled her mind. Ecra was always finding a way to get into trouble.

"I don't recall such things."

"Not you, never you." Mirtoff chuckled at the memory. "It must have been Ta'nan, even though she was the eldest, and as I recall very athletic, not a clumsy awkward little *Yép*. Like you."

"I was never a clumsy, awkward little Yép. You must be thinking of someone else." He sipped at his drink, trying to hide his smile, but the color filling his cheeks and ears could not be hidden. "That was so long ago it seems like a different life, much like our lives when Ka-shi was alive. Right, Suloff?"

"I wish I remembered her better. Sometimes I wish she was here." She glanced from Faa to her father and aunt. "I imagine she would be excited to meet the humans. I remember her reading me stories of life on other worlds." She shifted Faa in her arms.

"Yes, I believe your mother would as well," Erca said. He turned to Mirtoff. "I appreciate that you are worried, my sister, and you haven't gotten to spend much time with us, but how go your dealings with the humans?"

Mirtoff leaned back, letting the softness of the chair caress the curves of her body. "They are so different from us, and I keep having to ask myself: how open is too open? The moment we arrived here, their worldview transformed." She sighed. "Most of their reactions were not what we were told to expect. And now, trying to get the Speaker's House to support my actions is almost as hard as trying to figure out what these humans will do next."

"I'm sure that's not the case," Erca said. "I have no doubt you'll do what is right. You always do. That's how you became speaker general. You always do what is best no matter the cost, and people respect that."

"I don't always know."

"Danu agrees." Ecra watched Mirtoff closely. "He worries for you as much as we do. Why do you suppose he pushes you so hard to come to these meals?" He grinned. "It's so you can relax and rest."

"I know. Even tonight he was hurrying me along."

"You're not going to talk about work are you, Auntie?" Suloff sat in a side chair with Faa on her lap, rubbing his head. "I thought you came to get away from that?"

"You're right," Mirtoff said, amused by her niece. "Let us leave work at the door. How go your studies? Are you doing the Za'entra and your family proud?"

Suloff frowned. "I should let you and father talk about work instead." She rolled her eyes at the question and continued to rub Faa's head, much to his delight.

Both Ecra and Mirtoff laughed.

"It's good to be with my family." Mirtoff enjoyed another sip of the warm e'xin. She grinned at her brother, niece, and Faa.

*The human reception would come soon enough, and Mi'ko can handle it. There's no use worrying. Plus, he may enjoy himself, as may the others in attendance.*

The break from the Speaker's House and her life as speaker general was what she desired. She needed to feel what it was like to be a Nentraee again. She even allowed herself a fleeting thought of Danu and what he was doing during his off hours. Maybe she should have offered him to come to share a meal with them. He and Ecra got along well, and it would be nice to spend time with him outside of work.

She smiled at the ridiculousness of the idea and took another sip of her e'xin. She was sure he had better things to do than spend his off time with her and her family. She sighed relaxing deeper into the chair. This was perfect. Everything else would wait.

# Fifteen: Reception

TODD ADJUSTED THE knot in his lavender tie with shaky hands. He glanced over at Jerry, who had been watching him dress. "I'll give you a call later and tell you where to meet me." Todd tightened his tie. Unhappy with how the tie looked, he loosened it and redid it. "I'll get more info from Jim, but it'll be fine. They have our names, and we provided the security information they asked for. Still, get there early, just in case."

His light gray suit was his best fitting and complemented his now neatly knotted tie flawlessly. He straightened his collar and gave himself another once-over. He was happy with his appearance. His new haircut and his perfectly shaped goatee were amazing.

*Gotta look good for the Nentraee.*

He went over to Jerry, bent, and kissed his forehead.

"Wow! Don't you look sexy." Jerry reached out and pulled at Todd's tie. "Maybe, I won't let you leave. Keep you here for myself. I wouldn't want some hunky Nentraee to fall for you."

"Okay, you've convinced me." Todd started to untuck his shirt.

"Go on," Jerry said. Then adopted that teasing voice that Todd always hated. "Everything'll be fine."

"Shut up. This is a big deal."

"Uh-huh." Jerry rolled onto his side. "You've been driving us crazy with this Nentraee stuff for weeks. Now, go. I'll see you tonight. Love ya."

"Later, hon." Todd grabbed his keys off the nightstand.

He walked lightly to try to be quiet enough to not wake up Dan, but his shoes clacked on the hardwood floors.

Bianca ran across the dining room on one of her secret kitty missions. "Crazy cat," he whispered.

Before leaving, he scanned the dining room table to make sure he had his notes. He'd spent the last few weeks going over everything available on the Nentraee: reading government reports, media articles, and contacting companies that had already met with the aliens. His goal was to make sure CRiNE didn't screw up.

"Good luck today." Dan rubbed his eyes as he sluggishly made his way from the guest bedroom to the bathroom.

"Sorry, I didn't mean to wake you." Todd frowned at his shoes.

"You didn't; I gotta pee. See you tonight after the big dinner. I'll light a candle for you when I'm with my mom at mass...again." He frowned.

One of the reports Todd had read said that since the Nentraee arrived, every religion had seen an increase in attendance at services. He only hoped that folks wouldn't be joining the groups of religious protestors and xenophobes popping up.

"Sorry, Dan."

"It's not your fault. Just be safe today." He rubbed his eyes again. "Thanks for letting me crash here. I know it's made things easier on my family. Once my mom realizes they aren't the devil or whatever, I'll get out of your hair." He walked into the bathroom and closed the door.

*So much has changed.*

TODD BRUSHED OFF the white cat hair from his suit jacket as the limo bringing the Nentraee finally pulled up to outside the office. All the CRiNE staff was hovering in the lobby ready to get their first in-person look at the aliens. There was no way to stop the staff, so they didn't try. Varick, Todd, Lorena, and Grant stood ahead of everyone forming a barrier. They hadn't planned for this. Todd should have known better. Still, he pushed the team through countless, exhaustive practice meetings to ensure there were no blunders.

The four Nentraee exited the limo and slowly made their way through the double doors. They were tall—not freakishly tall, but they stood as tall as Todd. Even the females.

*Remember, don't touch them. Touching is an intimate act. They are formal. Small talk is not necessary. Also, they are polite but direct.*

Todd turned to Lorena. The color drained from her face. She took a deep breath and calmly leaned against the reception desk.

As the Nentraee entered the lobby, Todd didn't know where to look.

The eldest Nentraee male was the vice speaker. He appeared in his fifties by human standards. Todd recognized him from the photos in the reports. He was from the Ultween clan, was darker in coloring from the rest, and had handsome aqua eyes. Slightly chunky but not fat, his suit was pressed and neat but not as well tailored as the others. A lopsided bow that matched the color of his suit tied back his shoulder-length, brown hair.

If Todd was judging him by human standards, he would call him neither handsome nor unattractive. From the report, it was learned the vice speaker had a wife and three sons, and he was considered an accomplished businessman. He took a shaky breath.

The tall female next to him had to be his security guard, Vi-Narm. She was from the Dentraee clan. She would travel with the vice speaker everywhere. Todd didn't want to mess with her. Her face was made of hard angles, and she didn't smile. Her mouth was a perfectly straight line. She didn't keep her hair as elaborately braided or in nearly as high a bun as the other female Nentraee did, instead keeping it up in a tight bun to one side of her tanned face. She had no spouse and no family. From what the file said, the Dentraee clan were very religious, but Todd couldn't tell by looking at her.

The male with the reddish-brown hair and deep-olive complexion was of the same clan as the speaker general a Za'entra. Dan would call him *"muy caliente,"* considering his broad shoulders and sharply tied-back hair. It took a moment for Todd to recall his name. Weaqu. There wasn't a lot more in the file on him, which was kind of a bummer.

Todd's neck started to warm up.

The shorter female was from the Caleen clan. Their skin tone and facial features were the fairest of all the Nentraee clans. However, of the three other Nentraee in the lobby, she was as by far the least attractive. Her dirty blonde hair was styled up with heavy braids with several curls falling out of place. Her blue eyes were cloudy, and her skin was blotchy. It was unfortunate.

*It's the ridges in her forehead; they're really pronounced. More so than the others. They just look funny.*

Her name was something Cee. GanCee. Todd remembered finally. It would have sucked if he couldn't remember.

*At least I have their names in my file.*

He scrutinized the group again, taking in their appearance as a single group.

The lobby was completely silent as Todd and the others waited. A couple of coughs from behind him made the lack of noise even more noticeable.

*Why isn't Varick introducing us?*

Todd glanced at Varick whose mouth was quivering or trying to form words. Todd wasn't sure.

*Crap.*

"Welcome to CRiNE." Todd stepped forward. His voice shook as he gestured around the lobby. "I'm Todd Landon, Human Resources Manager. This is Varick Braun, our CEO…um, Chief Executive Officer." His hands trembled as he pointed to Varick. "This is Grant Nguyen, our VP, sorry, our Vice President of Marketing and Sales. This is Lorena Sanchez, our Vice President of Engineering."

The four Nentraee bowed.

Varick cleared his throat, scanned the lobby, and finally found his voice. "Yes, welcome to CRiNE. I'm Varick, as Todd said, and this is my team and my office. Welcome."

Todd closed his eyes for slightly longer than a blink.

*Thank God. I thought you would never talk.*

"I Vice Speaker Mi'ko Soemu." Mi'ko bowed. "This is Security Aide Vi-Narm." She bowed. "Me *Métkip* Aide GanCee." She bowed. "And in last place, Weaqu me *Jektíl* Aide." He bowed.

It was charming to listen to the Nentraee speak English; they seemed to often miss words or use the wrong phrase. Their lack of using contractions added to this charm.

After bowing, each member of the Nentraee delegation stepped forward and greeted the team from CRiNE with firm handshakes, which surprised Todd considering how they supposedly felt in regards to touching. Grant shot him a frustrated look as he was the first to be greeted in this way by the Nentraee.

Todd shrugged slightly, not sure what to say or do. *Best just to go with it.*

The Nentraee's stiff shoulders and timid faces showed discomfort. However, their handshakes were strong to the point of being painful. Todd flexed his hand when it was over.

Varick worked his fingers after the handshake and turned to Todd with a look that seemed to ask how Todd thought things were going.

Todd nodded in the affirmative.

The first moments of the Nentraees arrival were awful. Everyone was milling around, not talking. Still, seeing the Nentraee for the first time—actual, real-live aliens—was mindblowing. After the handshaking, the awkwardness passed. Todd had a big dopey smile on his face. Even the way the Nentraee moved was different, graceful, yet with a rigidity that made him wonder if they had steel rods running from shoulder to foot. One of the oddest things about them was their lack of body hair, other than at the top of their head. No eyebrows, no arm hair, nothing. Did they have hair anywhere else? Perhaps that was why they had long hair— to compensate for it elsewhere.

"Please, let us move to the conference room for our discussion." Varick gestured. "And allow the rest of my staff to get back to work."

Todd bit his bottom lip and sneaked a peek at Kati, who frowned at Varick but made her way back to her office with the rest of the staff.

Several people, including Kati, ran into one another with their heads almost craned over their shoulders to get final peeks at the Nentraee.

The CRiNE conference room was a meeting room and a demo space. It had built-in features that allowed the flat screen TV to lower so they could show demo videos and other interactive media. A couple of displays would come up and out from the high-gloss maple cabinets to show different applications for the company's software.

Todd adjusted his jacket. He tried to focus on the meeting but was more fascinated with the Nentraee—how they were so engaged, how they moved, how they sat, and how they grasped at each item mentioned by Grant or Lorena. He had almost hoped for a cultural snafu to spice it up.

Eventually, Varick leaned back in his chair. "Well, Mister Vice Speaker, it's getting late." His mouth turned up in an unnatural manner. "Why don't we continue our talks in the car on the way to the reception? I'm sure we can hammer out the rest of these details later."

The vice speaker nodded at GanCee, who would be heading up the CRiNE project.

"Vice speaker," GanCee started, "we can call ahead the other and let know we going to be behind schedule. What you like?"

Bowing, the vice speaker turned to his other aides. "We shall stay here and finish our talk and then go welcome. Vi-Narm, please contact Denes with the other members of our delegation and advise them of the situation."

Todd noticed Weaqu run his flawless fingers over the Nentraee version of a computer tablet. Weaqu shifted his broad shoulders. "Now please, Missus Lorena Sanchez, you certain that you able integrate the scan device with our current system? What about the waresoft? Will that able to adjust?"

*I guess it's back to business.*

"Of course, there may be issues; that's expected with a project of this nature, but nothing in the information you provided us indicates there will be an issue with your current systems," Lorena said. "As for the software, we will need your assistance with the translation matrix, but everything else should integrate easily enough." She flipped through her notepad and made a few hasty notes.

Todd caught the vice speaker's forehead tighten into what he thought was a frown.

*I wonder what that was about.*

"We work with companies all over the world," Lorena added. "Well, our world. We've never had an integration problem."

"It's one of our main selling points, which is why we're the leader in biometric security," Grant said.

It didn't take long before Vi-Narm was back to her seat, and everyone was again focused on the meeting.

*So much for leaving.*

FINALLY, ALMOST AN hour later, the limo pulled out of the CRiNE parking lot and headed off to the reception at the hotel. Todd texted Jerry once they left, so he knew to wait for him at the entrance of the Fairmont Hotel.

As they rode, Varick addressed Mi'ko. "You see, Mi'ko—I'm sorry, Mister Vice Speaker—our biometric technology and algorithms are very robust and can easily be modified to accommodate the Nentraee with whatever needs you have. We will, of course, need to work with your engineers to ensure the binary translation operates properly, and there will be extensive testing."

"Binary coding seems to be common between our two people," Weaqu said.

Varick adjusted his position on his seat. "We're very proud of our algorithms."

"And the hardware?" GanCee asked.

"Plug and play," Varick said, and the Nentraees' brows raised. "Um...well...what I mean..." He turned to Todd.

"Sorry, it's an American colloquialism. It means that we may not need to physically configure your devices, depending on compatibility. However, we'll need to—"

"Yes. Thank you, Todd," Varick interrupted.

The landscape and traffic passed. Todd kept having to stop himself from tapping his leg. He hated being tardy for anything—something his mother forced into him and Brad.

Varick continued to blather on regarding the technology as the vice speaker and the others listened intently. Todd thought about Jerry and Dan and how he now understood what they were getting at when all he did was talk about the Nentrae. He dusted off a fleck of dirt from his suit. They were expecting a lot of cameras and media at the event. Luckily for him, they would be focusing on the Nentrae and Varick. He planned to leave the limo last. So, with luck, he would quietly enter the hotel, find Jerry, get to their table, and stay out of the way.

Weaqu caught Todd's gaze. The edges of his mouth turned up, and his eyes sparkled. It was a surprisingly warm and full smile, different from the almost-fake ones they showed when they first arrived.

Todd returned the smile before Weaqu turned back over to Varick and Mi'ko.

He focused on studying Weaqu's features, scanning his body up and down, continuing to come back to his face.

"Is something wrong with me face?" Weaqu asked.

Todd snapped out of his gaze.

"You unpleased with my feature? Have I offended you in some way I not realize?" asked Weaqu.

Weaqu was sincere in his questions, and Todd couldn't fathom how he put himself in this situation. He wanted a good rock to crawl under.

"Oh, no. I'm...um... I'm...sorry. I didn't mean to stare. I..." he stammered as he spoke.

"You turning color. Is you okay?" GanCee asked, pulling out her computer device thing from inside her jacket.

Todd's face burned even hotter under the new scrutiny. He pulled at his collar as small beads of sweat broke out on his forehead.

"I apologize for Todd." Varick held back a chuckle. "Even though we've been studying your customs, as you can see we don't know everything. We aren't used to your appearance yet; that's all."

The vice speaker nodded, as did Vi-Narm. She examined Todd for a moment longer with a hint of a frown. Finally, she turned back to Mi'ko.

Weaqu's continued gaze made Todd uncomfortable.

"You are unique-looking to us as well," Weaqu said in a hushed voice. "Not altogether unpleasant." There was a slight raise of his brow.

Todd cleared his throat. "I'm sorry, it's very rude for me to stare, as you can imagine—"

A bright flash of white and yellow light enveloped the car. The light seared into Todd's vision, drowning his world in white. A sound like a jet plane taking off filled Todd's head—it was deafening.

Without thought, he pushed himself diagonally onto the vice speaker to cover him. The glass shattered around them. He did his best to cloak the vice speaker with his body and his suit jacket, but he was shifted off him as the limo lifted off the ground and flipped over.

Everything moved in slow motion; the glass shattering, the car tumbling, everyone inside getting tossed around like candy being emptied from a box by an impatient unknown child.

The limo came to a crashing stop. Todd heard a crunch and felt pressure in his leg as he landed on top of the vice speaker. He couldn't let anything happen to the Nentraee. The vice speaker was too important.

As if from a distance, he heard the screaming and yelling around them. After a few seconds of shock, he yelled, "What the fuck was that?" It was barely a whisper over the screaming from outside. "Is anyone hurt? Mister Vice Speaker, are you okay? Please, God, be okay." He pulled himself off the vice speaker, who was covered in cuts and had disheveled hair.

"Yes." The vice speaker shook his head. "I fine, but what?"

The vice speaker started talking in his language to the other Nentraee. His words got louder the more he spoke. The vice speaker pushed debris off him and continued speaking louder as he signaled to the others in the vehicle.

"Varick, are you okay?" Todd scanned his boss. Varick had landed on the other side of the vehicle. His eyes weren't open. Todd examined his body. Nothing seemed to be stuck into or out of him though there was so much blood he wasn't sure.

*All the blood is red.*

He fingered around Varick's neck for a pulse. He found the pulse, but it was weak.

*He must be unconscious.*

"We need to get out of here." Todd glanced to the partially broken window. There was a quick pain in his leg. He kicked the rest of the glass out with the leg that didn't have a tingle to it. In the back of his mind, something didn't seem right, but he didn't have time to think. As much glass as possible needed to be cleared. Shrugging off the tattered ruins of his suit jacket, he laid it out to cover the shattered remains of the window. Glass crunched under his knees when he crawled out. He shifted to the side, witnessing the surrounding chaos.

*It's madness.*

Smoke and dust blurred Todd's vision, making it difficult to breathe. Screams rang out from all around. Gray figures ran in every direction. What he could see through the smoke seemed to be in ruins. No road, no buildings. Todd coughed a few times to clear his lungs. A field of gray surrounded him. He remembered this—from his dream.

He stopped focusing on the gray because it distracted him from what was happening outside the vehicle. He needed to get the others out of the limo and help them.

*Keep them safe.*

"Mister Vice Speaker...Mi'ko, give me your hand," he called back into the car. A hand grasped his. He pulled the vice speaker through the broken car window. With a struggle, Todd leaned the vice speaker against the side of the limo to rest. At least for the moment.

The vice speaker was quiet as Todd tried to pull out his security aide, Vi-Narm, from the vehicle window.

His leg pounded, but he paid no attention to it while he helped Vi-Narm to crawl out. Todd heard a different kind of yelling from behind him. It was loud and angry, but he couldn't make out what it meant. He was too engaged in his actions, and the growing pounding in his leg was becoming challenging to ignore.

Vi-Narm's eyes grew large, and her mouth started to open. Todd peeked over his shoulder and saw a human shape running toward them.

*Oh shit!*

The cloud of gray was fading, and he could see outlines of people running away, except for the person sprinting to them yelling, holding something in his hands.

*Something's wrong with him. Why are people running from him? He's not coming to help.*

Vi-Narm was still partly in the limo and unable to do anything. She was still half in and half out, trying to pull herself up. Todd looked around, seeing the figure get closer. He turned to the vice speaker. Then back. This couldn't be happening, but it was, and it was up to him to stop it.

*He's coming to kill the vice speaker.*

Todd pointed to the man. "Stop! Stop him!"

Todd faced the vice speaker, who sat against the car. His eyes were slightly opened, but he had a vacant look on his face. Todd grabbed the vice speaker's arms and pulled him down to shield him from what was to come.

There were loud popping sounds. Todd tightened his body around the vice speaker to cover as much of his body as possible. The noise reverberated all around. Then the second explosion came. Debris pierced his shirt, then his skin. Todd was expecting there to be pain, but instead, he felt only pressure and dampness on his back. To his mind, the second explosion had been much smaller. Within seconds of the flash, it was over.

Todd listened, still covering the vice speaker, not allowing him to move. He checked the immediate area; the blaring of sirens and police calling out instructions and orders cut through everything.

An officer ran up to him and the vice speaker. "Don't move; we're going to get you out of here," he said shaken but strong. "How many hurt?"

Vi-Narm pulled herself out of the car. She was covered in gray filth. She had several cuts on her face. Her tight bun had fallen and hair spilled over her shoulders. GanCee, Weaqu, and Varick were still inside. Todd shook his head, trying to focus. Everything was getting cloudy and confusing. The pounding in his leg and back was getting worse; he tried to pay attention to what was happening around him.

He turned to the police officer. "They need help. This is the vice speaker and his aides. You have to help them. Don't worry about me. I'm not important, just make sure they're all right. I don't know how badly they've been hurt, but you have to help them." He rubbed his eyes; things were so cloudy. "What the hell happened?" demanded Todd, his face getting hot.

Vi-Narm, in a cold professional tone, said, "The driver of this vehicle and Weaqu are dead. GanCee is hurt, as is Mister Varick Braun." She helped Todd move off the vice speaker to free him so she could check him for herself.

*Did she say dead? Weaqu and the driver were dead?*

Todd scanned the disaster area; there was nothing but gray ruin and carnage. Wet, sticky blood was splattered inside and outside the car. "There is so much blood. Please get some help!" he yelled at the police officer. The police officer was doing something, talking to someone, but Todd couldn't make any of it out. He tried to focus, but he didn't see anything—it was a haze.

Mi'ko and Vi-Narm were speaking in their language and staring at him. Vi-Narm had pulled out something that looked like a gun, but even that was grainy in his darkening vision. He couldn't keep anything in focus.

"It'll be fine," Todd said, forcing his attention on Vi-Narm and Mi'ko. "I won't let anything or anyone else hurt you. None of us will." He turned to the officer, grabbing at his leg to get his attention. "Will you?" he demanded, and the officer nodded.

"We've got this," the officer said. He was covered in a similar gray dust.

Forcing his body to move, Todd finally saw more police and other rescue workers coming. The horrid smells of burned flesh filled his nose. He coughed again, spitting out the filth and smoke. It may have only been minutes, but it seemed like hours. Some emergency workers made their way toward Todd and the destroyed limo, while others cleared out the uninjured and secured the area.

*They need to work faster. If they won't help, then I will.*

He strained to rise but couldn't. For some reason, he wasn't able to stand. Someone grabbed him.

"Get off me," Todd shouted. GanCee and Varick needed help. The driver of the limo required assistance, or did Vi-Narm say he was dead like Weaqu? He couldn't remember. All these other people needed help. He tried to move again to help Vi-Narm and the vice speaker, to make sure they were safe.

*This is hell.*

Finally, he could make out his rescuer's face. It was Vi-Narm's hands on him. "Do not move. You hurt. Mister Todd Landon, you need stay still," she said, as he tried to listen to her. "Mister Todd Landon, you cut badly."

Inspecting his leg, he noticed there was a piece of metal as long as his forearm sticking out of it. He didn't feel it.

His gaze bounced around, checking his own condition. He was soaked in blood, and his clothes were tattered.

"I'll be okay; it's a little glass and a few cuts," Todd insisted, straining to move his injured leg. "The vice speaker, GanCee, and you. We have to keep you safe; we have to help the others. I'll be fine. We need to help the others."

A quick tickle of a sensation from deep within him pushed forward, a sense of darkness and cold was becoming harder to push away. He wanted to move his leg again but found it increasingly difficult. He watched the confusion and chaos around him. It was becoming so cloudy, not from the dust or smoke, but from his own eyes.

The police officer, Vi-Narm, and the vice speaker were talking to him, but he wasn't hearing their words. Vi-Narm had put her hand on his leg to stop the bleeding. He experienced the pressure and pain instantly. He closed his eyes against the pain, the blurriness, and the chaos. Once his eyes opened again, everything would be clear.

# Sixteen: Sorrow and Loss

*BEEP...BEEP...BEEP...*

*That's a strange sound.*

Shifting, Todd found his body wasn't responding the way he wanted.

*Beep...beep...beep...*

*It sounds like... I'm not sure.*

His eyes fluttered but stopped before they opened.

*Beep...beep...beep...*

*Annoying.*

Changing positions was impossible as only resistance met his efforts.

*They still need help.*

A heaviness hovered over him keeping him from moving.

*No more screaming. The air doesn't reek of death or gas fumes.*

Light slowly crept through his eyelids as their seal broke and his surroundings came into view. He was in a room.

*What's going on? I'm not on the ground. How did I get here?*

Memories flashed through his foggy brain: the inside of a limo, driving to the reception, then an explosion. A bright flash of light and screams. Bodies lying scattered and buildings in ruins.

*What happened? Where am I?*

A hospital room. He was in a bed. The scent of bleach burned his nose.

*What's going on? Where is the vice speaker and the others?*

More and more of the room came into focus. He blinked, his vision clearing. Cards, flowers, and balloons filled every open spot.

*How long was I out?*

"Hey," a familiar voice said. "You're awake. How ya feeling?"

Blinking a couple more times, Todd located the source of the voice.

Sitting in a chair next to a portable bedside table sat Dan. He had dark circles under his eyes. He put his tablet next to an empty soda can and half-eaten burger and fries.

"Dan, where's the vice speaker and the others? What's going on? There was an explosion—"

"And like any typical drama queen, you passed out," Dan interrupted and leaned in; sadness lingered around his eyes, betraying the soft smile on his lips. "You had everyone worried, girl. The doctors said you lost a lot of blood. Lucky for you, the police and paramedics were there quickly."

"How long?" Todd asked.

"Doesn't matter," Dan said.

"How long?" Todd's voice was firmer.

Dan lowered his head. "Six days. It's been six days." He shifted his gaze to the monitors.

Todd's gaze followed Dan's to the displays. There were more cards and flowers on an additional dresser. He reached up, carefully avoiding the tubes in his arm, to rub his chin; it was bare.

"Sorry," said Dan, scooting closer. His voice was soft, barely more than a whisper. "That butch-ass goatee had to go. Kati and I had no intention of trying to shave your face around that thing. Mainly because of how fussy you are over it."

The rest of his face was clean-shaven too.

Dan's eyes dodged Todd's as he spoke. "Actually, Miss Thing, you're quite the hero." He cleared his throat. "Mi'ko, that Nentraee Assistant Head of the Speaker's House, or whatever, wouldn't be alive if it wasn't for you jumping on top of him. You slut." He replaced the frown on his face with a half smile. "You got all the glass and debris in you. Nothing hit him."

Dan's words played around in Todd's foggy mind, but they took time for his dulled brain to process. The explosion seemed so quick. He wasn't even sure he remembered what happened.

"What were you thinking?" Every line and wrinkle stood out on Dan's face, making him appear fifteen years older.

"I wasn't." Todd finally found his voice, still processing everything. "I mean, I just reacted. I saw the light and knew I needed to do something. To cover him with my body." He shifted his arm, but the tubes hindered him. "It was so fast." He met Dan's stare. "Are they okay? Dan, what the hell happened?"

Dan was quiet.

"What...where is...?" His stomach lurched, Todd's dull gaze bounced around the room. "Dan, where's Jerry? Why isn't he here?" Quickly, he examined the room for anything of Jerry's. A jacket. Something that showed he was there and would be back, but all he caught were Dan's eyes. "Dan, where's Jerry? He should be here; he wouldn't leave you to take care of me. Where is he?"

Dan inhaled slowly.

"Why isn't he fucking here?"

Dan's expression softened, and his eyes grew damp. "Todd, the attack." He licked his lips; his gaze never left

Todd's. "A group of terrorists, or something, maybe one or two. Everyone's still trying to figure it out. They had explosives and suicide bombers. No one knows anything for sure yet. Everything in a two-block radius of the Fairmont Hotel is in ruins, and the Fairmont is gone."

Dan's voice was soft and flat. "Todd, a big chunk of downtown is gone." He bit his lip. "What wasn't blown up in the blasts will have to be torn down. You guys were lucky you were running late so you weren't at ground zero when it went off." He swiped the back of his hand across his eyes. "The news says it was a truck bomb or some shit like that, but they don't know. There is no way it was a truck bomb." Dan shook his head. "Anyway, they're not sure. The terrorist planned to kill the vice speaker."

Todd's vision went fuzzy as his brain put the information together bit by bit.

"There were very few people who survived at the site."

Todd tried to get out of bed, but his body wouldn't listen, betraying him.

*Jerry's here, he's fucking around. Dan and Jerry are messing with me. I'm going to get up...*

"Dammit Dan, where the fuck is Jerry?"

He knew the answer.

The words slowly started to form in Dan's mouth.

Talking just over a whisper, Todd said, "Dammit, Dan. This isn't funny." He didn't want to hear it. He couldn't accept it. He wanted Jerry to walk into the room with a big dopey grin on his face. Jerry needed to open the hospital door, sipping a diet soda, and give him a "what?" sort of look.

Every part of him went limp as if someone pulled the drain on his energy. Jerry had been at the hotel waiting for them. Tears clouded his vision, and he began to tremble, and his heart sank so deep it was like it dropped to the floor. The room spun, as his grief overcame him. "You and Jerry need to knock this shit off and..."

Dan pushed out of his chair and sat on the edge of the bed holding Todd's hand. "Honey, they didn't even realize what hit them. Todd, it was quick. No pain. I promise you, Jerry didn't know; he didn't suffer."

Struggling to lean forward and rest his head on Dan's shoulder, Todd lay there crying, hindered by the equipment that monitored him. He wanted to rip it from his body. What was the point? If what Dan said was true nothing mattered anymore.

"Todd, I'm so sorry. I don't know what to say." Dan's voice broke. "Your parents–"

Todd opened his eyes, seeing his family by the door.

His mother rushed over and wrapped her arms around him. "Todd, honey, it's Mom." The hug pulled at the tubes in his arms, and it hurt, but it was nothing compared to the pain of losing Jerry. She kissed his forehead. His father and brother silently moved over to the bed and sat as he cried. He didn't know how long the tears flowed.

"Oh baby, it's good to see you're awake." His mother reached for his free hand and held it. "We're so sorry. It's been awful. Jerry's such a wonderful... We met his parents, the Bakers; they're here too. We've been worried about you."

His mother checked him and fussed over him, adjusting the blankets.

He burned on the inside; pain and anger pumped through his veins. He wanted to lash out, but it wasn't their fault. He stayed quiet, burying it.

"They left a little while ago to get some rest." His mother continued to rub his arm. "We've been taking shifts."

Her voice became shaky, the strength draining away. "Even your coworkers have been here off and on." His mom's soft cheeks lifted in an exhausted smile. "We finally had to send Katherine... Kati...home. She wouldn't leave your side. I think the hospital staff was happy to see her go. She'd been hard on the poor nurses. I felt sorry for them." His mom turned to Dan. "Dan finally managed to get her to leave."

Dan's forced smile lifted a bit more.

Slowly, Todd came around, as more of his new reality became clear. He wiped the tears from his eyes as best he could, even though they still fell. "This isn't happening. Mom? Civilized people don't act like this. We don't act like this. No one acts like this, blowing things up. They weren't hurting anyone. They just got here. Why would anyone do this? We don't do this; there has to be a mistake." He bit at his lips, the lack of hair as unfamiliar as the reality he was being forced to understand. He needed someone to tell him this was a nightmare.

He turned to his father. "Dad. Please tell me this isn't happening?"

"I wish I could," his father said. "What's important now is that you get better." He glanced at Dan. "Do you mind giving us a minute?"

Quickly and quietly, Dan got up from the bed. "I'll see you later. Don't worry about anything. I've been taking care of things for you." He rubbed Todd's hand awkwardly. "Is there anything you want me to bring from home?"

Todd's mind was empty. "No, Dan, thank you."

Dan moved to the door right as the nurse walked in. "Excellent, Mister Landon, you're awake. Brad, Mister and Missus Landon, how are you today?" The nurse scanned Todd's charts and went on checking the monitors and readouts.

"We're much better now, Cora," his mother said.

"Now that Toddy's awake," Brad said. "The little faker was starting to make us worry."

Cora didn't glance up from her paperwork. "Very good." She smiled. "I'll tell the doctor you're awake. I'm sure she'll want to see you." She continued absentmindedly tending to the machines around Todd. "Well Mister Landon, now that the worst is over, once I confirm with the doctor, we can feed you real food. How's that sound? Is there something special you'd like?"

"I'm not hungry," Todd managed to say. He was giving as much attention to her as she was to him.

"The doctor will be by later to see how you're doing." She checked her watch and made a few notes on the chart. "Mister Landon, everyone's been asking about you. People will be excited to hear how you're doing. You should eat. What about some soup?"

"I don't want anything!"

She placed the clipboard in the hanger at the foot of Todd's bed. Her pleasant smile faded. "Of course. Well, ring the bell if you need anything."

He stared at her with a blank expression as she left the room.

Todd's father was pale, and his eyes were red. The creases on his face were deeper than they had ever been. "This is a lot for you right now, and, well, we're happy you're okay and getting better, but don't get angry with the nurses. They've been amazing and are just doing their job."

Todd was silent.

*I don't know what I need. I don't know what's happening. I need someone to tell me this isn't real.*

"Todd, we're so proud of you." His dad started speaking faster, and his voice shifted, becoming louder to fill the space. "There's been people from the White House checking on you. Even President Zachary called. Twice." He raised up two fingers. "The Nentraee...well, the Nentraee are amazing. They've offered to use all their resources to help find out who did this; even their medical teams have offered to help us. To help you. Boy, they were pissed; they have zero tolerance for this sort of thing. Like any civilized people. The government has the city on lockdown for now. But, the news is saying that it was a bunch of lone-wolf types—anarchists. But if the people at fault are found alive, the Nentraee asked if they can prosecute them per their law. I don't think that will happen, but who's to say? Right? It's still pretty fresh right now."

Todd focused on his father. Anything to get his mind off Jerry.

"No one has taken credit yet, the bastards, and several countries and terror groups have come out with very strong condemnation statements about the attack. The reaction has been unlike anything before."

With a stern glance from his mom, Todd's dad stopped.

Brad turned to Todd. He picked up a few of the cards and started telling Todd about the people from around the world who had sent him well wishes and other things. Todd was barely listening to any of it. His thoughts were on Jerry and how empty his whole body was right now.

*I never got to see him. I never got to say goodbye.*

"Saving Vice Speaker Mi'ko Soemu is a big deal," Brad said. "It got worldwide attention. They finally had to stop sending these to your room and bring in security." Brad held up a card. "The hospital is holding them for you until later if you want them." His lips raised to a grin. "We're so proud of you and what you did. You're amazing, totally amazing."

Staring at them as they continued to talk at him, Todd's mind couldn't focus. They told him about his condition. How after the explosion, when he blacked out, he was pulled from the wreckage and taken to the closest trauma center for treatment. The doctors had to remove glass and debris from his back and his leg. He had a leg fracture and some very deep cuts. Luckily, none of his arteries had been cut, and they were able to patch him up. There would be some scars but no permanent debilitation.

Todd needed time to process. All he wanted was for Jerry to be with him, talk sense to him, but Jerry wouldn't be there. Todd's rock was blown to bits.

Attempting to swallow, but with no saliva, he still managed to speak. "It was just a reaction. Mi'ko was sitting there; I saw the flash and covered him," his voice was shallow and gravelly. He scanned his body: his stomach was caved in, any definition in his chest now gone, and his legs were covered in bandages. That was nothing compared to the emptiness in his heart.

"Is there something we can get for you? Do you need anything? Are you in pain?" his mother asked again.

"Dammit! Quit asking me that. Unless you can bring Jerry back, I don't want anything."

*Jerry. I need Jerry.*

Todd turned to his mother, seeing the hurt and the pain on her face, on all their faces. "I...I need time to digest this. I'm sorry. I really want to be alone right now. I...I don't want to seem ungrateful. I need time to myself to process."

"Of course," Brad said. "Come on, let's give Toddy some air. We'll come and see you later." He stood up and motioned toward the door.

Brad pulled at his mother's arm to stop her fussing. She fixed Todd's hair, then the pillow. Finally, Brad got her to move.

"Take care, Button," his dad managed to say as he walked to the door.

"Get some rest, honey," his mother whispered.

She was on the brink of tears, and Todd realized she would cry once she was out of his sight.

"Listen, Toddy, I expect you up and out of that bed when we come back. None of this being lazy crap. Landons aren't lazy SOBs." Brad's voice cracked.

Todd lay there, gazing at the window. He replayed his and Jerry's last phone call. He always said, "I love you," but he couldn't remember doing it this time. Did he? Three words and he couldn't remember saying them once that day.

# Seventeen: The Choices We Make

THE TREES SWAYED in the breeze outside of Mi'ko's window. His family's living quarters had an amazing view of the ship's gardens with its tall trees, fields, and small stream. That was something his people got right, making sure that the living quarters had a view of nature from their long-since-destroyed home world. The idea of modifying their quarters to allow for a balcony was something he and Laina had discussed. However, with both their jobs and their lack of time, there was no need to waste the resources for such a luxury.

*It might be nice.*

He inhaled a deep breath, clearing his thoughts. The view from his office mocked him. The little blue planet that they had attempted to work with, and where they had put all their hopes, sat there taunting him. He could no longer look at that world.

Mi'ko had decided to come home. His thoughts still plagued him. His people had wanted to work with the humans, tried to create an alliance with them, and an attack on his life was how they responded.

His arm and chest were still bandaged. The medical attention on Earth was adequate, but he was relieved when his own doctors examined his injuries. Plus, he wanted to be with his family, mainly his wife. Laina would put up a strong front. In reality, his family soothed him more than he soothed them.

A stabbing pain ran up his arm as he moved to fix the tieback in his hair. He hated it unkempt, falling to the sides and covering his ears. Even if he couldn't get the bow to sit right, he wanted it tied. It was disrespectful to have unkempt hair. This time, the bow had come completely out, and he wouldn't ask for assistance. There were some things a male had to do on his own.

After a second failed attempt, he tossed the bow on his desk, frustrated. His hair bounced off his neck and ears.

His thoughts flashed to the lost Nentraee; Weaqu and GanCee's remembrances were pleasant enough, and both were recognized with commendations by the Speaker's House. All the others dead in the attack, including the two members of the House of the People and the son of General Gahumed La-Enn, were given the same honor. Weaqu and GanCee were so much more than his aides; they were friends, almost family, and his heart ached for them.

"Why would they do such a thing?" he protested to the empty chair.

*That planet, those creatures, they're not ready for us. They aren't ready for the opportunities we bring to each other.*

He didn't want to recognize this at first; none of them did. His gaze fell; that wasn't completely true. General Gahumed did. She realized something like this would happen.

*The barbarism is too much to overlook. Our people are in mourning, calling on us to leave. More extreme Nentraee want retaliation—blood for blood.*

His own thoughts joined those that wanted to leave this solar system. All their worries and concerns had played out.

Again, a twinge of pain plagued his arm. He turned back to his device so he could work on this declaration. It would be taken to the Speaker's House for approval, and when passed, it would be presented to the speaker general for final ratification. His jaw tightened and quivered.

*It's as good as done.*

Still, he struggled to finalize it. Mirtoff couldn't write the declaration herself. It had to come from a member of the Speaker's House. After Mi'ko had talked with her, they agreed it would be best for him to write it, taking into account her comments and wishes. The declaration had to come from the one who had been the target of the attack.

Yes, General Gahumed lost her son and was pushing to write the declaration, but it was because of her anger she could not provide it. Gahumed wanted blood and would try to push for a military response. It would, without doubt, lead to war. A war the humans would lose, and then what? The humans would have a ruined world, and his people would be responsible for genocide.

His declaration was to cease ties with the humans and leave their world at once.

He stood and began to pace. "We shouldn't have come to Earth," he muttered through his scowl. It was in the best interest of everyone to go, and Mirtoff agreed.

Mi'ko marched back to his desk and sat. "Such a waste." He marked the document as he continued to review it. Each edit to the declaration caused his posture to crumple.

The door to his office slid open revealing Laina dressed in a rich white gown with hints of gold throughout. The lightweight gown played on her dark features and her pure green eyes. Her hair was wrapped up with gentle wisps falling along the sides of her face.

*So beautiful.*

He offered her a slight bow.

"You're working too hard, and I won't have it," Laina said. "We've discussed this already. The doctors said you should rest. Now come to bed. It's late." She brushed a tuft of hair off her face.

Mi'ko put the declaration down. "My work can't wait. The speaker general is expecting it, and as vice speaker, it's—"

She cut him off with a motion of her hand. "You could have died, Mi. Then what would we have done?"

*Things can't wait.*

"Our children still need you despite them being out of *emisaration*, and you need your rest." The ends of her mouth went flat. "I understand how important your work is. But with all that happened, you need the break. That's final." Her face was tight with worry. "This silly declaration of yours will wait. Now come to bed."

"Silly?"

"Yes, Mi, silly. Your health is more important. Anything our speaker general needs will keep until you are healed."

Mi'ko dodged her gaze as he spoke. "I know, my love. I do, but our people, this planet was a mistake. They're too violent. The attack happened in one of their most secure and stable countries. In a city that has never seen violence on this scale."

"You have to rest. Your body is still healing."

"No." He banged his hands on his desk, his ears warming. "I'm bringing forth a motion to leave here before more of our people die. This was our fault as much as theirs; we should have never come here."

Her frown turned to worry.

"We should have never trusted them to protect us." Mi'ko's tone softened. "I should have never forced our people into going to that reception. General Gahumed La-

Enn is infuriated and more distraught than I've ever seen her. I can't blame her. She lost her only son. Her only child. What if it was Mi'cin, Hir-shif, or Hir-ko?"

Laina's voice was calm. "It wasn't them. Instead, it was almost you. If not for that human, you would not be here."

Mi'ko picked up the tieback and tried again to retie his hair. An angry bolt of pain stopped him.

Laina stepped away from the door and allowed it to close as she glided over and tied his hair back for him. "My husband, ask for help when you need it. Don't be like other males. There is no need to be so proud when we are in private." She sat on the edge of his desk, and lifted his chin with her hand. "This human who saved you...doesn't that hold any weight in your debate? Even your own security escort was saved by him. What does that say about the humans?"

"My love, both Mirtoff and I are in full agreement. We will be leaving this place. It will be announced tomorrow. Maybe someday when they mature, we'll come back."

Her eyes narrowed, and her lips pinched ever so slightly. "Mi, you can't be serious. Am I the only one to see logic? Mirtoff is agreeing to this rash decision?"

He nodded.

"Our people died. I understand, but so did theirs," Laina said. "We have to stay; we can't run away. Not from this; not like frightened *Yéps*. We have nowhere to go, and the ships—"

"We'll find another place."

"Our fleet won't last, and if the ships do, for how long?" she asked. "Even with the repairs, we are able to make here. It almost took all our resources to get here, and we don't have enough to find a new planet. Being on Earth is a risk we must take. We have no choice."

Mi'ko rubbed his bandaged arm. "They blew up their own people to kill us. To kill me: they murdered over a thousand, they destroyed a part of a city, and their government claims to have found them all. They say it was an isolated group."

She shook her head.

"They have no respect for life," Mi'ko said. "Outwardly, they accept our help to investigate, but they block us at all opportunities. The ones responsible killed themselves in the attack. How can we work with these beings when they would sacrifice themselves like that? What if one of them comes to a ship and blows it up? How many more are out there?"

He turned away from her and saw the trees again; they seemed so calm. "They are cowards and barbarians. We can't risk more of our people's lives. Their history is riddled with these kinds of acts."

Laina huffed.

"No." Mi'ko's voice raised, but there was no color in the tips of his ears. "We must leave. We have no choice in the matter. We can find more resources on the way, as we have in the past." He massaged his ears. A hint of disappointment was directed toward himself as well.

"No Mi, you're wrong. You forget the human who saved you and the others who rushed in to help. Hundreds. They were everyday people—people who risked their lives to help us."

"My love—"

"Mi, listen to me," Laina interrupted. "They didn't run away from the danger; they ran toward it. You didn't see them, but we saw the images play out live for all to see. That was no act of cowardice. Their people reacted with outrage; it was monumental. They are as angry as we are. If anything, this attack has made many of them more resolute. Even stronger. To leave would be an insult to those who died. How will they be able to greet J'Veesa then?" She touched the side of his face with her hand, forcing him to turn back to her.

He met her gaze, his hair now tied up in a perfect bow, no longer falling off his shoulders. "There was one man, and the outcry wasn't for the Nentraee that died, but for their own people." His tone was more defensive than he wanted. It didn't matter—he was tired, frustrated, and by all rights, upset.

"You're wrong, my love. We mourned together. These humans may be barbaric by our standards, but how different are we?"

Her face tilted to the side, and a hint of light from behind gave her a glow. The vision melted his heart.

"Sometimes all it takes is one person." Laina turned to the books on the shelf across from him. She crossed over and pulled out one, scanning it rapidly. "What of our history, our past? We were not that much different. We brought our world to the brink of destruction, and we were able to repair it. It was only by a cruel act of fate that we had to leave. Again, my love, sometimes one man is all it takes."

"You can't judge the value of an entire planet on a small group of people, or even one man, no matter how noble his actions are," Mi'ko said. "There are so few of us left, and once we're gone our culture is dead. What happens if more of us die because of incidents like this? Our histories may be similar, but what did it cost us?"

Laina put the book on his desk. "What happens if Colony Ship Seventeen loses pressure again? Instead of us being able to fix it, what if it implodes? Ten-thousand people dead." She opened the book. "What if our agricultural ships turn barren, and we can't feed our people? One hundred thousand dead. What happens if a nanite containment field fails, and there is nowhere to evacuate the people involved? One hundred dead. These are the risks we face every day. Some are greater and some are smaller, but they are risks, nonetheless."

She sat on the edge of his desk again, reached out, and touched the side of his face with the back of her hand. "You can be so emotional. That isn't always the best thing, my love."

He pursed his lips.

"But it is part of why my love for you has lasted these years." Laina inhaled and peered deeper into his eyes. "We can't judge an entire planet on the actions of a small group either."

*Using my own words against me. Calling me a hypocrite without using the words.*

She tapped the open book and squeezed his good arm. She went to leave but turned back at the door. "Come to bed when your mind is clear. But tomorrow you rest, or I'll order a tranquilizer for you." With that, she slid out of the room.

Mi'ko ran a hand over the open pages of the book she left for him. It was a book on the history of their people prior to the Clan Wars. A passage caught his eye.

*"Special Envoy Dra-mic of the U'Xraee clan sacrificed herself to save the leader of the Dentraee clan. After the senior cleric of the Temple of J'Veesa was beheaded as an example of disloyalty to the faith. The clan elders were at a regional meeting of the clans to debate membership of the Denmaee clan into the Dentraee clan. Fifty members of the..."*

When he finished, he turned to his declaration. "We cannot risk our lives on a planet that has no value for life. There is too much at stake..." He scowled. He pondered what he just read and turned to the other books on the shelves. They were filled with Nentraee history and stories.

He considered his own words. Was he overreaching? Was he blaming them for one incident? He glanced out his window, thinking of the little blue planet that waited out there for his next move. He picked up the datapad, and with a sigh, he deleted the declaration. He opened a fresh file and began to write.

"We cannot judge a planet on the actions of a few, nor can we overlook our own history. Are we any different from these humans? The actions of one human..." Mi'ko continued to write. He was no longer stumbling over the words; they were flowing freely.

By the time the document was ready, the hours had melted away. He knew the arguments he would now face. But after reviewing their history, he realized they were no better than the humans, and the idea of running away didn't sit well with him. Despite his emotions, he had to convince Mirtoff and the others, and that wasn't going to be easy.

TAPPING HER FINGERS on the council table, Mirtoff's shoulders dropped, as did her eyelids. Sleep had not come easy since the attack. Her words and internal thoughts haunted her. Was she doing the right thing? Did they have another choice? She rubbed her temple, but she couldn't focus.

The council doors opened. "Ah, Mi'ko." Mirtoff stopped tapping and pushed the datapad over to Danu. They had been discussing the upcoming Speaker's House meeting. She picked up her cup of tuma and took a sip. Her posture relaxed as she studied Mi'ko.

*All the fighting and negotiating with the Speaker's House is over. The final piece, the declaration, is here at last. Thank J'Veesa.*

The Speaker's House would be meeting later in the day, but it was good he was here so they could talk.

*He looks rested.*

"Madam Speaker, I need to talk to you." Mi'ko's body seemed stiff, and his arm was still in the sling.

She thanked J'Veesa every day that his injuries weren't worse. The only positive thing that came from this attack was that his tieback was perfect—something she was sure Laina had a hand in.

"Vice speaker, I see I'll need to chat with your wife for keeping you from your duties. Was the extra day of rest necessary? For what? A small cut and a few bruises," she teased. Mi'ko and Vi-Narm were the only two Nentraee to survive the vicious human attack.

*They murdered twenty-eight of their own good people.*

She turned to Danu. "Please excuse us."

He bowed and faced Mi'ko. "Mister Vice Speaker, I'm glad you're recovering well."

The Chamber Hall was one of the grandest places in the entire fleet. The design was pure Benzee; it had high ceilings with smooth curves throughout. Granite mosaics of ancient events and landscapes covered the floors. Much of the hall was original and from their home world; however, the parts that could not be saved during the evacuation had to be reconstructed to fit the space. Even so, the Chamber Hall could hold several of their transport shuttles.

Ancient, hand-painted portraits of past leaders filled the walls, their watchful eyes serving as reminders of past struggles. Mirtoff's would be added at the end of her term to forever keep a vigilant eye on the Nentraee people. The hall and the paintings reminded the government what actions they took now would never be forgotten and would help shape the future of all Nentraee.

Gazing from face to face of the past leaders inspired Mirtoff and forced her to always think about the future and how her people would continue on.

*I wish you were all here now. Am I doing the right thing?*

"The declaration is ready for your review." Mi'ko passed it over to her. It was assembled as a traditional scroll with leather straps.

Mirtoff forced a grin. Once they approved it, Mi'ko would seal it with the vice speaker's traditional mark melted onto the leather fastenings. It was an antiquated tradition she found charming. "I don't need to read it. We've already discussed the details."

"Not this one, Madam Speaker." Mi'ko massaged his wounded shoulder. "I want you to read it before I present it. My feelings have changed."

Her brows raised as she picked up the final ceremonial document. She undid the straps and read it. Her confused expression changed as she absorbed the declaration. Her heart pounded angrily in her chest as her eyes grew larger.

"Mi'ko, this is a late boat on a river." She pushed the document back to him.

He refused to take it, and it dropped to the table almost knocking over her cup of tuma. She put her hand on top of it to stop it from falling over.

"Madam Speaker, I don't agree. I have spent hours going through our legal books and historical records. There is nothing that says we can't do this. In fact, it was very common—"

"Enough!" She cut him off. "It was very common before the Clan Wars." Her tone was dangerous. "Before the bastards nearly destroyed us, and our world—oh yes, I understand Mi'ko." Her stare bore into him. "I understand too well our history, and I'm trying to avoid repeating those mistakes." She pointed at the document. "But this. You even agreed coming to Earth was a mistake; one we can now fix."

*How dare you. You betrayer!*

"General Gahumed is ready to go to war." She slammed her hands on the table. "War, Mi'ko! The Rádo was stationed and ready to launch a full attack on New York as punishment. Almost nine million humans would have died." Her ears were hot with anger. "It's by sheer force of will that I'm able to keep her steady, and therefore, keep the military from attacking. Your resolution, the resolution to leave, was the only thing keeping us from a path of blood."

Mirtoff took a breath. "Now you're changing your mind and doing so only hours before the Speaker's House is to meet. You're making a fool out of me. Surprising me in this manner is reminiscent of our past leaders. Did you find that in our history books as well? Gahumed will definitely call for a vote of removal. Not just of me, but you as well." Her hands shook.

*How can you do this to me? You're my closest friend. It's because of me this happened.*

His betrayal mocked her as he stood there. She had insisted on only using human security. Only Denes and Vi-Narm were sent, and now, one of them was dead. Mirtoff wanted to trust the humans, and this is how they repaid her.

"Mirtoff, please. That was not my intent," said Mi'ko.

She scowled at him and he bowed.

"This is your choice, Madam Speaker." He paused. "Please understand that I cannot support us leaving, not any longer. If a vote of removal is called, I will not support it, and it will not pass. I assure you. Madam Speaker, we cannot judge them on the actions of a small group of cowards. To do so, we will let them win. And that is weakness. There is more at stake than you and me." He pointed to portraits of the past speaker generals. "How will history judge us and this moment?" He stopped. "I'm sorry."

She pushed past the chairs, banging them into the table, and stood eye to eye with him. "Mister Vice Speaker, I expect you to support me on the original declaration to leave Earth as we discussed. Remember, you are not the only one who understands tradition and history. I can use it as well. So can the other members of the Speaker's House, especially General Gahumed." Her voice softened. "If a call for removal succeeds, General Gahumed La-Enn will be named Speaker General, and J'Veesa help the humans then."

"What of the humans now?" he asked. "They suffered a greater loss than us. Consider how they are responding. All one has to do is watch their media feed, and our own, for that matter."

He picked up a datapad from the table. His fingers danced over the display. He pushed the information to her. "They are pulling together in ways no one ever expected. They didn't realize there would be an attack. Their religious leaders are calling for prayers for both our species. Their governments are putting aside grievances and offering support for those lost in the attack. Countless messages are being sent to us daily from their people saying how awful it was, and how we can't let these radicals win."

He swiped the images to the table monitor where she could not ignore them.

"These terrorists do not speak for the majority of the humans, and we cannot ignore them because we are angry and afraid. What message does that send? The Clan Wars would have destroyed us if brave females and males didn't put their arms up and stop it. Nentraee are similar to these humans. Madam Speaker, this might be a greater opportunity than we first recognized."

Mirtoff was quiet while viewing the information.

*Is he right? Can we risk it? Do we have a choice? Should he have come to me with these changes sooner? Why did he wait until before the meeting to surprise me with it?*

Mi'ko pulled the device away from her and tapped his fingers on it. He swiped the holographic image to the table showing her the ships that were still being repaired. "Plus, can the fleet last another ten or fifteen years while we search for another planet?"

"We've been repairing them," she huffed at him.

"I need you to hear this and to understand," Mi'ko pleaded with her, his eyes large. "You're not only our speaker general, but my friend. I recognize you feel betrayed." He licked his lips. "Madam Speaker, Mirtoff, please. Finish reading the declaration."

He put down the datapad and waited.

It took several moments, but she finally picked up the scroll and read it.

Her eyes lifted from the scroll as she closed it. "You assume this will make a difference, calling on our old traditions. Traditions, mind you, that haven't been used since before the Clan War?" She shook her head. "What of the humans? Do you believe they will understand this and the other suggestions you are making?"

Mi'ko adjusted the sling for his arm. "Madam Speaker, I will use the same argument I used with you. Everything is here on this datapad, including the estimates on how much longer our fleet can survive in space. All I'm certain of is that we try, and I need you to help me. We'll have more to convince than just General Gahumed, but tradition is on our side. Ritual is a strong ally, in particular Gahumed and her Dentraee Clan. As for the humans, I can't say, but they have as much to gain as we do with this offer. Plus, if my guess is correct, it might be the hand of peace we need."

"I allowed your words to convince me to change my mind on this world once before, and you were almost killed. Killed, Mi'ko! Need I remind you of that?" The tips of Mirtoff's ears were cooling off. They deflated slightly calming her even more. She was no longer shouting. "Not to mention those that did not survive, including General Gahumed's son. Now you are asking me to trust you again. At what price?"

She thought of her brother, Ecra, and niece, Suloff. She thought of her cádo, Faa. All the Nentraee that were counting on her. As with every choice she made, it came with its own burden.

What pushed her the most was that Mi'ko was right on one thing: the fleet. The ships were getting older and needing repairs more often. The chance of them lasting another five, ten, fifteen years was a huge worry. They had lost more people on the decaying ships—including her brother's mate—than during this human attack.

She scrutinized the declaration, then Mi'ko.

"What you ask me to do..."

"I know, Madam Speaker. Trust me, I know. If I thought there was another way..." he trailed off.

She collapsed on the chair. "What we're doing...what I'm doing, I do in the name of all the Nentraee we lost. Not just those lost in the attack, but those lost during our travels in space...those left behind to face certain death when our planet was destroyed...and those that were lost during the Clan Wars. I do this for them...to honor them. It may be the only way that some of our people will survive." Every part of her body slumped, even her elaborately braided hair. She rested her head on her intertwined fingers.

"If this doesn't work, or if they want blood, I will provide it." Mi'ko bowed. "I will accept the responsibility. I will ensure it is my blood, not yours."

Seeing the resolve, she was sure he reviewed all the Nentraee protocol books on how this was handled. How the arm of gratitude would be extended. There would be a lot of work involved; they were facing a battle with the House of the People and the Speaker's House. The confrontation would take their combined political prowess to overcome. "And I suppose you have someone already picked out."

Mi'ko shifted, the weight of their existence now showing on his face. "Yes, I do, and believe it or not, you may thank Laina for the idea."

"I'm sure there are a great many things to thank Laina for," Mitoff said. "Something tells me she had a strong hand in changing your heart." She examined her cup and the last of her tuma. Then she pushed it aside.

# Eighteen: New Opportunity

"TODD? MISTER LANDON, sir? Are you awake? Is this a good time?"

He turned his aching body, not wanting to deal with another doctor or nurse. How many of them were there anyway?

"Todd."

The voice sounded familiar. Jerry! He opened his eyes and lifted his head, but Jerry wasn't there. Instead, he saw Mi'ko and Vi-Narm. Some man in a plain brown business suit that he didn't recognize—and didn't care about—stood next to the two Nentraee.

Todd pushed away the tray of mostly uneaten food. Everything was in a fog. He didn't remember the food being brought in, and he didn't remember forcing any of it down.

Sitting up, he attempted a smile. Ignoring the man in the dull brown suit, he turned to his guests, who were dressed in similar suits to what they had on the day he first met them. The difference today was they had on cloaks. Mi'ko's was dark blue and Vi-Narm's was a deep red. But what stood out was the lopsided tieback in the vice speaker's hair wasn't lopsided like it had been the day of the attack.

Todd swallowed hard.

After a moment, he noticed one of the vice speaker's arms was covered by a bandage and in a sling. "Mister Vice Speaker, Vi-Narm, it's good to see you're healthy. How're you doing?" Todd pointed to a couple of chairs. "Please come in and sit."

"We are fine, Todd Landon, thank to you," said the vice speaker in his awkward English. "You risked you life for mine, and we are very grateful." A polite smile adorned his face.

The man in the suit approached Todd. "Mister Landon, I'm White House Chief of Staff, Greg McNeil." He stuck out his hand. Todd ignored it, and McNeil self-consciously withdrew it and shoved it deep in his pocket. "It's a pleasure to meet you. I've been asked by President Zachary to personally check in on you and see how you're doing." He smiled. "Also, I'm here to ensure that all your needs are taken care of, and if there is anything that we—or I—can do for you."

Todd's vacant eyes moved past the man blathering on. *Why is he here? What is he after?*

"Both the Nentraee government and the people of Earth owe you a big thank you. The president apologizes for not being here in person." McNeil's voice was calm and polite. "However, when you're up to it, he would like to thank you personally in Washington at the White House. You are quite the hero, Mister Landon."

Finally, Todd started to concentrate on him. Mister McNeil appeared to be in his later forties or early fifties. In his youth he might have been a handsome man, but now his lined face bore testament to the harsh years of public service.

Sighing, Todd shifted, and the familiar twinge of pain wracked his leg. He digested what the man said. His anger built, a mix of physical and emotional pain. Seeing McNeil smiling at him like an idiot, Todd wanted to reach out and punch the smile off his face.

His words came out tight and icy. "I'm sorry, Mister McNeil. I don't think the president would want to meet me."

"Of course, he would," McNeil said. "How could President Zachary not want to meet a hero? Specifically one of your caliber."

Lifting his injured leg, Todd tried to find a comfortable position. There wasn't one.

*There is nothing comfortable about my life anymore. It was all blown to hell.*

McNeil was about to speak when Todd stopped him cold with an icy glare. He wanted to lash out. Someone had to hurt as much as him.

*Because of people like you, I lost everything. Because of people like you and the president, I'm in a hospital in pieces. Because of people like the president, Jerry's dead.*

"You see, the president doesn't like people like me, sir." All the hurt and frustration of losing Jerry boiled up inside of him, and he vomited up that hostility toward McNeil. "You know, he isn't a big fan of us fags, and we aren't fans of him either! Does the president realize that? Does President Zachary comprehend that the man he wants to personally meet and thank is a fucking faggot? Or is he too stupid to understand such things?"

His voice trembled, and his eyes started to moisten. "I'm sure that would make his day! Does the president know that the man he wants to meet and thank sucks dick? Does he get that I lost my husband in that fucking explosion? A man I wouldn't have been allowed to marry if he had his way. A man who shouldn't have died if our great and powerful country was doing its job. A country under his watch. Does he understand any of that? What does the president really have to say?"

He needed a sip of water but took a breath instead. McNeil opened his mouth to respond, but Todd rolled over him. "Am I going to get some fucking flag and then be brushed back into the closet after a nice photo op showing the world and the United States how he supports all of us? Even the fucking faggots!" His brain finally kicked in and stopped his mouth. Tears of sadness and anger streamed down his face.

*How could they let this attack happen? How could they not have known someone would try this?*

Todd didn't want to deal with McNeil anymore, but he couldn't stop glaring at him.

"Mister Landon," McNeil said, completely unfazed by any of Todd's outburst.

Todd grabbed the napkin from his tray of food and wiped his eyes.

McNeil continued, "The president and his wife have asked me to send their deepest sympathy for the loss of your husband. He is aware of your situation and the sorrow you are undergoing. He would like to meet you when you are up to the trip. You don't have to decide now; think on it, and we'll be in touch."

Reaching out, McNeil touched Todd's good leg, giving it a squeeze, and started to walk out of the room. Before he left, he turned and met Todd's gaze. "Mister Landon, what you just said doesn't fall on deaf ears. I promise you. You are still raw and hurt. It's why I was sent specifically. Feel well soon. I, too, am very sorry for your loss." He left the room.

Todd threw the spent napkin at the door and changed positions before realizing both the vice speaker and Vi-Narm were still standing there. His face was as hot as embers in a fire, his heart hurt, and his stomach sank. He felt like he did when his folks walked in on him masturbating. If he could be struck in the head by lightning, now would be the perfect time.

"Oh, shit! I'm so sorry...I mean...I...I forgot you were here." He wiped tears from his eyes with his hands, trying to regain some form of dignity. "I'm so sorry. What I said was...wasn't appropriate for anyone, least of all you. I'm sorry."

Vi-Narm said nothing. Her face was an emotionless wall.

Adjusting his bandaged arm, the vice speaker said, "Todd Landon, my family and I are very thankful for what you have done." He paused, studying the room and Todd. "It is our sorrow news to tell you that Weaqu and GanCee both died from their wounds. Their families also send thanks for the attempt to save them." Both he and Vi-Narm bowed. After a moment, they raised their heads.

Todd wanted to interrupt the aliens. He wanted to say that he didn't do anything, that it just happened.

But the vice speaker continued. "Todd Landon, in our cultural, these types of deeds are something we regard highly." He stopped and turned to Vi-Narm, then back to Todd. "How do I explain this to you?" He paused. "You are not a hero to me and Vi-Narm. You are a hero to all of the Nentraee. Not because I'm one of the heads of the Speaker's House, but because you value others' lives as equal to you own." He took a step toward Todd. "Actually, greater than you own. What you did was something very few people would do, even in our cultural. For that we are, I most of all, am in you debt." He bowed.

Todd's face grew hotter, and he went to rub his goatee, but it wasn't there, so he rubbed his chin instead.

The vice speaker shifted on his heels. "I know in you culture, this is soon, but in ours, I am required to present this offer to you as promptly as possible." He turned to Vi-Narm. "Which is why I here today when you are not fully well. Once we heard you were awake, and after I gained approval from my government, I was duty bound to come see you." He checked the door to the hospital room. "I might add you government was no pleased with the new security measures taken, but they allowed it."

Todd glanced over to the closed door that McNeil had exited from. Was there something more out there that he didn't know? Not like he had left the room.

Continuing, the vice speaker said, "I have come to offer you a position within our government to work for me." He stood taller and adjusted his bandaged arm. "You would be a special liaison between our two peoples." He paused. "You would report to me and work with us. You would be involved in all our affairs." He motioned to Vi-Narm. "This offer has been approved by the speaker general, the Speaker's House, and the House of the People."

Vi-Narm moved forward and presented Todd with what appeared to be a roll of parchment tied with a strip of leather. He hadn't noticed her holding anything before. A seal rested on it. This seal was on all documents he had looked at before the accident. But nothing he reviewed before was this elaborate with an intricate carving that he didn't recognize.

Vi-Narm outstretched her arms, holding the parchment scroll out to him, her head bowed.

Todd wasn't sure what to do. Vi-Narm wasn't moving, and Mi'ko watched him. Slowly, he reached out and took the documents. They were heavier than he thought, and the texture seemed grainy like sandpaper. He wasn't sure where to lay the bundle, so he put it on the bed next to him, hoping it wasn't an insult.

Vi-Narm raised her head and stepped back.

The vice speaker added, "Our Speaker General, Mirtoff Esmi, is anxious to meeting you, as are many of our people, including me family. Todd Landon, this is a very rare honor."

Todd couldn't have spoken even if he wanted to. His throat was parched. He reached for the cup on his tray, but it was right out of his grasp.

The vice speaker moved for the cup and handed it to him. "Todd Landon, I do not expect an answer now, nor is one appropriate. Please do consider this offer. It will be a great opportunity for both of us people, especially with the days ahead."

How the vice speaker's gaze met his and how serious he appeared told Todd this was important. It was something special, even for them. There was much more to this offer than what he was being told. It seemed as if the vice speaker's own personal honor and duty depended on that scroll.

Not sure what to say or do, he finished off the water and put the empty cup on the opposite side of his body away from the documents.

*Is that why McNeil was here? Is that why the president is "excited" to meet me?*

He finally found his voice. "I don't understand. Because I supposedly saved you, you want me to work with you and your government? That seems a little much. I mean, we have diplomats for that sort of thing. They've been trained for this." He focused on the rolled document. Suddenly, the room turned small and quiet. "Wouldn't flowers and a card have been enough?"

"Mister Todd Landon, we don't use plants in this manner," said Vi-Narm, "but if you would like, we can arrange that. We still have much to learn about your culture and your customs."

Todd barked a laugh, which surprised him. Laughing for the first time in what seemed like years actually felt good. What struck him the funniest was Vi-Narm's appearance. Her left eye was raised, her lips were down, and her hand went up to her braided hair, adjusting it. It was nice to see that he wasn't the only one out of place right now. He had her totally confused.

"That was my attempt at a joke. A very bad joke and I apologize." Todd's laughter waned as he reached out and picked up the documents. "Thank you for the offer, but I don't—"

Vi-Narm stepped forward and waved off his remarks. "Mister Todd Landon, nothing more should be said on this now; you need recovery. Consider it. Say nothing now without thought. Everything is there in document in you language to review."

Todd was silent, taking to heart what she said. He didn't want to offend them.

"Mister Vice Speaker," Vi-Narm said, "we keep Chief of Staff, Mister Greg McNeil, waiting. We should let Mister Todd Landon rest. I sure Chief of Staff, Mister Greg McNeil, will need to return to his duties."

Both the vice speaker and Vi-Narm bowed.

"Be well, Todd Landon. May you rest peacefully," the vice speaker said.

Todd watched them leave his room and turned to the window, seeing the blue July sky. "God, this sucks," he muttered.

# Nineteen: Apologies and Invites

PECKING AWAY AT his laptop he remained quiet. Todd barely noticed Kati enter the living room and sit on the chair opposite him. Bianca jumped up on her, hunkering down to take a nap.

"Have you thought more of the Nentraee's offer?"

Todd shrugged.

"Todd, it's been months. You don't want them to just say screw it." Kati rubbed Bianca's head.

Todd sighed as he massaged his shoulder.

"Who wouldn't love to have an opportunity like that?" Kati's said in a raised voice.

Todd lifted his face from the screen briefly, then went back to his laptop.

"Dammit, Todd, All you do is play on that damn computer. You barely eat. You don't even open your mail. These last few months..." Kati lowered her voice. "It's like you're only half alive. I realize you're recovering...but fuck."

He stared at her with his face drawn from exhaustion. All his clothes were baggy, including his shirt, which he was currently swimming in. She clearly wasn't going to give up talking to him, so he finally gave in.

"Kati, I'm alive," he said. "Trust me, the pain is a daily reminder. And I haven't given any thought to the Nentraee's offer because there's been too much going on with the memorial and Jerry's family. Not to mention the legal crap and my physical therapy. It's been a never-ending nightmare."

Leaning back on the chair, she studied him.

"Plus, the dumb-ass media, who I wish would go away and leave me the hell alone," he grumbled. He'd had to call the police a few times—some of the more aggressive journalists had gotten into his backyard, destroying Jerry's plants. They almost broke through the back door before the media interest finally started to wane.

He shifted again. He could never get his leg comfortable, but at least the baggy sweats didn't bother him. His leg was still wrapped up, but nothing like it was in the hospital. The cut had been so deep over a hundred stitches were needed to put it back together. His femur was fractured and was taking longer to heal than he'd hoped. But, the doctor said progress was good. At least the pain was fading. The physical therapist said he wouldn't have a limp as long as he pursued his therapy religiously.

"Come on, Todd. Some of the interviews you enjoyed, and they treated you nice." Kati shifted Bianca. "Don't be a jerk. You had fun at the party the office had for you. Not to mention the visits from the governor and the mayor. Come on, that was pretty epic."

"If you can call a drug haze enjoyable." Todd sighed. "And yes, some of the media was respectful." His voice had a flat, indifferent tone. "It happened so fast and the medications I was on— I hardly remember any of it."

The memorial for Jerry was the hardest part.

The funeral, per Jerry's wishes, was simple. Everyone shared stories about him. Todd played Jerry's favorite songs. No one wore dark or depressing colors. The hardest part for him was giving the life sketch and not getting overly emotional. He even managed to get a few laughs. What made it the more difficult was not having anything to bury, or not much of anything.

He'd used the excuse of the pain in his leg and the medication he was on to force Jerry's family to deal with all the arrangements. It wasn't his finest hour, and he regretted it now.

"What about going to Washington?" Kati asked. "Are you going to do that at least?"

"Well, I haven't heard back from them, and I'd be surprised if they didn't just let it all drop. The media moved on, so why not everyone else?" Todd said. "I was harsh to that McNeil guy, but if I get invited, then the way I see it, I don't have a choice. If I don't go, it'd be disrespectful."

Todd moved his leg slightly and a twitch of pain shot through his body. As if to remind him of how much of an asshole he was. He winced. "I wouldn't call me back after something like that. I sounded like you."

Shrugging, she gently pushed Bianca off her lap. "Jerk. Well, of course he was pissed by what you said." She dusted off the cat's hair. "Still though, I don't suppose it'll matter. I'm sure he's used to that sort of thing given who he works for."

After stopping his fidgeting on the sofa, Bianca took the opportunity to jump up on his lap.

"All I know is I wasn't thinking, plain and simple." Todd rested a hand next to the cat. "I voted for the jerk. I realized what I was getting. Still, he was better than the alternative." He shook his head. "I should have never said those things."

Dan flitted into the living room. "And what are you two girls talking about? Me, of course?" He flounced on the chair, crossed one leg over the other, rested his hands on his knee, and batted his eyelashes.

"Oh, yeah baby, come and give me some of that funky lovin' of yours." Kati faked at trying to grab him.

Dan hastily changed his position. "Gross—you're a nasty ho."

"And you're a snarky bitch, who's gonna get popped one of these days."

"Dan, watch it. I've seen her rip apart bigger men than you." Todd was so grateful for the both of them. They had gone above and beyond.

"Yea, watch it bitch." Kati winked, in a very deep, butch voice, putting up her hands to mimic cat's claws. "And I ain't no ho."

Dan laughed. "Trust me, girl, I know. I've seen who you date." With a raised eyebrow he scanned up and down her body.

"Anyway." Todd inhaled the aroma from the kitchen. "So, what's for dinner? Something smells good."

"Meatloaf and taters, my precious. I just finished things up in there. You know, if I'd realized I was gonna be your house boy, I would have brought my thong."

"Now that's an image I can do without." Kati rolled her eyes.

Dan had saved Todd from staying with his family, a debt he could never repay. "Thank you for staying here and helping me. I owe you. I love my family, but I can't handle them here twenty-four seven, you know. Like my mother wanted—"

Dan held up his hand. "God forbid. Trust me, *chico*, I get it. Plus, I couldn't bail on you after everything you and—" He broke off and started again. "You've done for me."

"It's okay. You can say Jerry's name. He was your friend, and it's good to remember him. I need to remember."

"Now, Miss Thing, don't go getting all serious and sentimental on us," Dan said, fluttering his hands near his eyes and forcing a big dopey grin on his face.

"That's what friends are for. Right, Dan?" Kati looked back to Todd. "Plus, when you're working for the Nentraee, and you will be working for them, you'll get us both fabulous jobs with them. Of course, I only want to work with them if they have a man that resembles John Bon Jovi or Brad Pitt. Can you manage that for me, Pooky Bear?"

Dan snapped his fingers. "Oh girl, you got that right." He held up his hand to her for her to high five.

She obliged.

Rubbing his sore leg and contemplating the rolled Nentraee documents he had in the den, he sighed. The coolest thing was after he broke the wax seal, it had changed from red to blue. Once he rolled it up, the seal reattached itself as if it hadn't been broken but stayed blue. It was incredible.

"Sugar Lips, it would be an amazing move," Kati said. "Plus, it would be a change of scenery; it'll get your mind off other things." Her eyes grew larger and her eyebrows raised. "I read the documents, and the Nentraee were being all formal and shit. Then they sent you that offer letter that could choke a horse—well, or a man who was the size of a horse." Her index finger tapped at her chin.

"You would be crazy not to take it," Dan said.

"Wait. You both read the document and the offer letter?"

Dan and Kati nodded.

*That would explain why the seal faded from the blue it was to now almost white. I'd thought it just changed over time.*

"I can't believe you two."

They shrugged.

Todd's eyes narrowed at Dan. "Speaking of decisions, have you figured out what you're going to do? I'd like to get my guest room back at some point, and you still won't wear the French maid outfit," he teased. "I don't need a resident hobo."

"Bitch! I've been waiting for your sorry ass to heal," Dan said. "Then I thought I'd get a place here in San Jo' and continue the travel and tour thing. With the Nentraee opening up a couple more of their ships for visitors and them not wanting to book the tours online, there is a lot of money to be made." He pulled at his shirt collar. "Or that's my hope. So, there." Dan stuck out his tongue at Todd. "I've been taking care of business while you've been meeting all the 'A' list people. You nasty-ass ho, don't even—"

The phone rang, interrupting the conversation. Todd slowly reached for it.

But Dan snatched it up and spoke into the phone with a high-pitched female voice. "His Excellency Savior of the Nentraee and Keeper of the Galactic Peace, Todd Landon's Palace. This is his servant Crystal Chandelier. How may I service you today?"

Todd grabbed a pillow and threw it at Dan's head.

Kati chuckled.

Dan's face paled. His voice dropped even lower than normal. "Oh, Mister McNeil...no, sir...you have the right number. Ah, sorry, sir. Yes, Todd's here...sorry, sir. I thought you were the...um...here, let me pass you to Todd." He hastily tossed Todd the phone, and it landed on Todd's hollow stomach.

Todd picked up the phone and glared at Dan.

Dan's face was awash with mortification and he mouthed the words, "I'm so sorry."

"Hello, this is Todd. Mister McNeil, hello, how are you?"

There was a pause.

"I'm sorry for my friend. He has a very rare condition of dumb-assness. We don't normally let him answer the phone or talk to civilized people." He scowled at Dan while Kati snickered.

"Um...well, sir..." Todd turned his face from both Kati and Dan.

He listened.

"All right, yes, okay, Greg. I haven't had a chance to consider it. There has been a lot of stuff going on. It's indeed an honor."

Another break.

Both Kati and Dan moved in closer, not quite crowding him.

"Of course. I'm definitely, seriously considering the possibility."

He nodded.

"Well...um...you see, Greg, I wasn't sure I'd still be invited after the horrible things I said to you, which I'm so sorry for. I was out of line, and there is no excuse."

He waited.

"That is very kind of you to understand. Thank you." He shifted to face Dan and Kati.

He paused.

"In that case, I would love to come to Washington, DC. Thank you."

Dan and Kati faced each other, then turned back to Todd.

"That is too kind. Thank you."

There was a final pause.

"Definitely, I'll let you know. Have a good afternoon too. Bye." Todd clicked off the phone. Before he could put it down, questions flew at him.

# Twenty: Ultimatums

"IT'S SO BEAUTIFUL here," Laina gazed out of the hotel room's picture window. "I wonder if they know how lucky they are?" It was a fall day, and the trees were a colorful array of golds, reds, and oranges. It reminded her of their home in OoNowa.

Mi'ko had worked so hard toward this day. She wanted him to succeed, for this to work. Not just for him, but for the Nentraee. She understood that all their futures, human and Nentraee, were now tangled together and nothing could change that, not even everybody's combined stupidity.

"I doubt it. We never did. We took it for granted, even after the Clan Wars. Just like they do now."

Laina turned to her youngest son. She hadn't expected him to answer.

"Forever the optimist, Mi'cin," Laina said, the afternoon sun warm on her face.

She was proud of the male he'd grown into, despite his pessimism. His soft brown hair and his broad shoulders reminded her of her deceased brother.

Mi'cin brought his foot up and crossed it over his knee. "I'm saying that it took our planet blowing up before we realized what we had. These humans don't seem any different in the way they pollute their land, water, and air." He adjusted his collar with a steady hand, loosening it, causing his dress cloak to shift.

"What do you know of our home world? You were only a child when we left." Laina floated over to him, and then fixed his collar, finally dusting off the lint. His clothing seemed to be tailored for him, unlike Mi'ko, who never had his tieback right. *Males.*

"I remember the purple mountains that we could see from the house in OoNowa and going to the ocean for the day." His eyes narrowed on her. "I remember more than you think."

"As well you should. Never forget our home, Mi'cin." Mi'ko walked the rest of the way into the hotel room. The dark gray dress suit Laina had picked for him flattered his soft form, and the deep blue cloak was clasped at the shoulders with large blue stones. He commanded authority without needing to say a word.

Mi'cin stood and bowed. "Hello, Father."

Laina drifted over to her husband, before stopping to fix the tieback that held his hair.

*I want my males to look perfect today.*

"Is everything worked out for tonight?" She touched his cheek, seeing the worry in his eyes. It had been a hard-fought battle within the government, but he had pulled it together. She couldn't have been prouder of him.

"It is. The president of the United States of America will make the greeting, then the speaker general will address the people and the media. She will announce the new position and give the special envoy the *Kap'erin*. It will be a big moment for our people. Once the media are satisfied, we'll move on to the private dinner where I'll introduce you to our special envoy." The lines on his face softened. "Given the amount of planning that went into this, including the assurances we had to give the other world leaders, everything should be perfect."

Mi'cin sat back on the couch, resting his hands on his knees, a tight expression on his face. "As well planned as—"

Laina stopped him with a stern look. He put a hand to his heart as a sign of surrender.

"Fine, fine. Where are Shif and Ko?" Mi'cin asked. "I thought the whole family had to be present at this magnificent and glorious event? The moment that will change our futures."

Laina frowned at her son.

Mi'ko sighed. "Hir-shif and Hir-ko are waiting for us downstairs in the lobby with security. There was no need for them to come up." He walked to the chair and picked up his wife's cloak to help her with it. "You're beautiful tonight, my love. I adore how the light bounces off the flecks of your dress. You have such elegance." He reached up and touched her hair. "Perfectly braided and in one of my favorite patterns."

"You flatter me, Mi'ko." Liana touched his cheek again with the back of her hand.

A knock at the door interrupted their conversation.

"Come in," Laina said, as she clasped her cloak then took a step away from her husband.


VI-NARM ENTERED THE room followed by two humans. "Mister Vice Speaker, I'm sorry for the interruption, but we have a situation. We must speak with you." She turned to Laina and Mi'cin. "If you don't mind joining the others in the lobby, security will escort you." Her English and her tone were strong.

Laina motioned for Mi'cin and he stood. "Don't be long," Laina said, and she and Mi'cin both bowed. They made their way to the door. Laina's eyes met Mi'ko's briefly before leaving the room, and he offered her a reassuring gaze. She bowed again and left, closing the door behind her.

Mi'ko scrutinized Vi-Narm and her two guests. Vi-Narm had spoken in English and was getting better the more she practiced. He was still having issue with the language. English was not easy to speak or fully understand.

"Chief of Staff, Mister Greg McNeil and Secretary of State, Miss Martha Webster, what seem to be the issue? I thought we had worked everything out between the governments?" Mi'ko spoke slowly and focused on his pronunciation.

"Mister Vice Speaker, as you know, we have been trying to work with your request, but…" Secretary of State Webster stopped, and her boxy, deep-gray skirt suit shifted, revealing the white shirt underneath. She reached up and adjusted the neckline. "Vice Speaker, may I be blunt?"

Mi'ko's head tilted slightly.

*Have you ever been anything but blunt?*

He turned to Vi-Narm and then back to the secretary of state. Vi-Narm stood tall and rigid as the secretary of state shifted on her feet.

"Of course, Secretary of State Miss Martha Webster." Vi-Narm spoke on behalf of the vice speaker. Her tone was shaky but firm.

Martha clicked her fingernails together, then stopped, grasping her hands together and holding them in front of her. "We don't feel your choice for this post will adequately represent our country and its people. Not to mention the entire planet. The president, as well as the UN Security Council, have further doubts."

Mi'ko was exhausted by these humans. He sat heavily on the couch, shaking his head at the floor. He took a breath before he spoke, his tone icy. "Secretary of State, Miss

Martha Webster, both you president and our speaker general has been over this. We went as far to speaking with you UN Security Council on the matter, at you insistence. An agreement was met."

His ears started to swell and warm. This was getting annoying, and it had to stop. "The only way, and let me emphasize our position, the *only* way we willing to consider stay here is on this condition. We have assured you this will no affect our diplomatic efforts with you country or any other. The speaker general has stated so personally."

He turned to Vi-Narm. Remembering their conversation, his ears tingled with anger.

*You had similar words with me. Why are the two of you trying to sink my boat?*

Vi-Narm didn't trust Mr. Todd Landon or agree that this was the right world for them or that honoring a human in this way would help their relationship. Luckily, her opinions on this matter were irrelevant. Once Mirtoff announced the special envoy position to her people it gave them hope. Mirtoff and the rest of the Speaker's House had witnessed the excitement of their people. He was happy to see Vi-Narm supported him now, standing there straight and tall, her arms to her side and her palms down. She was a statue. He couldn't ask for better support than this.

Mr. McNeil spoke up. "Madam Secretary, Martha, we've done our due diligence. There is nothing in the files that says Todd Landon would be anything less than stellar in this position. Even several members of the Security Council have agreed his education—"

The snort from her small, flaring nostrils cut him off. "It isn't for us to question. We're here to support and represent President Zachary. The president now feels differently, as does the Security Council."

When she focused back on Mi'ko, her face grew softer, and her tone seemed more civil. "Now Mister Vice Speaker, we have a list of several other civilian personnel who we believe better represent our world and who we feel would be—"

"Enough!" It was Mi'ko's turn. He was done. He had fought with the Speaker's House, with the Speaker General, and he had fought with the House of the People. All he had done was fight, and he did not want to fight with this female anymore. "Madam Secretary, enough!" He stood, and the tips of his ears ached from the burn and puffiness. "Our decision is final. If you governments are no willing to cooperate, speaking behalf of my speaker general, tonight we announce that through much talk and based on the attack that occurred in you city of San Jose, we cannot and will not stay on the planet for fear of our safety. Since you government has no yet been able to find those who did the attack, an attack that almost took my life and did take lives of twenty-eight of my Nentraee."

The room froze as Mi'ko stood there, daring her to challenge him. The announcement tonight would be made on the spot, locking the Nentraee into this course of action. This was too important for them and to him. Yes, it took him opening his own eyes and looking to their past to move them into their joined future. To see her try to block the appointment of his special envoy, a human, not even a Nentraee...

*No.*

This would happen even if he was the only one who recognized how important this was to all their people. Nentraee and human.

"Martha, you can't let this happen. Not over Mister Landon or his personal life." Greg broke the silence. "If the Nentraee want him, then who are we to say no?" His tone was intense. "If you and the president stop this, if you allow this to happen, the president will have my resignation in the morning, and I assure you there will be several others following. Not to mention the outcry from around the world. Can the United States afford to be known as the country that ruined our first contact with an alien race? This is politics at its worst, and frankly, I hate it!"

"Mister Vice Speaker," The skin around Martha's eyes hardened. "It was only a minor concern on our part. Of course, we'll honor your request. We only wanted to make sure all options were reviewed, and you were comfortable with your choice, and you didn't make this offer because of some tradition we hardly know anything about. After all, this is a very important post, and we didn't want you to think you had to do this out of some kind of obligation."

"Of course, Madam Secretary Webster." Mi'ko bowed. "I assure you we are very please with our choice. I and my people have complete faith in Mister Todd Landon. After all, the man did save my life and the life of my aide, Vi-Narm."

"Of course," Secretary Webster said with a polite smile that didn't reach her eyes. Her fingernails clicked together again. "I apologize for any misunderstanding, and I hope you won't think ill of me. After all, we all want the same things. Now if you'll excuse me, I need to see to the details for the rest of the address."

"I understand," Mi'ko said. "It is possible there have been miscommunication on both our part. It is my hope that, with the help of Mister Todd Landon, such poor communication will fall to the past."

She marched to the door, her body moving in a stiff manner that seemed abnormal for humans—at least the humans he had seen. They tended to bounce when they walked, like Mr. Greg McNeil did.

Mi'ko turned to Vi-Narm and then back to the secretary of state and decided now would be the time to assess this relationship. If he had learned one thing, it was to test these creatures. It seemed that with humans, their words did not always match their intentions. "Madam Secretary of State, Miss Martha Webster, please inform you government and the other governments Mister Todd Landon, once officially given this post, will be considered the honorary top-level special envoy for you world. As such, he is important to us and will, of course, be extended all rights and privileges that we, the Nentraee people, can afford him. Also, he will be addressed as Mister Todd Landon, Special Envoy to Mi'ko Soemu for Terran Affairs. Or Special Envoy Landon for short, if they prefer. We expect this from anyone who address him." The air seemed much cooler in the room as she turned to acknowledge him and his request.

"Absolutely, Mister Vice Speaker." The smile was back. It appeared as if her mouth was going to envelop her whole face. "We'll be certain he's addressed as such, and you have my personal guarantee that Mister Landon will be afforded appropriate privileges to this very *honorary* position." She opened the door and then stepped out.

Greg turned, grinning from ear to ear.

Once the door to the room clicked shut, Vi-Narm's shoulders lowered, and she shifted on her heels. "Are you sure this is a wise choice?"

Mi'ko walked over to the window, massaging the tips of his ears. "It is beautiful here, Vi-Narm. The colors are amazing. All I'm missing are the purple mountains." He stopped for a moment to take in the trees, the sky, and the clouds, then continued. "Mister Todd Landon has a psychology degree and went to one of their universities. He has broken no laws, no criminal record, and from what we have seen of him, is an outstanding example of all that is decent in these humans." He turned from the window. "Plus, I like him. He speaks his mind, and that is something I find very refreshing. It seems to be a quality unique among these beings."

"His own people will make it very difficult on him." Vi-Narm pulled out a datapad, tapping it and scanning the room. "Do you think he's aware of what he'll be up against?"

Mi'ko was quiet.

"You saw their secretary of state—she does not want him, and I wouldn't doubt it was her trying to force this change." She nodded, appearing happy with what she saw on the device, so she put it away. "Not to mention some of the other world representatives aren't pleased. There is his personal life, one that is not fully accepted on Earth."

Mi'ko adjusted his dark-blue cloak, and examined it. Tradition and honor were held in his cloak, and yet it would be lost on most of these people tonight, except possibly Mister Todd Landon. He seemed to have an understanding unlike the rest. Not seeing them as aliens but as equals— even without fully knowing it. "I'm sure he can handle himself. Anyone who will sacrifice himself to save others going against the nature of self-survival is certainly stronger than others would think. And as for his personal life, that is these humans' problem, not mine. Don't you agree?"

# Twenty-One: Final Thoughts

MIRTOFF ADJUSTED THE braids of her hair, her thoughts only half there; she needed a break. She needed a moment of peace. She was hoping time with her brother would give her that, even briefly.

"Madam Speaker," Danu said, "it's almost time for the reception. If you want to visit Ecra, you need to leave now"

He approached Mirtoff, a datapad in his hand. "I've been reviewing the final details for the night's events, as well as the security measures—both human and Nentraee. We're not taking any chances."

Leaning back on the sofa, she raised a hand to her mouth to stifle a yawn. It had been a hard few days. Faa laid half on the sofa and half on her, swishing his tail.

*I could stay here like this and enjoy the peace.*

Danu handed her the device, and she scanned the fleet updates. It was agreed she would stay in orbit until just before the event.

Faa picked his head off her lap. "Provider, is Faa coming?"

Mirtoff rubbed the top of his head. "No, little one, you get to stay here with Ecra and Suloff. I don't suspect the humans are ready to meet you yet."

Faa jumped to the floor. He shook his head back and forth, fluffing up his fur.

"Okay, Faa wait here." He turned back to her. "Faa love Suloff. She gives good scratches."

Grinning at him, she rubbed his furry head. "Of course, little one. I'm sure you'll have a nice time with them."

Faa's big, green eyes watched her. His left ear flopped over itself. "Okay." He walked to the opposite couch and hopped up on it, curling his tail around the front of his body. "Faa have nice time."

"Very good." She stood and dusted off her suit, picking off some of his fur and letting it float to the floor. She moved to the mirror to scrutinize her hair, making sure the braids were tight and in place. "Did you confirm with the vice speaker? Is everything ready there?"

"Yes, he and his family are waiting for you in Washington, DC. It will go smoothly." Danu's tone was determined.

"And the gift?" She watched him in the mirror.

Danu lifted his head from his datapad. His face brightened, and he offered her a polite bow. "It will be ready for you to present. I will hold it for you myself." Head tilted, he opened his mouth but paused before continuing. "Should we have told the humans? So they aren't caught off guard?"

Mirtoff stopped fussing with her hair and turned away from the mirror. The thought had crossed her mind, but given what she had learned of the humans, it wasn't out of the social norm for them to present each other with gifts. "No, I don't believe so. From what we understand, this is a very common ritual for them. Plus, this is a monumental moment for our people. There are some traditions I'm not willing to overlook to make the humans comfortable. We are to remain quiet about it until we offer it to him. He needs to witness our sincerity...my sincerity."

"Of course." Danu swiped the last of the files on his datapad over to her device.

Mirtoff saw the new reports on her screen. "Very good. Please inform my brother that I'll be there shortly with Faa." She checked her braids again. "If you could give me a few moments, I'll be right out."

He bowed. She took a moment to watch him in the mirror as he departed the office.

Once the door closed, her posture slumped, and her face fell. Danu was sure to have picked up on her worry, but he wouldn't say anything. No one close to her would. Everything depended on this idea of a special envoy.

Mirtoff glanced over to Faa, and he peeked back at her. She smiled for him, but his eyes narrowed, and he said nothing. Turning back to her datapad, she scanned the additional notes for the human reception. Then she put it down with a huff.

*This needs to work. I can't fight with General Gahumed any longer, no matter the obstacles the general presented. We need to work together for this to be right. It wasn't perfect, but it was the best plan, and Ecra and Suloff are excited at the prospect.*

"Please let this be right," she said, closing her eyes, lifting her head to the ceiling, and offering a quick prayer to J'Veesa.

"Provider, it be okay. You very good; it will be fine." Faa watched her.

Somehow, he always understood and said the correct words to lift her spirits. She knelt and picked him up. "Oof."

He happily murred in her arms.

"Thank you, Faa."

Fas twisted in her arms, his big eyes on her and his tail swishing.

"What do you think? Do you agree we should stay here?" Mirtoff said.

Faa nestled his head into her shoulder, a happy mur coming from him. She held him a few more seconds before she put him down. "You keep growing, and I won't be able to pick you up anymore."

"Faa grow no more, Provider. Faa promise."

She chuckled as he walked to the door and sat. Her heart lifted, and her limbs felt lighter.

She grabbed her ceremonial cloak and put it on, the weight of it recognized by every part of her body. "Let's get you to Ecra."

Faa nodded, and they walked out of her office together.

WHEN MIRTOFF ARRIVED, Ecra had made them both a cup of tuma, and invited her to sit and relax. Faa had disappeared with Suloff.

"You don't need to be so worried," Ecra said. "Everything will be fine, sister. He will appreciate the gift, and the humans will be welcoming."

"Who said I was worried?"

"I can tell when you're worried; you've been fussing with your braids." He took a sip of his drink. "Relax, it'll go fine."

"Easy for you to say, little brother. You don't carry the weight of two races on your boat. I need this to work for everyone." Mirtoff tried to leave the doubt behind her. She was glad Todd Landon had taken so long to accept the offer. The additional time was needed for her to appreciate the idea and see the value as Mi'ko did. The time gave them additional ability to evaluate the appointment and create their gift for him—the special Kap'erin. Even Gahumed had stopped her protest, which Mirtoff thanked J'Veesa for. Of course, it didn't mean that Gahumed would make it easy, and Mirtoff's instincts told her that the general was planning something.

"I cannot consider a better boat for our fates to be on. You have father's kind heart and mother's determination and strength."

"And what if—?"

"No, sister, no what-ifs. None can distinguish the future but J'Veesa nor should they. J'Veesa's will shall come to pass no matter what we try to do or how we interfere. It is the way of the universe. You witnessed it on Earth with what happened to the vice speaker and the human. These are events that, if stopped, would have come to pass in other ways. We're on this course for a reason, and you're leading because it is where you belong. Not even General Gahumed La-Enn can fight it, though she might like to." Ecra's eyes did not leave her.

She allowed his words to wash over her. The choices she had to make were becoming easier and allowed her an air of comfort. He was right, of course; the universe had a plan, and this was but a small part of it—J'Veesa willing. She took a sip, and the spiced coolness slid down her throat. "When did you get so wise?"

"I've always been wise according to Ra'pia. You've just never had the need to listen to me until now." He smiled at her. "Between you and the humans, the arm of peace has been greatly extended. Have faith in that, dear sister."

She touched the side of his cheek gently with the back of her hand. He returned the touch. "Thank you," she said. "You know I expect this to be a new start for us, and I believe this new beginning starts tonight."

"And the special envoy?" Ecra asked.

"I suspect Mister Todd Landon will surprise us."

"Good. Now go. Go share a meal with these humans. Show them the strength and determination that we witness in you every day. Go meet our new Special Envoy, Mister Todd Landon. Make him feel welcome and demonstrate your good will and your kind heart." He stood and pulled his sister to her feet. "Welcome him to not only our clan but to our people."

Something about his expression, the way his eyes focused on her, how his mouth turned up, reminded her of their father. Mirtoff placed her hand on his cheek. "Thank you."

# Twenty-Two: Simple Questions

TAPPING HIS HAND on the side of the chair, Todd peeked at his cane next to him as Andy from the office of the chief of staff explained what was going to happen this evening. He had been with Todd since the morning, making sure he was comfortable and properly briefed for the night's event. He was a bit nerdy and a bit preppy at the same time with a close-trimmed beard and brown eyes.

"Most importantly remember when you talk to the president to address him as 'Mister President' or 'Sir.' Don't bow to him; you're American, not Nentraee." Andy checked his papers. "Well, Mister Landon, that's everything. The whole process is simple. After the president's announcement, the speaker general will address the media, both theirs and ours, and then she will introduce you as the Terren envoy."

"It's Special Envoy to Mi'ko Soemu for Terran Affairs," Todd corrected him flatly.

It wasn't that he lacked excitement about the new position. He was thrilled. But he wasn't sure what it meant. The Nentraee said they would explain more once he started. Some government officials and more than a few military-types weren't pleased with his lack of answers and even less with him being selected, but he had no control over that.

He turned to the files on the desk, focusing on them. Based on the reports and the information that Vi-Narm sent him, the role was similar to an aide or an assistant. Nothing that special. Yet everyone was acting like it was the most important thing in the world. Why?

"I don't understand," Todd said. "This position wasn't in the information they provided. This type of aide doesn't make sense to me. It's not part of their cultural structure. Not that I found."

"Mister Landon, all I've been told is that it's important to the Nentraee, so it's now important to us and you." He reviewed his notes, checking a few more items off.

Todd shrugged. Maybe it's related to something from their past. "Yeah, I suppose."

His heart still ached for Jerry, but life was moving on. Even back home, they had started rebuilding and repairing the area of the attack. "Andy... sorry... Mister Miller, do they have any more ideas of who was behind the attack in San Jose? I mean, I realize they say it was a couple of lone wolves working together, but isn't that strange? It's been over three months, and nothing has been found."

Andy's attention moved from his notes to Todd, and Todd continued. "Isn't that odd?" He shifted in his chair, adjusting his leg. "Isn't there a way to trace the materials that were used? And what about witnesses?" He shrugged, a slight frown on his face. "We knew who attacked us within hours of nine-eleven. What's the holdup?"

The pleasant expression on Andy's face changed; his smile grew, and his eyes widened. It seemed fake. "Mister Landon, I don't have any information on that. At first, everyone thought it was Al Qaeda or ISIS. However, they were ruled out. Since the Nentraee got here...well, those terrorist groups sort of went into hiding, didn't they?" Andy shifted his stance, adjusting his suit jacket. "The whole bloody Middle East went quiet. Everyone assumed when the Nentraee showed up it scared them since they perceive power as strength." He stopped and grinned. "And the Nentraee definitely have power, don't they? With their technology, they could have easily attacked the planet if they wanted, but they didn't." He closed his notepad. "Well, anyway, Homeland Security has been investigating, and I'm sure that they'll find who's involved. They always do."

Images of the attack rushed back to Todd's memory. He could smell the burning and taste hints of blood on his tongue. How could it go from being national headline news and the subject of special reports to not even having a brief mention in the local news? Even the protests were getting less and less coverage as everyone went back to celebrity gossips and scandals.

"Mister Miller, I'm sure it sounds crazy to you, but do you think there's more to this whole thing? Is it possible something's being covered up?"

Andy's face contorted as if he had been slapped. After a second, he politely smiled. "Todd, people see conspiracies all the time. It doesn't make them real. I'm a simple man who works in the Office of the Chief of Staff. I'm so far removed from the inner workings of the White House that I would be the last person to be told anything. I can assure you that every effort is being made to find who killed those people in San Jose."

Andy went over his notes again. "The car and driver will be here at five p.m. to take you through security and to the reception. Unless there's anything else you have for me?"

Todd shook his head in the negative.

"I should check in and inform them that you are all set," Andy said. "If you need something immediately, your security team will be able to assist you." He headed to the door.

Todd picked up his cane and walked with Andy to show him out.

Andy turned to him. "You can also call me. You've got my cell and office number."

Todd nodded, not sure what else he could possibly need. The hotel suite was bigger than his house, and the staff had been incredible to him. He hoped everyone got treated this well. Either way, The Willard InterContinental had been amazing, and he hoped he would get to come back.

"Thanks." Todd watched Andy scurry off to the elevator. "Now what?" Todd mumbled. He scanned the suite as he headed back over to the files on the desk.

*What am I doing here? This is insane. No. This is a great opportunity. One Jerry had to die for in order for me to get.*

Todd tapped his fingers on the desk and glanced over at the telephone. He picked it up and dialed.

"Hello, this is Katherine."

"Hey Kati, it's Todd." He forced a relaxed tone. He was nervous over the night ahead of him and wanted a little reassurance. The choice was to call either Kati, Brad, or his mother, and he didn't need his mother to worry or to hear Brad tell him to chill out and enjoy it.

"Hey there, Sexy Buns. Are you ready for your fancy party tonight?" Her tone was instantly uplifting.

"To be honest, I'm scared to death. It's nothing like what I thought it would be. There are all these rules on how to stand, what to say, what not to say." He took a breath. "And those are only for the president. It's a lot, and I'm not sure I'm up for it."

"Oh my God," Kati snapped. "Stop being a pussy."

He rubbed his sore leg absently. "What if I trip in front of the cameras or say something stupid and mess things up? What if I cause an intergalactic war? And did I mention the security? They gave me secret service. There are people outside the room watching over me. It's creepy as hell. I'm sure they did something to my cell phone. The reception sucks, and I'm stuck using the hotel phone."

Kati stifled a snicker.

"Kati, I'm serious. I'm just some inadequate guy who…" As he paused, his every fear came to the surface. He wanted to run and hide. But security would probably catch him and make him go to the White House event.

"Listen, Todd, no one is going to care about the size of your penis and how inadequate it might be…"

"Dammit, Kati. I'm serious, I'm freaking out here. I've had this guy from the Office of the Chief of Staff here with me going over protocol. He just left. It's nuts." He tried not to yell into the phone.

"Muffin, honey, sweetness, listen to me. No one understands that stuff. There isn't one single person on our whole planet that gets it. I bet that there isn't one from the Nentraee that does either. Everyone is making it up as they go along. You're not the only one scared. Everyone has their doubts. So suck it up and deal with it. Because, if I had to choose between you representing me and some dusty, crusty, talking suit or political jerk-off, I'd pick you in a heartbeat."

Todd remained silent.

"Honey, all we can do is our best. These people who create all this protocol and these rules do it so they have something to fall back on when the shit hits the fan. What you—Todd—what you do, will shape things to come. When all is said and done, people will write books about you, and your dealings with the Nentraee. Some of it will be what not to do—"

"Gee, thanks."

"Get over it. It's true, but most of what will be written will be what to do. Hon, you need a little faith in yourself, and you'll do fine. If you still want to hide, and if I have to transport there, or whatever, I'll kick your fat ass. And today I'm wearing the right shoes for it."

A chuckle escaped from Todd's mouth at the image of Kati and her shoes trying to kick him in the butt. "I don't want to fuck it up."

Laughter filled the other end of the phone. "Like you would be the first. You won't; you'll be fine. Trust your gut, it hasn't steered you wrong so far. And if you do mess something up, roll with it and make it appear intentional. Every move you make do with confidence, and no one will know that you screwed up. Sweet cakes, you're going to do great. I have faith in you."

"Thanks, Kati."

"Good. Now that the crisis is solved, when you're at the White House, can you snatch up one of those—"

"I'll see what I can do. Thanks again. See you soon."

"Good luck, dumb-ass, and enjoy," Kati said with a chuckle.

"Bye," Todd said then hung up. "Fun. Right. Like explosive diarrhea is fun." He grumbled and raked his hand through his hair as he lifted his head to view the beautiful, coffered ceiling. He felt his chin and face; he missed his goatee, but not having to deal with trimming it and trying to keep the lines perfect was a time saver and one less stressor for him. Still, he missed it.

"Relax. She's right. You're gonna be great." He heard a familiar voice from behind him and an even more familiar laugh. "You need to lighten up and enjoy. Move with intent and confidence, and they'll never see how nervous you are. Stop trying to hide from this. You can't hide anymore, hon; it's time to grow up and face the world."

Todd turned to the voice. Jerry stood there beaming from ear to ear, a soft glow around him. A surprised grin stretched across Todd's face. He should be in shock, but how could he be? It was so familiar and welcoming. Part of him hoped Jerry was watching out for him no matter how ridiculous it was. However, to see him...even if it was a manifestation from his subconscious, it didn't matter. He got to see him.

"Do you remember when we went diving, and you were sucking down the air?" Jerry asked. "After the first dive, you got so worked up that you didn't want to do the second dive. The dive master had to get in your face and tell you to loosen up. He had to remind you that diving was supposed to be fun, and you needed to chill out."

Todd rolled his eyes. "I'm still suspicious about those tanks. I think they were leaking air."

Jerry's grin widened. "Whatever you say, Mister Man. But what happened during the second dive?"

"I relaxed and didn't focus on the air gauge and how fast I was using up my air supply."

"Right. You focused on the scenery and having a good time. That ended up being one of your best dives. It's the same thing. If you're convinced you're going to fail, then you're going to fail." Jerry walked over to him. "They wouldn't have picked you if they didn't find you capable. The ones who don't think you can... Well, it'll be even better when you prove them wrong."

"I wish you were actually here with me to be a part of this. I miss you so much."

"I'm here." Jerry pointed to Todd's heart. "Even though I'm not real. I'm still here with you."

There was a tapping at the door so Todd turned. "Just a sec." He glanced back to where Jerry was standing. He was gone.

*They're right. I just need to relax and enjoy. Whatever is gonna happen is gonna happen.*

"Let's do this." He grabbed his cane and made his way to the door.

*It's time to get my party on.*

# Twenty-Three: The Kap'erin

FROM HIS SEAT on the stage Todd examined the guests and media in front of him. There were so many cameras and lights, he was sure he'd have a suntan by the time the guests moved into the reception. In between the blinding camera flashes he noted how formally everyone was dressed.

*It's a black-tie event, and I'm a part of it. I hope I'm dressed all right.*

Todd thought the White House would have bigger rooms. They were currently in a staging area and would be moved into the East Room for cocktails and then into the State Dining Room for dinner. He wasn't sure what to expect. He appreciated how much work had gone into the event. It was organized chaos. The Secret Service stood at attention in tuxes as the Nentraee Security wandered around the crowd in their businesslike security outfits. Neither side was taking chances tonight.

When he'd first arrived at the White House, he was immediately escorted to his seat by Secret Service agents, which he appreciated. His sore leg made standing for long periods impossible. It amused him that he had yet to meet either the president or the speaker general. Part of his briefing explained the purpose of the reception.

It was nice to see Mi'ko here. Mi'ko stood with a female Nentraee and three younger, male Nentraee—presumably his family. Vi-Narm wasn't too far away; she eyed Todd quickly, then turned away.

Todd could have brought a guest, but he hadn't been sure who. The only person he would have wanted to bring was Jerry, and that was impossible, so he figured he would come alone. A decision he now regretted.

As the president spoke, his wife regarded him adoringly. She wore a stunning navy-blue dress that hugged her curves. Todd wondered who designed it.

The secretary of state, like the others, watched the president. At one point, she turned and caught Todd's gaze, a slight frown crawled over her whole face. He got the message and stopped people-watching.

"And now, ladies and gentlemen," the president said, "it's my privilege to introduce the speaker general of the Nentraee people, Mirtoff Esmi." President Zachary joined in the rumble of enthusiastic applause as Mirtoff moved to the podium.

Mirtoff bowed to the president. Leader to leader, they were a match in that they both seemed impossible to disturb. Not the media, not the cameras, not even the crowd. Her posture was perfect, her shoulders leveled, and her head and neck held in a straight line. Her auburn hair was elaborately braided and pinned up. Her pointed ears and high, ridged forehead made it impossible to see her as anything but alien.

*She's still pretty, and her dark eyes are like a pool of melted chocolate.*

Todd adjusted how he sat in his chair, making sure his leg was comfortable.

"President Zachary, I thank you." She offered him another slight bow. "On behalf of my people, I thank you and the government of the United States for its hospitality. Who among us would have thought only a short time ago any of us would be here tonight? A new beginning for all. At this moment, our two histories join to become one."

There was more jubilant applause.

"This new beginning would not have been possible without the hard work and dedication of many people." The crowd broke out into another round of clapping, and she waited for it to die down before continuing. "If possible, we would honor all who have work to make us welcome on you world. Unfortunately, we cannot, so I ask that you accept my personal gratitude."

Todd thought the thunder of the crowd was a bit much; however, considering all that had happened, people were probably being overly polite.

Mirtoff turned her focus on Todd, and his face instantly heated as every eye was on him.

"We have decide to honor one among the many who we consider represents that which is the best in us all. In hopes that he will help us to understand you better, and that he will help you understand us. Opening doors and extending the arm of friendship for all. It is with the greatest of respect and honor that I present this man to you tonight: Mister Todd Landon, Special Envoy to Mi'ko Soemu for Terran Affairs."

Todd stood with a death grip on his cane as thunderous applause reverberated around the room. He tried to move with confidence and intent over to the speaker general. He bowed. Bowing was a Nentraee tradition, one that Andy had told him would be acceptable in this context. "Consider it their version of a handshake," he had said. Todd took a breath and raised his head.

After ambling over to the president, Todd shifted hands on his cane, careful not to fall. He shook the president's hand, noting that he, too, was careful.

"Good luck, Mister Landon. We're counting on you."

Todd gulped. *Be confident.* He wanted to throw up. "Thank you, sir. I mean, Mister President." It was all he could muster; everything else Andy told him was forgotten.

Todd turned back to the speaker general, who had stuck out her hand. She looked as awkward as when he had first met the Nentraee at his office all those months ago. Touching skin for the Nentraee was an intimate act only done between couples and family. His face lightened at the gesture, his smile grew larger, and a sudden lump took up residence in his throat.

*Relax and breathe, and for the love of God, don't cry.*

"You honor us, Mister Todd Landon. We welcome you. I welcome you," she added as Todd took her hand and gently shook it.

She faced her aide, and he walked over carrying folded material that matched the deep blue color of Mi'ko's. "As a symbol of you position, Mister Todd Landon, that you will hold in our government, may I present you with our *Kap'erin.*"

Her assistant, Danu, bowed, holding the neatly folded *Kap'erin* in his outstretched arms.

Todd's eyes grew large. *What the hell! No one mentioned a gift. What the hell am I supposed to do now? There was no mention of a gift being presented to me. How am I going to hold it and my cane? Great. I'm going to look like a fool in front of everyone.*

He noted the flashes of cameras. He glanced at the president, who was grinning and clapping as well.

*Bullshit! You had no idea this was coming. Why are you standing there clapping? This wasn't part of the plan.*

Jerry's soft voice spoke in his head, "Roll with it. It'll work out."

If the president of the United States faked it, so could he. "Thank you, this is very kind; you honor me."

"No, Mister Landon, you honor us with you acceptance of our gift. Now, allow me to bring forward the man whose life you valued enough to save. He will officially present this gift."

Todd stood with what he hoped was an appearance of modesty. He peeked over to the president's handlers.

*They're worried. Of course, they are. This wasn't on the agenda. Idiots!*

He took a breath. *Focus.* He blocked everything from his mind and concentrated on the vice speaker.

Mi'ko stood up and walked over, then bowed his head to the president, and then to the speaker general and took the cloak from Danu. His lips grew into a calm smile, making his eyes soften. "This *Kap'erin* represent our people and our tradition. Each of the seven embroidered symbols represents one of the seven clans from our world. They are combined on this cloak to show unity. It unites us." He pulled the cloak open for it to be viewed.

Again, Todd was blinded by the flashing of the cameras.

The cloak had a wide embroidered collar with silver stitching. Two large silver clasps were at the top, and each clasp had a deep-blue stone embedded in the center. There was no hood. The embroidery continued the entire length of the cloak to each of the symbols.

Todd counted eight, not seven. It was beautiful.

Mi'ko moved to fasten the *Kap'erin* on Todd. He draped the cloak over Todd's shoulders and affixed the clasp on the right and left lapel of his suit jacket where they attached. "As a show of unity, this Kap'erin has an additional symbol on it, one we have chosen to represent you human clan and you Earth."

The symbol was embroidered in some kind of silver thread and was in the shape of three stylized heart symbols that met at their curved tops surrounded by a circle.

*What does it mean?*

"Wear it with great honor and pride, Mister Todd Landon."

Once the *Kap'erin* was secured, Todd slowly turned around and faced the cameras. The flashes and clapping seemed to last forever.

Mi'ko backed off.

Todd, President Zachary, and Speaker General Esmi stood for pictures. Any previous awkwardness now passed. Once finished they were able to retreat into the East Room, away from the media.

Mirtoff's aide, Danu, offered to take the Kap'erin. Todd accepted the offer, then relaxed, feeling lighter. He sauntered over to a server, who handed him a glass of white wine. He managed to hold the wine in one hand and hang onto his cane with the other. There were no seats, so he would have to stand. He hoped the wine would help a little with the mounting discomfort in his leg.

"You're not used to this are you, Mister Landon?" a pleasant and confident voice said from behind him. He turned to see the president standing there with the first lady on his arm.

"No," Todd stammered. "I mean, not really, sir. I mean, Mister President. Sorry."

President Zachary grinned. The First Lady's pleasant full-lipped smile also greeted him. He instantly relaxed. Her voice was polished and had an air of amusement to it. "Not to worry, Mister Landon, you're doing fine. I suppose your hiding in the corner is on purpose given your nerves?"

*It's not hiding; it's out of the way.*

"The presentation of the Kap'erin threw everyone off," the first lady said. "I thought Andy's head was going to pop right off. The poor man. We should have expected something like that. The Nentraee are a gracious people. The welcome gift they presented Richard and me with…" she paused, but then, with an amused tone, continued. "Well, let's just say it'll have everyone talking." She was as welcoming and gracious as people claimed. "I find in those situations that if I smile and tilt my head, that's all they're after. Well, that and a few dozen answers for their questions."

"Alison, you're more than a pretty face, and you know it." President Zachary put an arm around her waist. "Mister Landon, don't let this woman fool you." He patted her waist. "She may appear as delicate as a flower, but behind that soft smile is the mind of a political shark. I learned years ago to never get on her wrong side."

Todd nodded and took a sip of his wine. "I'll keep that in mind. Mister President, I wanted to thank you for—"

President Zachary cut him off with a firm look and wave of his hand. "Mister Landon—Todd, if I may—it is we who should be thanking you. What you did meant a lot to the Nentraee, obviously, but it also put the United States ahead of the other nations in our dealings with them. That's extremely important to our country. That blasted attack on our own soil. It made us look bad, but what you did and now this." He glanced around the room and then clapped his hand on Todd's shoulder.

Todd wasn't sure what to say to that. He forced his eyes to meet the president's. "I did what was right. I wasn't thinking. I just acted. I wish…" He shifted his stance, his mind filled with thoughts of Jerry.

The first lady picked up on the fallen conversation. "We were all saddened by the losses, and we are sorry for your personal loss. It is a pain I wouldn't wish on anyone." She reached out and touched his hand, as it rested on his cane. "For whatever it means to you, we were both very sorry your husband was killed. It is a tremendous loss."

Todd blinked away the dampness that threatened his eyes. "Thank you. That's very kind of you." He needed to change the topic. He cleared his throat. "It's amazing, Mister President. We are lucky to be here, especially now. It's a whole new world. History is going to remember all of this. It's a monumental time." Shifting, he forced his chin up. He would be dammed if he was going to show weakness in front of the president and first lady.

"I'm glad I'm not the only one who agrees with that. I hope we get to see more of you." The first lady touched her husband's arm.

"Please enjoy the dinner, Todd. We'll speak more I'm sure." President Zachary rested his hand on his wife's.

"Thank you, Mister President." The first couple walked off to greet and talk with the vice president and her husband.

"You handled that nicely. They liked you. They don't normally talk that long with guests, at least on the first pass. Of course, you aren't just any guest." Greg stood off to Todd's side holding a glass of wine.

Todd sipped his wine before speaking, "I sounded like an idiot."

"Not in the least." Greg held up his glass. "Welcome to Washington, DC, and welcome to the White House, home of all the idiots in our country and those we import from overseas." His face lit up as he spoke. "If you want to observe a true idiot, look over there at the Speaker of the House."

He pointed, and Todd casually shifted. The Speaker was laughing at something. "That man laughs at his own jokes that I can assure you aren't the least bit funny. I can't tell you how many times I've had to hear 'pick a cod, any cod.'" He shook his head.

Todd sipped his wine again, watching the Speaker amuse himself while the people he was with smiled blankly.

Greg turned back to him. "You know I have to admit, after our first meeting, I never thought you would come here."

Todd's neck and face warmed. "Oh, God, I'm still mortified about that. I...it was all so fresh and so raw and you...you..."

"I walked in with a big red target on my suit. I don't blame you. I don't. It was a difficult time, I'm sure, and because of the Nentraee's short timeline, our government didn't have much choice."

Greg stopped a waiter carrying a tray. "Ah, the mini Beef Wellingtons, try one." He picked up a napkin and nabbed two of the hors d'oeuvres.

Todd balanced his drink in the hand with his cane, then took a napkin and one of the hors d'oeuvres offered to him. The server walked off. He took a bite of the beef, savoring the warm, lightly spiced flavor. "Wow."

"They're amazing. I love them. Luckily, so does Allison, so they're always on the menu for events like this. She's got amazing taste." Greg popped a whole one into his mouth and washed it down with a sip of wine.

Todd finished the rest of his nibble and then moved the wine glass back to his free hand. "About that day...I wanted to ask. What did you mean when you told me that what I said didn't fall on deaf ears...are you?"

"Ah, famous last words. They've come back to haunt me," Greg quipped. "No, Todd, I'm not of your...ilk..."

Todd winced at the word. Greg didn't seem to notice, and Todd let it go. He doubted Greg meant anything by it.

"But my younger brother was." Greg's tone changed slightly, his voice became soft and reflective. "My brother was the baby, and we protected him. Growing up, he was *sensitive*; that's what my mother would say. Anyway, we did our best and watched out for bullies and so forth."

Taking another bite of his second mini Beef Wellington, Greg continued. "But we weren't able to protect him from everything. Once my brother got sick, there wasn't any more hiding. We had to face the fact that he was gay. His partner, or 'roommate' as we told the neighbors, was the first to die. We stood by and watched his family come in and strip the house of everything. They even took the bed. Why? I have no idea. Maybe to be spiteful. Add insult to injury." He shook his head. "No matter how bad my brother thought we treated him, and we treated him pretty badly, we were saints compared to them."

Greg finished off his wine in one gulp, sorrow and regret filling his eyes. "I suspect what killed Allen wasn't AIDS; it was when they were legally able to sell the house from under him. They kicked him out and left him homeless. No one would hire him. He was starting to show symptoms of the disease."

Todd had heard stories like this before. It wasn't uncommon even today. "Didn't you try..."

"No. We...I let it happen. Something I'm still ashamed of." Greg grew quiet as he led Todd a bit more out of the way. "I told myself there was nothing to do. I wasn't the only one; we came up with excuses. It wasn't till the last year when he was in the hospital that I couldn't take it anymore. I had to help him. He was my baby brother, and I loved him. I know it doesn't sound like it, but I did. I couldn't let him die on the streets forgotten. So, I moved him into my house. We hired a private nurse, but by then the fight was out of him. Allen spent his last few months as comfortable as possible, but more importantly, he didn't die alone. We were with him." He sighed. "That's why I told you what I did that day. I didn't want you to assume I was blowing smoke. Probably more info than you wanted, but..." He shrugged.

"So the president knows?"

"That's why he sent me. Well that, and I requested to go."

Todd scanned the room, stopping on the secretary of state.

"I didn't..." Greg followed Todd's gaze to the Secretary of State, then he focused back on Todd.

"What?" Todd asked.

Greg's face went flat, his lips vanishing into a thin line. "You should be mindful. Several people in the presidential cabinet and some of our allies weren't happy that the Nentraee picked you for this post. Our allies lessened their objections when the Nentraee assured them that their dealings with those nations would not change. However, there are still people in our government and overseas who wanted to see someone they trusted in the post."

"Is that all? Tell me something I don't know." Todd laughed. "I've seen the articles, and I've gotten the nasty phone calls. And there are some *terrific* negative social media pages. You should check it out. It's kind of funny. Anyway, I can handle it."

Greg inhaled softly, checking over his shoulder. "I hope you can. Be careful and watch your back. These people can be sharks."

"Mister Todd Landon," the vice speaker's familiar singsong voice said.

Todd froze.

"Mister Todd Landon, I would like to present my wife, Doctor Laina Soemu."

"Oh...ah." Todd stumbled over his words. He was startled, almost dropping his cane and empty glass of wine.

Greg was calm with a cheerful expression on his face, his voice filled with Washington charm. "Mister Vice Speaker, a real pleasure to see you again. Doctor Soemu." He offered a polite nod in her direction.

Mi'ko bowed in return. "As with you, Mister Greg McNeil."

"Lovely to meet you, Doctor Soemu," Todd said, glad that Greg bought him a minute to recover from his potential blunder.

Dr. Soemu's dress flowed over her body, hugging her curves while the conservative cut and rich shades of emerald presented an image of strength and elegance. Her hair was arranged in an elaborate, formal braid, ending in a bun on the top of her head.

*How long does it take her, or any of the females, to do that?*

Laina bowed toward Greg and then turned to Todd. Her green eyes ran over him. "The pleasure is mine, Mister Todd Landon. Please, may I present our twin sons Hir-shif and Hir-ko, and our youngest son Mi'cin."

The three young males bowed to Todd. It was such an odd feeling having people gesture that way, but it was their custom and Todd wasn't about to disrespect them.

"I'll leave you to get acquainted." Greg offered a respectful nod to Mi'ko and his family.

Todd's heart pounded in his chest as Greg headed off, a devilish smirk tickling his face.

"Not to worry, Mister Todd Landon," Laina said. "We will not eat you, as your movies might suggest. You have my assurances." Her expression was playful, and she had a beautiful grin on her face.

The twinkle in her eyes put him at ease. He chuckled. "I'm sorry, was I that obvious? I wasn't expecting..." He glanced at the floor and then focused on his new boss and his family. "I'm sorry, I'll work on that."

"You will understand that I could not keep my family from meeting you any longer, Mister Todd Landon," Mi'ko said. "I apologize if we seem forward or abrupt. We are still get used to these American human customs."

"No, it's an honor to meet you. Thank you for the wonderful gift of the Kap'erin. It's beautiful. I didn't want to give it up."

"I pleased that you appreciate it. There was much debate, I can assure you." Mi'ko placed a hand where the clasp of the cloak would have gone. "As for wearing the Kap'erin into the reception this evening, we did not consider it a proper setting. We are no familiar enough with you tradition in such matter." He nodded and added, "However, you will have plenty of other opportunities to wear it."

A waiter came by and offered to take Todd's empty glass. The glass now gone, he was able to shift the cane and his stance to something that lessened the pressure on his injured leg.

Taking a calming breath, Todd scrutinized the Nentraee family. It was time to see if his studying had paid off. "Let me see if I can remember you correctly."

He surveyed Mi'ko's family, one member at a time. "Doctor Laina Soemu, I know that you work on one of the life science ships as a doctor. I believe your field is bio-nanotechnology and you're the head of the research." He caught a small nod from her. "You'll be talking to some of the medical schools on how the Nentraee use nanotechnology to repair damaged organs and to cure internal diseases." His body relaxed. "I'm sure our scientists are excited to meet with you."

"Very good, Mister Todd Landon. You honor me. Yes, the technology is exciting. We have been using nanites in medicine for seventy of you years. It field you world is starting to explore." She shifted her stance, standing taller. "We are hope that we can adapt this to treat several forms you cancer as well as other illnesses. However, this will take time and study. Sadly, it will not be a fast or quick process."

"Understandable." More at ease, Todd faced the twins. *It's like a game. Let's see how many of them I get right.* "Hir-ko, you're in life sciences?" He turned to the second twin. "And Hir-shif, you're teaching on the speaker general's ship?"

The two men's mouths turned into smiles. They both appeared to be younger versions of their father.

Hir-shif stuck out his hand, offering it to Todd.

*Wow. They are making an effort to adapt to our culture. It mustn't be easy.*

"I the one in life sciences. My focus is biochemistry, Mister Todd Landon. Thank you for you effort. It will be interest to see how the chemical reactions required for life to exist and function on both our worlds are different and the same."

The shaking of hands almost caused Todd to fall over and lose his arm in the process. Hir-shif let go of Todd's hand. His eyes grew large, while his mouth opened in worry. "Please forgive me. I sorry. I was not sure of how much effort to use. I hope I did not cause you harm."

"It's fine. We're all still learning." Todd adjusted his suit jacket and straightened up. "You almost make me wish I were a scientist, Hir-shif, so we can talk more on your field of study. Unfortunately, science was never my strong point."

"Not to worry, Mister Todd Landon. I would be happy to sit with you and explain it. The field is exciting, and I would very much like talk a human about it. Since you have no expertise in subject that would also be helpful to me. I am sure most human will not understand this and the practice would be very helpful. If I can make someone like you to understand then I would be able to make many understand." He stopped. "I apologize. I do not mean to say you unintelligent."

Todd blinked a couple of times, and his mouth slightly opened. "I...um...I never thought you did."

"Mister Todd Landon, Shif sometimes think everyone is interested in biochemistry when that is no the case." Hir-ko turned from Todd to his brother and back. "Have grown up with him and listen to him speak of nothing more, I can assure you it is no interesting." He shook his head. "I am the educator, Mister Todd Landon. I am also the eldest twin, so I have had to endure my brother far long than anyone else." His cheek raised in a hint of a smirk. "Now that events on Earth have calmed, I will be visiting a school here you might know: Cambridge University. Have you been there?"

They shook hands. Hir-ko's grip was much softer and the shaking less violent. "No, I'm afraid not. It's one of the top schools on our planet, though."

"I understand." Hir-ko adjusted his suit jacket. "It is supposed to be an excellent school with high standards; that is why I am visiting. It is unfortunate you were not able to attend. I am sure you had the intelligence for it." He shifted his stance. "My visit will focus on the curriculum. I am eager see if it is similar to ours. It will be nice to share teaching techniques cross-culturally. I hope human and Nentraee teachers have much to share and learn."

"I'm sure it'll be interesting." Todd turned to the youngest of Mi'ko's sons, who had quietly watched the exchange. Mi'cin absolutely got his good looks from his mother. He had the same brilliant green eyes. Mi'cin didn't appear young, maybe in his middle twenties. "You must be Mi'cin. I believe you're finishing a degree at the university, correct?"

Mi'cin bowed, instead of shaking hands.

*I guess not all of them are big on handshakes, but that's fine. Shaking hands is our custom, not theirs. Still, he's kind of cute. Nice eyes.*

"Yes, that correct. You are the man who lost his mate and whom my father put all his hopes. I trust you do not disappoint him or the rest of my people."

Todd was taken aback. In general, Nentraee were supposed to be polite in their conversations and not so direct. *So much for those reports.*

Laina's eyes narrowed with disapproval. "Mi'cin."

"Please forgive our child, Mister Todd Landon." Mi'ko also glowered at his son. "He tends to speak his mind when it is best to not do so."

The bow that tied the vice speaker's hair loosened, and Laina fixed it.

*Ah, that's sweet.*

"No, it's fine. I like a man who speaks his mind freely. I've been accused of the same myself." Todd straightened up. "Mi'cin is correct in his assessment. I hope I don't disappoint you and your family. Well anyone really."

He tried to keep the atmosphere light, even though he winced inwardly at the mention of the attack and Jerry's loss. "It's an honor to meet you. I've been anticipating this for weeks. I finally get to put some of my Nentraee research to use. I'm excited learn about your culture and share it with my people."

"Thank you, Mister Todd Landon." Laina's face filled with far more warmth and graciousness than Todd felt on his own.

Laina's expression stiffened, and she focused on Todd. "On behalf of our children, we want to thank you personally for the continued life of my husband and my children's father that you have give us. It is rare to find a brave man and rarer still to find one who values the life of another as equal to his own. You are going against nature to ensure his life continues. For that, we are grateful and understand we can never repay you. We also share with you the sorrow of you personal loss. We only hope our joy helps ease you pain." The family bowed to Todd.

The room became silent during the exchange, as other people, forgetting their conversations, watched Todd and Mi'ko's family.

Todd was sure he was turning a deep crimson. He didn't know what to say or do—Laina's comments were sudden and awkward.

Todd cleared his throat, finding his voice. "Your thanks and your words are greatly appreciated."

Finally, they raised their heads, and the onlookers returned to their conversations.

Mi'cin's eyes narrowed on Todd. "I have a question, if I may? Is it true you mate was a male? I don't see any other couples like that here. Is that abnormal on you world? I find it ever curious."

Todd didn't think his face could get any hotter. The heat seemed to travel all the way to his toes.

The chimes sounded to call everyone in for the meal. He pretended he didn't hear the questions, and instead shifted on his cane and pointed to the door.

"We should head in." It was all he could manage to say at the moment. He had a fleeting thought of whether it would be bad form to crawl under a table and hide there for the rest of the night or until security kicked him out.

# Twenty-Four: Goodbye Party

TODD RAN HIS hand over the Kap'erin. It was soft as silk but heavy like wool. He put the cloak back on the closet shelf. He didn't want to hang it up. It might stretch out, so he made a special spot for it next to a few of Jerry's things he couldn't part with: Jerry's goofy Hawaiian print shirt and stupid San Jose Sharks foam hat. The rest had been given to charity.

The trip to DC had been short. He didn't get to see much of the city, which was unfortunate, but possibly for the best since he was alone. Maybe with the new job, he'd get the opportunity to go back and spend more time there.

Things were moving so quickly. It was hard to believe in a few weeks it would be Halloween. How would he explain that to the Nentraee? Maybe they wouldn't ask.

"Hey, Gimpy. You ready to go?" Dan held out Todd's cane.

"I can manage without it," Todd replied. With his leg not fully healed, he wasn't comfortable driving. Thankfully, Dan was willing to help out. He ambled into the living room, Dan leading the way. "I can't believe this is it, you know? My last day."

"Don't be so dramatic," Dan teased, running his olive-colored hand through his dark-brown hair. "You're leaving your job and starting a new one. A better one, I might add. One that will open up a hell of a lot more doors than the one you're currently in."

"I know. I'm getting it out of the way before I'm bogged down by government officials."

*I don't have a clue what I'm supposed to be doing with the Nentrae, so how can these dumbass bureaucrats tell me anything?*

"Don't think about it now." Dan handed Todd his jacket. "It's chilly out."

"Thanks, Mom."

"Bitch."

Todd shrugged on his jacket, and they headed out the door. He cast a glance at the house as he hobbled to the car.

*My last link to Jerry, and I'll be damned if I'm giving it up.*

"So, what are your plans now that things are back to normal, and I don't need a babysitter anymore?" Todd got in the car.

"Well, I have my little job. Plus, I've decided I should stay close to my family. My mom is still a mess. I don't know. She's just...Maybe I should take her over to the visitor center or up to one of the ships. Something, so she isn't so scared." Dan started down the street. "I've been checking out apartments. I found a great one on First Street, right near the lightrail and not too far from downtown."

"I hear the new memorial is sorted out." He wanted to make sure Dan understood it was okay to talk about it.

"I've heard that too. It'll be good, get things back to normal, fill in the void in the city. It'll help the healing."

"I should've been more involved." Todd sighed. "Not so withdrawn from it all. Hiding in the fantasy world of my games." He frowned. "I don't know how you and Kati tolerated me."

"'Cause we're saints."

Todd laughed, then faded into silence for the rest of the drive.

When Dan parked, and the engine shut off, Dan's brown-eyed gaze met his. "I was going to warn you at home." He hopped out of the car. "There's a going away party planned."

"Bastard." Todd brushed away Dan's offered hand of help to get out of the car. "Why didn't you say something?"

"Why? So you'd come up with some stupid excuse to not go?" Dan said. "Get over yourself. This is for your coworkers. It gave Jim the opportunity to buy a cake from Peter's Bakery. You know how much he loves that place. Plus, it'll give you that final opportunity to tell everyone to fuck off. Like you've always wanted." Dan pointed at the building.

"Dan, I want you to stay at the house," Todd blurted out.

"What? Why?"

"I'm going to need someone to take care of the house and Bianca while I'm working. I don't want to leave the house empty, and I can't take Bianca with me. I don't want to give her away. I'd feel too guilty."

"Ugh...such a drama queen. Look, *chica*, we can figure it out later. Now let's get you to your party."

"No." Todd stopped walking. "I need to know you'll stay in the house. Please." His eyes burned into Dan's, trying to show him how important this was.

"Fine, but we're gonna draw up a proper agreement," Dan said. "Now come on you have a party to go to."

Jim rushed from his desk outside Varick's office to meet them in the lobby and led them to the conference room, then opened the door for them. Before Todd had a foot in the door, all his coworkers were cheering and clapping. Kati walked up in a lavender suit, showing off her legs and heels. Her black hair was brushed straight and draped over her shoulder; she hugged him and whispered in his ear, "Play along and have fun, or else." She gave him a kiss on the cheek.

"Yes, ma'am," Todd whispered back.

"We're going to miss you around here," Varick boomed. "Who else could handle the shit I gave them, especially when the company started?"

Varick had the same off-putting sneer-grin he'd had the day he told Todd of the Nentraee visit and the reception. Varick had been lucky the day of the attack. He only had a mild concussion and a few cuts. He was out of the hospital the following day. To see him now, one would never have guessed he went through that.

*I wonder how he's coping?*

"And I'm going to miss you too." Todd shook Varick's hand.

Todd greeted his coworkers and made his way around the room. He noticed the cake and ice cream and a green wrapped box on the table. Seeing the smiling faces, he made an honest effort with everyone, shaking hands and forcing out smiles and saying with as much honestly as he could that, yes, he would, in fact, miss them too.

*I'm so lucky to know these people.*

He answered questions about the White House and the president. The most asked questions were on the Nentraee. His coworkers asked him what the Nentraee ate and how Mi'ko's family treated him. They wanted to know about the cloak the Nentraee gave him. Several people, including Grant, were disappointed he didn't bring it to show off.

Kati handed him a piece of cake. "Wow. This is it. I didn't think leaving was permitted. I thought they were going to wheel us out of here with the furniture. Together."

"Not like I'm vanishing. It's simply a new job. We'll still see each other, just not every day for nine hours a day." Todd took a bite of the cake, tasting the chocolate buttercream frosting and raspberry filling as it melted on his tongue.

"Oh please, you're going to work with them. Once you're up there on their ship you'll forget about us little people back here on Earth." She took a bite of cake.

"It's not like that," Todd said. "I'll be around, and you're still coming over for Thanksgiving." He turned to Jim, raising a fork. "Great job on the cake selection, Jim."

Jim waved back.

"You're keeping the house? I thought you were going to live with them?" Kati asked.

He pointed to Dan. "I even have a renter. 'Course we—"

"Listen up." Varick's thunderous voice echoed around the room, calling his staff to attention.

Everyone settled and gave him their attention.

"I'm not one for speech making. All I'm going to say is, Todd, we'll miss you, and you did a great job while you were here. Best of luck, and realize you'll always have a home. If those aliens tire of you or don't appreciate you, you're always welcome."

The group applauded. Jim cleared his throat and pointed to the gift on the table.

"Ah, yes. Almost forgot." Varick handed the box to Todd. "Just something to remember us all by."

Todd ripped off the green wrapping paper and opened the box. He waded through the yellow tissue and pulled out a T-shirt. On the front, it had his employee number, thirteen, with his last name above it. When he flipped it over, the back said, "Now Retiring" with the big number thirteen under the words. Todd snickered. The shirt was signed by everyone.

"Wow," Todd said. "Thanks, everyone. This is really nice. 'Course, you're not getting rid of me. You're still one of the first companies the Nentraee want to work with, so..." he trailed off, noting the smiles. This was so much harder than he thought. He knew each one of these people. He had conducted their new hire orientations when they started, and now they would continue without him. He shifted uncomfortably but smiled anyway.

*I shouldn't leave. How can I leave these amazing people?*

"Anyway, thanks."

The room buzzed as everyone continued to chat and enjoy the cake, but then they slowly headed back to work. Each of them offered him one more personal goodbye. When almost everyone was gone and there was no more cake or ice cream, he turned to Varick. "Exit interview?"

"Sure, if we must."

Kati gave him a hug. "You owe me dinner. And I want to come up to that ship and have you take me around. I'm sure there are a bunch of hunky Nentraee men up there for me to meet."

Varick cleared his throat. "Don't you have a job to do, Katherine?"

She pursed her lips. "Varick's right. Call me later, we still need to go for drinks."

Todd and Varick made their way to Varick's office. Walking was difficult for Todd, but he was determined to not use the cane. The physical therapist said he could wean himself off the cane but to use it when he got tired.

"It's not going to be the same around here." Varick sat and pulled out the last of Todd's paperwork and final check. "I still haven't found the right person for your job." He huffed. "I figured someday I would lose you to another company. I never thought I would lose you to another race of people. How do I compete with that?" The sneer-grin was gone, and his face seemed to droop.

"I was under the impression that you wanted me to take the position?" Todd lifted the last word making it a question, as he signed the documents in front of him. "At least, that is what I've been told."

Varick settled back in his chair, then crossed and rested his hands on his stomach. "Bah. Of course, I do, but it doesn't mean I don't want you here for my own selfish reasons." He opened his desk drawer and pulled out a poorly wrapped box. "This is from me and my family. I never got to thank you properly for what you did. That day in the limo. They say if it wasn't for you, we'd have been dead. Your yelling drew attention to the second attacker, allowing the police to shoot him and stop him. Without you..."

"It's not necessary." Todd focused on the box. He wasn't a hero; he was just some guy who climbed out of the car window first. They were giving him too much credit. Could he be the hero they saw? Was he able to push away the pain and the loss to be that man? All he had wanted to do was hide away, but he couldn't do that. He had to do right by his friends and family. He had to make sure that nothing like this would ever happen again.

*I may not deserve this, but I have to do it. I have to become the man they all see.*

"No." Varick's voice pulled Todd back to the here and now. "The insanely large bonus check I'm giving you isn't necessary." Varick leaned forward. "Nothing I do is necessary, but as the boss it's my prerogative." His voice was gruff but with tone of gratitude in it. "Well, open it." He slid the box toward Todd.

Todd picked the box up and slowly turned it over. The gift was light and wrapped in gold paper with silver ribbons and a bow.

*Let this be the start of the new me.*

Todd ran his thumbnail along the taped edge, cutting through the tape. Wrapping paper revealed a black and gold box. He opened the top and pulled aside the tissue paper.

A glittering pocket watch sat inside, beautiful in its simplicity, gold with a black accent band around the edges. The front cover had more gold and had scripted initials on it, a *T* and an *L*. He clicked it open. The face had four black diamonds—at the twelve, three, six, and nine o'clock positions. Todd closed it, feeling the weight in his hand. The chain was a thin braided rope.

"Varick, thank you. This means more to me than you can imagine."

"It's an A. Lange & Söhne. Not cheap, but German-made, so it's worth it." His eyes opened wider, as did his smile. "Claudia helped me choose it. Read the back."

Todd flipped it over.

*To my Counselor Troi, thank you.*

*VCB*

"Thank you." Todd's eyes blurred with tears and he quickly wiped them away. "I don't...You didn't have...How can I—?"

"You've done enough. I can't repay you for what you have given me and my family. You're a true hero." Varick waved off Todd's comments. "Okay, finish signing this stuff and get out of here. I have work to do." His voice cracked.

Todd glanced once more at the watch, clipped the chain to his pants, and put the watch in his pocket, noting the weight and sensing the ticking within the clock. This gift would remind him of who he wanted to become. Varick walked him to the lobby where Dan was sitting with the last of Todd's boxes.

"Ready?" Dan asked, standing.

Todd peeked around the lobby one more time. *This is it.* "Sure."

"Do us proud up there and be the man we know you to be. Now get out. We have work to do." Varick turned and thundered back to his office.

"MISS. WEBSTER, I understand. I really do." Todd sat on an uncomfortable conference room chair. His leg was stiff and bothering him, but he could almost walk at a normal pace again.

She had shown up with several of her minions, wanting to meet with him to review his position again. "Do you, Todd? We've looked at your background and your experience, and, truthfully, I'm not so sure. You have no experience in this field." A small, gold crucifix slipped out from under the collar of what Todd believed was a government-issued ugly suit.

"As you and your people keep telling me, along with Vi-Narm from the Nentraee, I'm a figurehead. A public face, hell, not even that public. I have no power, no authority. I'm an envoy, nothing more. I give the Nentraee a human face." His head rested on the tips of his fingers.

Todd couldn't figure out why she didn't like him. He shook his head. "Madam Secretary, I realize you don't approve of me. I believe your exact words were, 'a pretty face with no substance—a true PR stunt on the part of the Nentraee.'"

Her lips pinched together. "That was taken out of context by that CNN reporter, and you know it, as do the Nentraee."

Todd rubbed his mouth, hiding his grin.

*One point, Todd.*

Honestly, he loved seeing her reaction; something actually bothered her. She was supposed to be a genius, according to her bio, but he didn't see it in her. All Todd saw was a bitter, angry woman. "I know. I know," he said with a dismissive wave of his hand. Her smile slipped to a scowl. She brought the smile back.

*Two points, Todd.*

She crossed her legs, leaned forward, and smoothed out the wrinkles in her skirt. The clear glass conference walls behind her showed a busy office. "Have you reviewed the materials we sent you?"

Todd thought of the stacks of papers he'd received that were sitting in the den at home. It was busy work, and none of it made any sense; policy and procedures he would never even need.

"I've started, but as long as we're being honest, how much of it is actually going to be useful? I mean—"

"You started? You start with the Nentraee..." She stopped and picked a piece of lint off her skirt, taking a full breath before she continued. "I can't believe we're allowing you to do this. This is a mistake. We should've had more control over this."

*One point, Martha. I'm still in the lead. Bitch.*

Todd flattened his tie, spotting a piece of cat hair on it. Ignoring it, he stared at her. He felt the tick of the pocket watch and breathed. He'd had just about enough of this woman, and everyone telling him what was what. "A mistake. As I recall, Madam Secretary, the government didn't have much choice in the matter."

Martha frowned again, taking a deep breath.

*Three points, Todd, one point Martha.*

"I suggest, Mister Landon, you remember where your loyalties lie and review the information we've sent you. Everything that we've compiled will be useful, I assure you."

"Even the stuff on those xenophobic groups and religious protesters?" Todd frowned. How stupid could these nut-balls be? "Madam Speaker, they're nuts. They're nearsighted bigots."

Martha's eyes narrowed. "Do not underestimate the power of faith, Mister Landon. You have no idea what people of faith can accomplish when properly motivated."

Todd sighed, exasperated with this conversation.

"Try not to be this naive with the Nentraee. And please try not to embarrass yourself or your country or, God forbid, the entire human race."

*Three points, Todd, two points, Martha. Dammit.*

"I believe we're finished here." She walked to the clear glass door that led back into the main office area.

"As always, Madam Secretary, it's been a pleasure." Todd bit his tongue as she opened the door, and he closed his padfolio and stood up. He moved slowly to the exit, careful where he stepped.

"How's your leg?" Her tone changed—it was sugary sweet now that the door was open and others could hear her.

Sadly, he would need to get used to, and better at, dealing with people like her.

"Getting better." He walked past her, waiting for her to trip him, or at the very least, push him.

"It's such a shame your recovery has taken so long. I'm sure that must be difficult for you and your partner." Her eyes grew large, and her voice got a little higher. "Oh, I'm so sorry; it slipped my mind. Please forgive me. Such a shame you lost *James* in the attack. I can't imagine the pain you must still suffer."

Todd stumbled as he shuffled his feet.

*Set and match. Todd Landon loses.*

"Well, it was good to see you, Mister Landon. Best of luck, and, again, I'm so sorry for everything. And again, I'm so sorry for your loss. Such a waste." She patted his shoulder and offered what appeared to be the deepest and most heartfelt look of sympathy and sorrow.

He gave her what he hoped was a polite nod and walked off, trying not to shake with disgust. That woman was pure evil, and there was nothing about her he liked. He pushed the button to the elevator and pulled out the pocket watch.

*There are people who love and care for me. I'm not alone.*

He checked the time, then slipped it back into his pocket. Someday she would get hers, and he wanted to be there for it.

To be continued in *Conviction.*

# Glossary of Terms

A': Day

A'UNA: Benzee holiday, the day the Clan War ended; celebrated by all Benzee but mainly celebrated by the Za'entra.

A'A LUTA: Marks the day the Nentraee world was destroyed; a day to remember all those who died and were left behind.

ACTIONSHIP: A two-seater (pilot and gunner) attack ship.

A'DA MAGINA: Day of hope, celebrated to remind the people that there is always hope.

A' GODÁ FAOO: Celebration after the third right of fatherhood is complete.

A'KO HUNE: Evil little spirits who are known to haunt weddings.

A' MEV: Naming day. This is similar to a birthday. It is the day that the Nentraee are given their name and presented to friends and family. Normally a week after birth.

A'SOOTEE: Rebirth, when the Nentraee calendar begins.

BENZEE: Nentraee home world

A'ZEN: Day the Za'entra celebrate the final winning battle over Dentraee, Martween, and U'Zraee.

CANDRA: First moon of Benzee; closest in orbit; similar size to Earth's moon.

CÁDO: Companion animal to the Nentraee. They are a medium-sized animal that has limited intelligence and can communicate on a basic level.

COLO CO MO: A Nentraee dish—a combination of meat and vegetables over a noodle. Very popular but very expensive to make as both meats and vegetables are rationed on the ship. It has an almond and citrus scent but is spicy.

DAMUS WITH MĨ (MEES): A vegetable-based dish with a thick sauce and a flatbread. A common dish among the Za'entra.

DEN A'TAE: Four-day religious event to honor Jealug Bravisa.

DUSAL: Flying water bird that buzzes and can be annoying.

É'BOWUNÁ: Stone unity bowl, used in all Nentraee wedding ceremonies. Each clan uses a different type of stone decorated in various ways.

EMISARATION: All Nentraee children, when they reach age twenty-four, are considered adults with full rights: voting, É'mawee, etc. At this point, they are no longer considered children and can make all their own life choices.

É'MAWEE: Nentraee wedding. A two-day event where the families and invited guests of the couple come together to witness and speak. It is celebration of the couple and the family.

É'MAW Po: Family dinner hosted by the families of the couple getting married.

É'MAZEE: Day of joining—the actual day the couple is legally married.

É'MAZ PO: Couple's first dinner—the lunch or dinner hosted by the newly married couple.

É'TOK: Wooden token placed in the É'bowuná by each person in witness of the É'mawee. The token has a unique symbol on it that represents the person in attendance. They will place the token in the bowl as an indication of their support of the couple and the wedding.

E'XIN: A rich Nentraee wine, served warm. Traditionally served at weddings or very special events, now it is enjoyed on other occasions. It has a fruity chocolate flavor.

GĨ: (1) A flying lizard-type animal; (2) A medium range passenger shuttle holding between ten and fifteen people, used mainly by government personnel.

GODÁ FAOO: Rights of fatherhood, there are three stages. Once the third right is granted, the only way Godá Faoo can be revoked is if the father has a child by another woman.

IZ-CUS: A flowering plant. Instead of petals, it has pink sweet-smelling berries. The berries are used as a perfume or deodorant.

IZ-GOOT: A flowering plant with large lavender blooms with spiky green leaves. Smells like ocean mist.

IZ: A flowering plant

Ĩ-TA (EES-TA): Vulgar word used to describe the Za'entra, meaning half blood. Commonly used prior to the Clan War. Now it is considered very offensive by almost everyone.

Ĩ-NO (EES-NO): One of the worst, most vulgar terms in the Nentraee language. The English equivalent would be "Fucking Bitch."

JAREEDAN: A leafy plant that has a strong lavender scent.

JEALUG BRAVISA: Formal reference for the Nentraee deity.

JEKTĨL: A high-level accountant or controller for a dedicated project.

J'VEESA: Common reference for the Nentraee deity.

KAP'ERIN: Ceremonial cloak, dress garb, used by the Nentraee. Often embroidered in gold or silver with the symbols of the seven clans. The military Kap'erin differs in that it will only be embroidered with the signet of the specific branch of the military.

KAROO: Silver-laced ear cuff worn in the left ear by some Za'entra. It started as a way to remember those lost in the Clan War, now it's a fashion accessory. Some were passed down over the years, but most are new with new designs. There is no one single design. They can vary.

KĨ: Largest class of military ship in the Nentraee fleet.

KUMNAS: An Ultween thick dip. A combination of nuts with oil and spices.

LAGU: Chopsticks used for eating, normally used in the left hand.

LÁOO: A tieback for longer than normal hair, used by males of the Altraee clan to keep their hair in a neat ponytail. The strands are braided around the hair, ending in a standard knot.

OMLANGA: Nentraee dish—a flat noodle and meat dish made like a casserole with the equivalent of cheese and spices. A common dish among the Za'entra Clan. Now, however, after the Clan War, only served on A'una to celebrate. This has a meaty, sweet, spicy scent.

MENTRA: Largest planetoid of Benzee. It also has the farthest orbit.

MÉTKIP: Position or title of a meeting keeper and note taker. Similar to a secretary.

NABUTIMABA: Tallest tree on Benzee, can grow to heights of 200 meters. Most grow between 90 and 120 meters tall. Has a nutty scent.

NAYUS: The Nentraee spirit or soul

NA-TRAEE: The title for the Dentraee spirit finder or talker. This is the priestess the Dentraee use in the event that the body cannot be found or entombed properly.

NENTRAEE: The race of people from the planet called Benzee. There are seven clans or races, each with different physical features.

RÁDO: Name of the Kĩ-class battle cruiser that is the flagship of the Nentraee fleet. It is also home to the General Command offices where military command in maintained—the command center for the fleet and the most heavily protected.

SAGVARWA: An Ultween dish. A sausage filled with meat and various spices and dried fruit. Often served with kumnas for dipping.

SALRA-KÉ: Nentraee dish—meat wrapped in either a leafy vegetable or thin bread with a thick sauce. A common midday meal for the Dentraee.

SEYAS: A baby cádo

TA-OOLEE: Offering for the dead.

TÉ: A large spoon-type device with one very sharp edge used in conjunction with the Lagu—normally used in the right hand.

TIEBACK: A piece of cloth or leather used by Nentraee males as a hair tie to keep their long hair in a ponytail and out of their faces.

TUMA: Nentraee coffee; this drink is traditionally served cold and has a sweet spicy flavor. The scent is similar to chocolate-covered chili peppers.

U'XTRA: Second moon, smallest, oval shape.

WÁ: Largest water mammal, similar to an Earth dolphin but larger and lacking the long snout. The Wá look like a combination of a shark and a dolphin.

YARUS: Tree, similar in size and color to a Japanese Maple tree, but with purple leaves and bare bark.

YÉP: A term used to describe troublesome children.

VAK YÉP: Slang. A little bastard or a weak little male.

XĨMÉ: Small blue-feathered raven-type bird that flies in groups of five or seven.

# Glossary of Races

ALTRAEE: Benzee clan, race of people whose features are very similar to that of the Martween, but their stature is closer to the U'Ztraee. They have a skin tone this is tan-red. They have dark hair: blacks and deep browns. Their eyes range in the family of greens. They have high cheekbones.

Some males wear a modified tieback (a Láoo) that braids around their ponytail keeping the hair tight and neat. Normally finished in a tight knot.

CALEEN: Benzee clan, race of people who are one of the most powerful and influential clans on Benzee; much of Nentraee culture is based on the Caleen. Their features, including their hair, tend to be some of the fairest of the clans. The race typically has blue and green eyes.

DENTRAEE: Benzee clan, race of people who are very religious and conservative. Their features are the closest to the Caleen, sharing many of the same features. Only their skin color and hair color differ, having aqua eyes and skin tones similar to the Utlween.

Can be very traditional and religious

Started the Clan War with the Za'entra. Clans that supported them at the start were the Martween and U'Ztraee

MARTWEEN: Benzee clan, race of people, most populous clan on Benzee prior to the evacuation of the planet. The shortest of the clans and they tend to have features that are more delicate than the other clans with midrange coloring. Eyes tend to be darker like the Za'entra as is their hair color.

One of the clans to start the Clan War.

ULTWEEN: Benzee clan, a race of people whose features are much darker than most of the clans with the exception of the U'Ztraee. Their eyes tend to be in shades of aqua and they have mostly brown hair. Their race has the most subtle forehead ridges of all the Nentraee.

U'XTRAEE: Benzee clan, a race of people whose features are the darkest of the clans and their eye color is the lightest. Their hair tends to also be the darkest. They also tend to be the tallest of the clans and have the hardest forehead ridges of the clans.

One of the clans to start the Clan War.

ZA'ENTRA: Benzee clan, race of people whose hair is an auburn or darker in color and their features are darker. They also have the darkest-colored eyes. Dark-brown eyes are the rarest. They tend to be an exotic-looking clan. Because of their mixed blood, some of the ridges on their foreheads will be more pronounced than others.

Some males and females wear a silver-laced ear cuff (karoo) in their left ear. It started as a way to remember those lost in the Clan War, and now it's a fashion accessory. Some were passed down over the years, but most are new with new designs. There is no one single design; they can vary.

They are a newly recognized clan. Prior to recognition, they were listed as half-breeds. Neither of their clans wanted to include them. They were outcasts until the Clan War, when they revolted and demanded to be recognized.

# Acknowledgements

This book would not have been possible without the support of several people including my amazing writing group and beta readers. The time and dedication you put into me and this story is appreciated and will not be forgotten.

A special thank you to fellow author Barbara Russell—you have been there since day one and you continue to support my writing and me.

Thank you to the real-life Dan. Your military expertise was a great help and I couldn't have done this without you.

# About the Author

M.D. Neu is a LGBTQA fiction writer with a love for writing and travel. Living in the heart of Silicon Valley (San Jose, California) and growing up around technology, he's always been fascinated with what could be. Specifically drawn to sci-fi and paranormal television and novels, M.D. Neu was inspired by the great Gene Roddenberry, George Lucas, Stephen King, Alice Walker, Alfred Hitchcock, Harvey Fierstein, Anne Rice, and Kim Stanley Robinson. An odd combination, but one that has influenced his writing.

Growing up in an accepting family as a gay man, he always wondered why there were never stories reflecting who he was. Constantly surrounded by characters that only reflected heterosexual society, M.D. Neu decided he wanted to change that. So, he took to writing, wanting to tell good stories that reflected our diverse world.

When M.D. Neu isn't writing, he works for a nonprofit and travels with his biggest supporter and his harshest critic, Eric, his husband of nineteen plus years.

Email: info@mdneu.com

Facebook: www.facebook.com/mdneuauthor

Twitter: @Writer_MDNeu

Website: www.mdneu.com

Blog: www.mdneu.com/blog

# Other books by this author

*The Calling*
*The Reunion*
*A Dragon for Christmas*

# Also Available from NineStar Press

# Connect with NineStar Press

Website: NineStarPress.com

Facebook: NineStarPress

Facebook Reader Group: NineStarNiche

Twitter: @ninestarpress

Tumblr: NineStarPress